The Undertaking

Rob Johnson

XERIKA PUBLISHING

"THE UNDERTAKING" COPYRIGHT

For Penny Philcox

With much love and very many thanks for all your support over the years and for your incredible talent and seemingly unlimited patience.

ACKNOWLEDGEMENTS

I am indebted to the following people for helping to make this book better than it would have been without their advice, technical knowhow and support:

Rob Johnson (a different one); Penny Philcox; Colin Ritchie; John Rogers; Dan Varndell; Chris Wallbridge; Nick Whitton; Patrick Woodgate.

And last but not least, my eternal gratitude to my wife, Penny, for her unfailing support, encouragement and belief.

COVER DESIGN BY PENNY PHILCOX AND PATRICK WOODGATE

Special thanks as always to Penny Philcox for the cover artwork and to Patrick Woodgate for the original design.

1

There was no denying it. "Max Dempsey and Partners: Funeral Directors" had taken a major financial nosedive, and we were at our wits' end what to do about it. Maybe it was because we were all novices at the undertaker game or it was simply because a lot fewer people died in the middle of summer, but that was the harsh reality. If business didn't pick up soon, we'd be staring into the abyss of what economists might call "totally screwed".

That's me, by the way. Max Dempsey. My real name's Simon Golightly, though, which was absolutely fine when I was a bank *manager*, but didn't sound right at all when I was embarking on my subsequent but short-lived career as a bank *robber*. Equally, it didn't seem appropriate for a funeral director either. Go lightly? Not quite up there with "rage against the dying of the light", is it?

Anyway, it was only about four months since we'd taken over the undertaker business from my erstwhile friend, latterly bitter enemy and now deceased Danny Bishop, when this guy walks into the funeral parlour and all he says is, 'Do you collect?'

Never mind a 'Good morning' or even giving me a chance to put on my well-practised sombre undertaker expression and ask, 'How may I help you?', just 'Do you collect?' There was maybe also a hint of an American accent.

'Collect what?' I said.

'Bodies.'

'*Seriously*?'

Just so you know, that was the voice in my head and not what I actually said, and to be clear, it's only ever the one voice in my head, and I only usually hear it in times of great stress. I'm not crazy, if that's what you're thinking.

'*Of course we collect them,*' the voice went on. '*What, do you think they all just wander in and pop their clogs right on the floor here? How bloody convenient that would be.*'

'We do collect, sir, yes,' I said aloud. 'Is there a particular deceased you have in mind?'

The guy looked like he didn't understand what to me was a perfectly simple question. He also looked like one of those typical gangster types in the old film noir movies. Black greased-back hair and a matching pencil moustache (but without the grease as far as I could tell) and wearing a light-coloured trenchcoat that reached down almost to his ankles and with the collar turned up. He'd also been overly heavy-handed with the aftershave, so I took a step back out of range.

When he still didn't answer my question, I decided that a gentle prompt might help. 'A family member perhaps?'

'France. Do you collect from France?'

'Well, it's not something that we usually—'

'These are the details,' he said before I could finish the sentence and thrust a folded sheet of paper at me.

I opened it up but had no sooner begun to read when he waved a thick brown envelope in front of my face. 'Your fee. Half now and half when the job's done plus any unforeseen expenses.'

As a funeral director, it would have been undignified to check inside the envelope, but it certainly felt like a generous amount of cash – unless the notes were all fivers, of course.

'Naturally, I'll need to consult with my partners before—'

'You need to understand that this is a vitally important undertaking, and one thing that you *must* guarantee is that you will bring him back in a coffin that you will take with you to France.'

'Oh yeah? And what else are we gonna bring him back in? A decommissioned telephone box?'

'You'll need this as well.'

The guy fished in the pocket of his trenchcoat and pulled out a cheap-looking mobile phone.

'There's only one number on this. Mine,' he said, prodding the phone at my chest. 'But do not use it unless in an absolute emergency. Got it?'

I nodded meekly and took the phone from him. 'Is it fully charged?'

Of all the multitude of questions buzzing around inside my head, that was definitely the most stupid and by far the least important. Nor was there any opportunity to get even one of the more important ones out of my mouth because Mr Mysterious had turned on his heel and swept out of the parlour in less time than it took me to open my gob.

'I'm not sure Alan and Scratch are gonna be too

9

happy about this,' said the voice in my head.

'And you think I am?' I said.

* * *

It came as no great surprise that the voice had been right about Alan and Scratch's reaction, and although none of us were exactly enthusiastic about taking the job, we'd eventually agreed that our pockets and the business itself were well overdue for a much needed injection of cash. And so it was that the hefty dollop of moolah we'd be getting was the clincher and the one and only reason that we were now bobbing about on the open sea across the English Channel.

I'm not keen on boats, I have to admit. Whether it's a pedalo on the lake or a massive ferry on the open sea, I always reckon it's gonna turn out like that *Perfect Storm* movie I saw with George Clooney. Maybe I should rephrase that. I don't mean I was watching the film at the cinema with George sat beside me or that we were slobbing it on the settee at home, watching it on the telly while we shared a bucketful of popcorn. Not a bit of it. What I meant was that Mr Clooney *stars* in the movie as the captain of a fishing boat that gets caught up in this horrendous storm, but I expect you knew that already.

Even now while I'm sitting here in the downstairs bar of a cross-Channel ferry with the sea as calm as a millpond, I'm still expecting a sudden gale to whip up the waves into a terror-inducing frenzy. And Scratch is no better than me. He's sitting opposite me with his eyes tight shut and his enormous hands gripping the arms of his chair so his knuckles are as white as his face. You'd have thought that somebody of his colossal stature wouldn't be scared of anything less than a nuclear missile hurtling towards him, but that's where appearances can be deceptive. He's got a good head and shoulders on me, and I'm about average height for a bloke, and his physique is entirely in proportion to his height. Then there's the shaved head – a vain attempt to disguise the rapidly advancing baldness – and a busted nose, so he looks like a right thug that you really wouldn't want to run into in a dark alley. But the honest truth is that Scratch wouldn't hurt a fly. Not unless provoked. And if that happened, you – or the fly – would be in serious trouble. As for his allergies, he should probably be in the *Guinness Book of Records*. Whatever it was, if you could touch it, smell it or swallow it, it was odds on that Scratch would come out in a rash. Hence the nickname.

Alan, of course, never missed an opportunity to take the piss whenever Scratch refused to eat or drink something because it would bring him out in hives or somesuch. On the other hand, Scratch had plenty of chances to get his own back on the frequent occasions when Alan was moaning about his recurrent neck pain. Apparently, this dated back to his younger days as an "almost champion" weightlifter when a serious neck injury forced him into early retirement. The flesh-coloured padded neck brace that he often wore was probably intended as some kind of badge of courage to remind everyone how badly he was suffering, except never in silence. Oddly enough, he wasn't wearing one today, and while Scratch and I had headed straight for the bowels of the ship and some alcoholic anaesthetic, he'd scurried up onto the deck like a hyperactive five-year-old.

'I'm gonna get some o' that sea air into me lungs

while you two wusses skulk down in the bar,' he'd said, but the very idea gave me palpitations.

For most of my life, I've been plagued with this thing called osmophobia, which is basically a morbid fear of smells. The doc didn't agree with me when I was first diagnosed, but I have this theory that it all kicked off in the biology lab at school. What with all the jars of dead frogs and what looked a lot like human foetuses the biology teacher insisted on having on display, the whole place reeked of formaldehyde. So, I jacked biology as soon as I could and did German instead. Dull but with a far more pleasant aroma. It doesn't have to be what most people would describe as *bad* smells that spark an attack, though. Even a whiff of jasmine or a certain brand of perfume would bring on the headaches, the nausea, the trembling and all the other shit, and I very much doubted that a lungful of sea air was going to do me a whole lot of good.

Thankfully, whisky had never been a trigger for my osmophobia, and I took another slug of my third double Scotch, trying unsuccessfully to block out the voice in my head, which was persistently nagging me about the terrible mistake I'd made.

'*The money's one thing,*' it said, '*but you've no real idea what you're letting yourself in for.*'

'Yes I do,' I didn't say aloud. 'It's a perfectly simple job. Pick up a body from France and bring it back to England.'

But once again, I knew that the voice had a point. There were too many unknowns involved and far too much "mystery" for my liking. What was it the guy had said? "This is a vitally important undertaking." What was so vitally important about it? It was a corpse, for God's sake. And I was only to phone him in the case of an "absolute emergency". What the hell was he expecting? That the ferry would hit an iceberg on the way back and was sinking fast?

'Oh, hello, Mr Mysterious. I know you said I should only call you if it was an absolute emergency, but I think this kinda counts. The thing is, you see, it seems we're all about to drown, so I'm afraid we won't be able to deliver the body after all. Sorry about that.'

I drained the last of my Scotch and foolishly turned my head towards the nearest window at the very moment the horizon had completely vanished.

2

In my brief experience as a funeral director, I've found that most people don't tend to stare at hearses. But that doesn't seem to be the case when you're queuing to drive one down the ramp from a cross-Channel ferry. Maybe what aroused the attention of the other motorists was that the three occupants of this particular hearse weren't wearing the customary black suits and ties but were casually dressed in T-shirts and jeans like we were off on a fortnight's holiday in the sun. Perhaps they were shocked at this gross disrespect to the deceased, but how were they to know that the coffin we were carrying contained nothing more than a few of our personal belongings?

'Pity it's not Paris,' said Alan, who was wedged between Scratch and me on the bench seat at the front of the hearse.

'Pity what isn't Paris?' said Scratch, braking sharply to avoid ploughing into the back of a VW camper van.

'Calais.'

'Well, I was never too hot on geography, but I'm pretty sure Paris isn't one of the Channel ports.'

'All I'm saying is that most ports are shitholes, and I've never been to Paris, so it'd be much better if the stiff we're collecting was in Paris instead of Calais.'

'Well, it isn't.'

'Yes, I know that, Scratch. It'd just be good to spend a bit of time doing the Eiffel Tower and all the other stuff they've got in Paris.'

'Like what?'

'I dunno. I've never been before, but it's a cast iron bet that it's got a whole lot more going for it than fucking Calais.'

I was painfully aware that this could easily turn into one of Alan and Scratch's frequent and interminable bickering matches, so I decided to nip it in the bud by pointing out that "stiff" wasn't the most appropriate word to use in our current line of work. Alan countered that he obviously wouldn't use it in front of any punters, but this was different, and we drove down the ramp in silence and followed the slow-moving queue of traffic to the customs check.

This turned out to be a right ball-ache, mainly because none of us had bothered to check up on the new post-Brexit rules on what you could and couldn't take into an EU country. As I mentioned earlier, we'd been attracting plenty of attention from our fellow travellers, so perhaps it was for the same reason that the French customs guy thought we looked sufficiently dodgy to give us the full going-over.

Of course, once he'd established that there wasn't a dead body inside it, he insisted that we take the lid off the coffin. There's no boot in a hearse since it's unlikely that the dearly departed would be bringing a suitcase with them, whichever way they were heading. As for the three of us, however, we'd hoped to make the return trip the same day but had taken the precaution of taking overnight bags and stowed them in the coffin just in case we were delayed.

Having rummaged through each of the three canvas holdalls and found nothing more than a few items of clothing and the usual bits and pieces, Customs Officer Clouseau then switched his focus to Scratch's "dietary essentials". These were crammed into a large plastic box that fitted snugly into the widest part of the coffin. Because of his multitude of allergies, he'd insisted on bringing about a week's worth of foods that he considered "safe" as an insurance against none of them being available in France.

Although we were utterly clueless about the new customs regulations, Clouseau had clearly memorised every one of them.

'What is in here?' he asked, picking up a large stainless steel Thermos flask.

'Soya milk,' said Scratch.

'*Milk*?' said the officer as if he'd just been told it was full of liquid nitrogen. 'Du *lait*?'

'*Soya* milk.'

The customs officer raised a heavy dark eyebrow and slowly unscrewed the lid of the flask. He peered inside, then sniffed cautiously.

'All dairy products are *interdits*. Strictly forbidden,' he said and proceeded to pour the contents of the flask onto the ground between his feet.

'Hey, what you doing?' Scratch shouted. 'It's not a dairy product. It's never been near a bloody cow in its life. It's fucking *soya* milk.'

He made a grab for the flask, but Clouseau took a step back out of reach and even made a move towards the gun on his hip.

'Whoa there,' I said, putting a restraining hand on Scratch's outstretched arm. 'Let's not overreact here, shall we?'

The officer eyeballed me for a couple of seconds before his hand moved away from his pistol, and he screwed the lid back on the flask.

'This you may keep,' he said and pointedly handed the flask to me rather than Scratch like I was his carer or something.

Ten minutes later, Clouseau finished his detailed examination of every tin, packet and bottle in the box and confiscated about two thirds of them, very possibly because he had no idea what most of them were but decided to err on the side of bureaucratic megalomania. To be fair to the guy, though, I didn't have a scooby what salba seeds and dulse flakes were either. Something else I didn't understand was why bananas were apparently OK, but apricots, plums and apples were a definite no-no. Still, ours was not to question why – although Scratch gave it a good go – and after Officer Clouseau welcomed us to France with a heavily sarcastic grin, we were finally on our way.

'So who's navigating?' said Alan, who'd taken over the driving as Scratch was too busy ranting about "bloody Brexit" and "fucking jobsworths" to concentrate.

'That would be me,' I said and unfolded the map of Calais we'd picked up on the ferry. Spreading it out on my lap, I checked the details on the sheet of paper that Mr Mysterious had given me. 'It's a side street off the… Rue de Val – en – ciennes.'

'Rude what?'

'Val – en – ciennes,' I repeated, tracing the word on the page with my finger.

'Yeah, that helps. So how the hell do we get there?'

'Christ, give me a minute, will you?'

I turned the map this way and that but failed to find the street I was looking for. In hindsight, it would have been most sensible to have sorted this out while we were on the ferry, but hindsight is a wonderful thing, of course. So too are sat nav systems, one of which Scratch had bought off a bloke down the pub in preparation for our trip. Unfortunately, though, when we'd fired it up we'd discovered that the nice lady who was ready to tell us exactly where we needed to go to reach our destination seemed to only speak Japanese. Or maybe it was Chinese. None of us were too well up on our Oriental languages, and in any case, there didn't appear to be any obvious way of getting her to speak English.

In a futile attempt to redeem himself, Scratch had suggested we used Google Translate to learn the Japanese (and/or Chinese) for a few words and phrases like "left", "right" and "straight on". Alan had then told him he was being a twat and pointed out that we'd also have to learn the words for "miles" and "yards" or even "kilometres" and "metres", not to mention "every sodding number from one to a thousand". And it was at that moment that the nice lady lost her power of speech altogether when Alan had hurled the sat nav unit to the floor and smashed the shit out of it with the heel of his boot. So the only guide we had now was the fiendishly unfathomable map of Calais, which was rapidly doing my head in.

'Some time today would be good, Max,' Alan was saying as we circumnavigated the same roundabout for what was the fifth or sixth time.

'Fuck's sake, Alan. I dunno. Just take the next exit

and pull over somewhere so I can get a proper look at the map.'

3

Even after we'd got to the Rue de Valenciennes, it took another twenty minutes or so to find the little side street we were looking for. The funeral parlour – or *salon funéraire* – was at the far end of it and at first glance was like any other small shopfront but with one major difference. Instead of shoes, clothes, books or whatever, this window display was crammed with a whole range of cremation urns, commemorative plaques, flower holders and a variety of other funereal paraphernalia.

As we opened the bright red wooden door to the left of the window, it set off a tinkling bell above it, and given the smallness of the shopfront, the interior was like the Tardis. The large open plan area was plenty big enough to accommodate an impressive assortment of coffins to suit even the most discerning of tastes. Soothing, sombre muzak played over hidden speakers, but there wasn't a soul in sight. On the other hand, this being a funeral parlour, there may have been the odd one or two floating about.

'Hello?' Scratch called out.

'I think you mean *bonjour*,' said Alan.

'Yeah, 'cos even if whoever's around is French – which I admit they almost certainly are – they're not gonna understand that "hello" means that there's somebody in their shop wanting some attention.'

'I'm talking about being polite, that's all.'

Scratch snorted. 'Oh, right, 'cos you're always so—'

'Do shut up, you two,' I interrupted and opened a door on the right, beyond which I guessed was probably an office.

It was, but it was currently unoccupied.

'There's another door right at the back,' said Scratch. 'Sounds like an electric saw coming from it.'

We all weaved our way through the display coffins until we were about ten feet from the door. The noise of the electric saw suddenly stopped, and moments later the door opened and out stepped a figure who looked like one of those forensics people that had just been checking out a murder scene. He was dressed in the same sort of white overalls with the hood up, and a paper mask and protective goggles obscured almost all of his face.

Clearly startled to see us, he managed a muffled '*Ah, bonjour, messieurs*' through the mask, then removed it along with the goggles and hood. This revealed a long, narrow face with a nose to match, and the tanned skin contrasted sharply with the layer of whitish dust which coated the few areas that had been unprotected by the mask and goggles. This two-tone appearance brought back a fleeting and definitely unwanted memory of the time several months ago when Alan, Scratch and I had spent many fruitless hours drilling into the vault of a bank only to find that we'd drilled into the wrong wall. But that's another story.

'*Pardon, messieurs*,' said the man and rattled out a couple more sentences in French, smiling broadly all the while.

Since Alan, Scratch and I had only marginally more knowledge of the French language than Japanese or Chinese, I had to ask the obvious question but refrained from shouting. 'Er, I'm sorry, but do you speak English?'

'But of course,' he said, his smile spreading wider. 'I was only apologising that I did not hear ze bell as I was in ze workshop, making a new *cercueil* – a new coffin.'

'So you make them here as well, do you?'

'Yes indeed. It is our *spécialité*. But how may I be of assistance today?'

'I think you're expecting us?' I said it more as a question than a statement. 'We're here to collect a... recently departed.'

The smile faded. '*Comment*?'

'A stiff,' said Alan.

'*Ah, oui, bien sûr*,' said the man, his smile making an instant comeback. '*Le stiff*. You must be Monsieur Dimpsey.'

'Dempsey. Max Dempsey.'

'*Je suis heureux de vous rencontrer*,' he said, shaking my hand with excess vigour. 'I am Antoine Lemery. If you please to follow me, he is in ze office.'

Antoine turned towards the front of the shop but stopped when I took him gently by the arm.

'He's in the office?'

'*Certainement*,' he said with the hint of a frown and a typically Gallic shrug. 'Where else would he be?'

Apart from the fact that I'd already been into the office and found nothing other than the usual desk, chairs and filing cabinets, there was something else that bothered me. 'He's not in, like, cold storage or something?'

Another Gallic shrug. 'There is air conditioning in ze office, but unfortunately it is broken.'

'So how long's he been in there?'

'Since yesterday morning.'

'And he's been in the office all this time?'

'Mostly, yes.'

I mean, it wasn't exactly a blazing hot day, but if the corpse had been out of some kind of cold storage for twenty-four hours or so, my osmophobia would certainly have picked it up.

'I was in the office a few minutes ago, and there was nobody in there then.'

'Perhaps he has gone out for a coffee.'

Scratch, Alan and I laughed nervously. Maybe this was the French idea of gallows humour.

'*Alors*. Follow me,' said Antoine and set off towards the office.

As we trailed along in his wake, Alan whispered, 'What the fuck's going on?'

Antoine opened the office door and stood back to let the three of us in. I tentatively sniffed the air. Nothing much more than the faint smell of wood polish. And still no body to be seen.

'Ssh, what's that?' said Scratch. 'Sounds like snoring.'

He hurried round to the far side of the desk and stood looking down. 'Jesus.'

Alan and I joined him, and there stretched out on the floor was the body of a very fat and very short man with his eyes closed and a peculiar smirk on his almost completely round face. He was using a rolled-up suit jacket for a pillow and wore a white shirt, splattered here and there with food stains, and a loosened maroon tie that had ridden up close to one ear. His chubby hands were clasped across his belly, which rose and fell with his slow, regular breathing.

'*Voilà*,' said Antoine. 'And here is your "stiff".'

'Except he's not, is he?' I said, rounding on him with not a little annoyance. 'In fact, he looks very much alive to me.'

'*I swear to God that if he does that little shrug again, I'd clock him one*,' said the voice in my head, but I ignored it.

'Ah, perhaps I misunderstood ze meaning of "stiff". Zis is not what you were expecting?'

'No, it bloody isn't,' said Alan. 'Why do you think we brought a hearse and a fucking empty coffin?'

'You did?'

'Yes.'

'Look,' I said. 'I think there must have been some sort of mixup. Are you sure there isn't another body that's been brought in that we're supposed to collect? An actual dead one, I mean.'

'*Non, monsieur*. Ze person who brought him in was very precise. "A man called Max Dempsey will come to pick him up tomorrow". He was an Englishman like you. Or maybe American. I cannot always tell ze difference.'

'And did he have a name?'

Antoine cast his eyes downwards as he considered the question, then slowly shook his head. 'No, I don't believe he did. *En fait*, he spoke very few words at all. Almost no more zan I have told you already.'

'Max, it really doesn't matter what the guy's name was,' said Alan. 'The point is, what the hell are we supposed to do now?'

It was an excellent question, of course, but right now I didn't have even a sniff of an idea what the answer might be. The information that Mr Mysterious had given me had been scant in the extreme, although...

'I could phone him, I suppose. Mr Mysterious. But he did say I was only to call him in the case of an emergency.'

'Yeah, well, I think this probably counts,' said Scratch, and I took Mr Mysterious's phone from my pocket and rang the only contact number on it.

I perched on the edge of the desk and listened to the ringing tone... and listened... and listened... and listened until a loud bleep told me that my time was up.

'No reply,' I said.

'Oh, that's terrific,' said Alan.

'Why didn't you leave a message?' said Scratch.

'Because there doesn't seem to be a bloody voicemail.'

'You sure you got the right number?'

'Shut up, Alan.'

I was rattled, sure enough, and I could well have done without Alan and Scratch's helpful suggestions. Maybe wherever Mr Mysterious was there was no signal, but then the phone wouldn't have rung at all, would it? Or maybe he'd left it somewhere and— I dunno. I'd give it a few minutes and try again.

'Perhaps you should leave it a few minutes and then try again,' said Scratch.

I was a nano-second away from giving him the verbal equivalent of a Tyson Fury uppercut when there was a weird snuffling sound from close to our feet. No, not snuffling. More like a cross between a horse whinnying and a whale blasting a jet of water out of its blowhole. Our very much alive dead man was emerging from his slumber.

Opening one cautious eye after the other, he squinted against the light, then belched loudly and appeared to be having major difficulty in focusing on his surroundings. The peculiar smirk that he'd had while sleeping now vanished, and his features twisted into an expression of utter bewilderment. With superhuman effort, he forced the bulk of his upper body up onto one elbow and gazed at each of us in turn through half closed eyes.

'Where the fuck am I?' he said at last and sucked at the inside of his mouth like it was in dire need of rehydration. He looked to be in his late fifties, and the faintest trace of an accent was Eastern European or possibly Russian.

'You are in a *salon funéraire, monsieur,*' said Antoine. 'A funeral home.'

'So am I dead then?'

Inconveniently not, I thought.

Antoine's chuckle was verging on the coquettish. 'No, *monsieur.* You are very much alive, and zese men have come to collect you as arranged.'

The man's eyelids flickered as realisation gradually began to dawn, and the peculiar smirk instantly returned. 'Ah yes. So one of you must be Max Dempsey.'

Yes, I suppose I must be, I thought. But at this particular moment I'd far rather be back as boring old bank manager Simon Golightly.

4

I can't say I agreed with Alan that Calais is a shithole, but the small backstreet hotel we'd checked into certainly was. Our two twin rooms were next to each other on the third floor with Scratch and Alan in one and myself and Oleg in the other. Oleg Radimov. That was how he'd introduced himself and, yes, he was indeed Russian.

After about the fifth time of trying to contact Mr Mysterious and failing, we didn't seem to have much choice except to do what we were being paid to do and get him back to the UK. The fact that he was *alive* hadn't been mentioned when the deal was made, although maybe Mr Mysterious hadn't realised that himself. Either way, he was paying us handsomely for the job with half the fee up front and the rest on completion, and there was no way we were going to miss out on that hunk of cash.

Even though Mr Mysterious had been pretty miserly with the details, one thing he'd been crystal clear about was that the "body" had to be brought over to England in a coffin, which was of course why he'd hired an undertaker in the first place. This had made perfect sense when I'd assumed that it was a corpse we were collecting but was obviously now a cause for some concern. If Mr M really did know that Oleg Radimov was very much alive, then what he was actually paying us for was to *smuggle* him into the country. My anxiety levels were off the scale. Knowingly bringing what was essentially an illegal immigrant into the UK was a crime that would have warranted the death penalty if the present government could have got away with it.

Then there was the issue of practicalities. Built like Danny DeVito's fatter brother, there wasn't a snowball's chance in hell that Radimov would fit inside the coffin we'd brought with us. And believe me, we tried.

'I don't suppose you've got a bigger coffin we could borrow?' I'd asked Antoine after we'd all broken sweat to unwedge Radimov out of ours.

'Borrow?'

'All right. *Buy.*'

'No, but I could make one for you.'

'How long would that take?'

'You are in a hurry?'

'Uh-huh.'

This time, the Gallic shrug was accompanied by the slow exhalation of breath through pursed lips as he made a mental calculation. 'It will be quicker if I can adapt a coffin I have already instead of building a completely new one, so perhaps midday tomorrow?'

An overnight stay in Calais was unlikely to feature on anybody's bucket list, least of all mine, Scratch and Alan's, but Antoine had recommended a "nice little hotel" not far away that was owned by a cousin of his.

Little? Yes. Nice? Not in your wildest imaginings.

Even a prisoner transferred here from Guantanamo Bay would have hesitated before giving it so much as a one star review on TripAdvisor. The whole place was a vicious assault on the senses. Everywhere reeked of stale cigarette smoke and damp, which did my osmophobia no favours at all, and the almost constant clanging of ancient plumbing would have been marginally more bearable if it had had some kind of rhythm to it.

The rooms we were in were scarcely big enough to fit two single beds and a couple of straight-backed wooden chairs, and the "en suite" bathroom in Alan and Scratch's room was minus a door but heavily adorned with patches of thick black mould. Taking a much needed shower was out of the question in both our bathrooms as the only available hot water was from the taps in the grime encrusted washbasins. As for the ridiculously narrow beds, Scratch had taken one look at his and announced that he'd be sleeping on the floor as he was severely allergic to nylon sheets. Alan had predictably ripped the piss out of him over this and pointed out that he'd probably have far more of an allergic reaction to whatever lurked in the poor excuse for a carpet, but he himself wasn't beyond complaining about the cigarette burn marks on the sheets and the total absence of pillowcases.

'*You used to have standards,*' the voice in my head was saying as I lay back on my own bed and stared up at the cracked plaster of the nicotine-stained ceiling. '*A good job, a nice house in leafy suburbia, a wife and two kids, not to mention—*'

'Yeah, a wife who buggered off with her Greek toyboy and took the kids with her.'

'*OK, so Carla did the dirty on you, but you're well*

rid of her if you ask me, and it's not as if you don't get to see the kids as often as you like – which is pretty bloody often now that the worst excesses of their teenage angst have begun to wear off.'

Well, that part was true anyway. I had a far better relationship with Brad and Emma now than I ever had when we all lived under the same roof.

'Take a look at yourself now, though. Christ almighty. First you're a bank manager who gets caught with his hands in the till, then a brief, spectacularly unsuccessful spell as a bank robber who then ends up as a fucking undertaker smuggling illegal immigrants and staying in a cesspit of a hotel that should have been condemned years ago. Proud of yourself, are you?'

Sometimes – very often, in fact – I wished that this bloody voice in my head could be a little more supportive instead of all the guilt-tripping and running commentary on my undeniable failings as a human being. In a desperate bid to tune it out, I forced myself to concentrate on the sound of the clanking water pipes, but even that was having to compete with Oleg's window-rattling snoring.

I glanced across the two-foot gap between my bed and his. He was lying in much the same position as when we'd first come across him in the office of Antoine's funeral parlour. Flat on his back with his hands clasped across his belly and a peculiar smirk on his round pink face. It was an expression he wore most of the time, whether awake or asleep, but what had he got to feel so pleased with himself about? Very possibly his frequent sips from his silver hip flask had something to do with it but couldn't have been the only reason. Perhaps it was because he knew he was on the verge of a new life in Britain, but what was he escaping *from*? He was hardly your usual refugee from some war-torn hellhole, so maybe he was a Russian dissident fleeing from Putin's ruthless response to anyone who dared to question him or his actions.

Naturally, we'd asked Oleg why we were having to smuggle him into the UK, but he'd remained stubbornly tight-lipped on the subject, and all he would say was that his orders prohibited him from revealing any details about his situation. As for my inevitable question of 'Whose orders?', his only answer had been to wink at me and take another glug from his hip flask.

To add to the inharmonious cacophony of the prehistoric plumbing and the loud explosions of Oleg's snoring, there was then the grating noise of unoiled hinges as the bedroom door burst open.

'We going out or what?' said Alan. 'I'm bloody starving.'

5

It was already dark when we left the French equivalent of Bates Motel and hit the streets of Calais. There were plenty of restaurants to choose from, but Scratch didn't fancy any of them. After half an hour, Alan had had enough.

'For God's sake, Scratch, there's no such thing as an allergy-free restaurant either in Calais or probably anywhere else on the planet.'

'You want me to end up in hospital, fighting for my life?'

'Course not, but if I don't eat soon, I'm gonna pass out from hunger, and I'll be the one needing intensive care.'

'What about that place we passed a few minutes ago?' I said in an attempt to defuse the escalating battle of wills. 'The menu had all sorts of gluten-free options, which dishes contained nuts and all that kind of stuff. That'd work, wouldn't it?'

Scratch grunted. 'Yeah, that's what it says on the menu, but who knows what goes on behind the scenes in some of these kitchens?'

'Right,' said Alan through gritted teeth. 'I think we've finally established that there isn't a single restaurant you'd be happy to eat in, so why are we still pratting about looking for a needle in a haystack when we know for certain that the bloody needle doesn't even exist in the first place?'

I could tell that Scratch was gearing up to launch his counter-attack, so I cut in with the only possible solution that sprang to mind and nodded at the plastic carrier bag he'd brought with him from the hotel. 'What you got in the bag, Scratch?'

He opened the bag and peered inside as if he had no recollection of what it contained. 'Just the things they let me bring through customs. Bananas, some dates, a few—'

'OK,' I said, 'so how about this for a plan? Stuff your face with some of those, and the rest of us can go where we want.'

'Brilliant,' said Alan and dived into the nearest restaurant without so much as a glance at the menu on the pavement out front.

Scratch continued to stare into his carrier bag as he considered my proposal, then agreed that my suggestion was probably the safest option and began to follow Alan into the restaurant.

I grabbed him by the arm before he'd gone a couple of steps. 'Hang on, mate. I don't think they'll be too happy about you eating your own food in there. Maybe you should stay out here and join us when you're done.'

'Yeah, fair enough,' he said and broke a banana off a bunch of half a dozen.

'You think they have vodka in here?' said Oleg, studying the pavement menu with his face six inches from the laminated card. His hip flask had long since run dry and he'd been deeply upset that our hotel bedroom hadn't been equipped with a mini-bar.

'I dunno,' I said. 'Let's go in and find out, shall we?'

The restaurant interior was tasteful but basic with more than enough space for the fifteen or so wooden tables, about half of which were occupied by chattering diners. Alan was seated at a table half way along the wood-panelled wall on the right and was already sipping at a large glass of lager.

'Glad you could join me,' he said without looking up from the menu he'd now decided was worth his undivided attention.

'Anything good?' I said, pulling back the red-painted wooden chair opposite him.

'Hard to tell. It's all in French.'

'Well, there's a surprise.'

'But do they have vodka?' said Oleg and planted himself heavily on the seat next to me.

'Depends what the French is for vodka,' said Alan.

'My guess would be "vodka",' I said and then flinched with embarrassment as Oleg clicked his chubby little fingers at a nearby waitress.

She was dressed in a white blouse and knee-length black skirt and was clearly none too impressed as she approached our table.

'*Bonsoir, messieurs, et qu'est-ce que je peux vous apporter?*' she said with the merest trace of a growl in her tone.

'Vodka,' said Oleg. 'Do you have it here?'

'Ah, so you are English,' she said, and this time her tone was more along the lines of "Ah, so now I understand why you're so fucking rude".

'No, I'm Russian. Do you have it or not?'

She visibly bristled, very possibly with the sudden

34

realisation that Russians can be just as obnoxious as the English. 'Dragon Bleu and Grey Goose.'

'Not Stolichnaya?'

'Dragon Bleu and Grey Goose,' the waitress repeated.

'Grey Goose then, and make it a double.'

She jotted the order on her notepad, then turned to me. 'And for you, *monsieur*?'

'I'll have the same as him,' I said, pointing to Alan's glass and attempting a smile that was intended to convey how ashamed I was of my companion's discourtesy and that I wasn't like that at all.

Judging by the sharp sniff and the way she flounced away from our table, I wasn't convinced I'd succeeded.

She didn't look as if she'd mellowed at all by the time she came back with the drinks and slammed them down in front of us, spilling some of my lager onto the paper tablecloth. I also noticed that there was an excessive amount of white foam at the top of my glass where there should have been lager. What she'd done with Oleg's vodka I didn't dare imagine.

'You want food?' she said.

We did, and all three of us ordered omelette and chips since omelette was about the only item on the menu that we recognised, and we were fairly sure that *frites* meant chips. Evidently underwhelmed by our choices of the gastronomic delights on offer, she didn't even bother to write the order on her notepad but made a tutting sound and sauntered off to the kitchen at the back of the restaurant.

'Is that his third banana or his fourth?' said Alan, looking past my shoulder at the front window. 'Any more and he'll start screeching like a chimpanzee and scratching his armpits like crazy. Mind you, he does that enough already.'

I swivelled round in my chair to see Scratch pacing up and down on the pavement, munching on a banana. There were two other people – a man and a woman – both peering in through the window and presumably checking out the place as they tried to make up their minds whether it was a suitable place to eat. They appeared to be in a lengthy debate about it and, strangely, kept returning their gaze to our own table. Moments later, their decision made, they came in through the door and sat side by side at a table at the far end of the restaurant and facing in our direction.

Out of the corner of my eye, I could see Oleg draining the last of the vodka from his glass and holding up his other hand as he was about to click his fingers at the waitress again. I took hold of his wrist.

'Please don't do that,' I said.

'Why not?'

'It's not very… polite. And in any case, it might be an idea if you ease off on the vodka for a while.'

Oleg scowled at me. 'What are you? My mother?'

'No, but I don't want to end up having to carry you back to the hotel, and besides, our job is to get you safely to England, and I don't want you dying of alcohol poisoning.'

'It would be a whole lot easier if he did snuff it, though, and what you thought you were actually being paid for,' said the voice in my head, and I couldn't disagree.

Oleg muttered something in Russian, then sat back in his chair with his arms folded across his chest like a petulant child who'd just been told, "No more sweeties for you, my lad".

'The apeman cometh,' said Alan.

I had no need to turn and see who he meant, of course, but I sincerely hoped he hadn't brought any of his dead banana skins in with him. For some reason, I didn't mind the smell of bananas themselves, but the *skins* made me want to gag.

Scratch took the chair next to Alan and plonked his carrier bag down on the table. From it came the definite stink of dead banana skins.

'You wanna put that on the floor?' I said, and he duly obliged.

'You know those two that just came in?' he said. 'I reckon they might be Russian.'

'And you know that how exactly?' said Alan.

'Well, I heard them chatting, and it wasn't in English or French.'

'Oh, so it must have been Russian then.'

'All I'm saying is it *sounded* like Russian.'

'OK, maybe Oleg could go and say hello and find out for sure. I mean, there can't be too many other Russians in Calais, so it might be nice for him to meet up with a couple of his fellow Russkies.'

'I do not think that would be a good idea,' said Oleg, still grumpy from being deprived of his next vodka.

'Why's that then?' said Alan.

'Because they might be here to kill me.'

I almost choked on a mouthful of lager. 'Kill you? What are you talking about?'

Oleg's smirk returned, and he laughed so loudly that several of the nearby diners turned to see what the joke was.

'Of course not,' he said. 'Whatever gave you such a ridiculous idea?'

'Er, I think you just did.'

Another laugh, but not quite so loud. 'Only my little

joke. You should not take me so seriously.'

Not take him seriously? Jesus. Given the level of mystery surrounding who Oleg Radimov really was and precisely why we were having to smuggle him across the Channel – alive when he was supposed to have been dead – my sense of humour had taken an extended holiday.

I glanced across at the two maybe-Russians. They were both in their mid to late thirties, and both wore almost identical black T-shirts under black leather jackets. The man had close-cropped dark hair with an unusually high forehead and a neatly trimmed goatee beard. The woman had shoulder-length bottle-blonde hair parted in the middle, a pale gaunt face with a jutting chin and prominent cheekbones and pencilled-in eyebrows.

They sat mostly in silence but occasionally speaking to each other from behind their hands and every so often flicking their eyes towards our table. The carafe of red wine they'd ordered remained untouched, their glasses empty. Something else that struck me as odd was that the man had an umbrella with him even though this was the height of summer and not the slightest hint of rain in the air.

'*There's something distinctly dodgy about those two if you ask me*,' said the voice in my head, and once again I had to agree.

'I need a piss,' said Oleg and struggled to lever himself up off his chair before half waddling and half staggering between the tables to the back of the restaurant.

I watched in trepidation as he came within inches of colliding with our waitress, who was balancing two plates of food on each forearm, and then barrelled his way through the swing doors beneath the sign marked "*TOILETTES*". Seconds later, the maybe-Russian guy was on his feet and followed him in, still clutching his umbrella.

'*I don't like the look of that at all,*' said the voice. '*You'd better go and check on Oleg and make sure he's OK.*'

'Me? Why me?' I didn't say aloud.

'*Well, I can hardly go, can I? I'm just the voice in your head, for Christ's sake.*'

What I'd meant was that either Scratch or Alan were far better physically equipped than I was to deal with anything that might involve violence, but they were busy bickering as usual and were seemingly oblivious to the danger signs.

As I got closer to the swing doors of the toilets, I heard a couple of shouts from within, then a dull thud and a shriek of pain.

I threw open the swing doors, and it took me a moment to take in the scene and several more to remind myself to breathe.

6

Holly Gilmartin checked her watch as she hurried along the damp tree-lined footpath on the north bank of the Thames. Wouldn't do to be late, today of all days. She'd only officially qualified to join MI5 six months ago, so why one of the top brass had summoned someone so junior was a complete mystery. And why not just meet him in his office? Why out here in the middle of a park that was little more than a stone's throw from HQ? It was also very likely to piss down at any moment and she kicked herself for having forgotten to bring an umbrella.

No doubt because of the imminent threat of rain, very few of the wooden benches that faced the river were occupied by tourists or office workers grabbing some fresh air as they nipped out to eat their packed lunches. Not that the air was particularly fresh in London at any time of the day, but the tide was at its lowest right now, and the mud of the riverbank was unpleasantly pungent.

Holly checked her watch once again and quickened her pace. Up ahead and set back by a few yards from the edge of the embankment was the memorial that Wyatt Bendix had described to her. Well, not Bendix himself. It was a memo from his secretary. In all of her brief time at Thames House, he'd never spoken a single word to her. Hardly surprising really since she was almost as low down the food chain as it was possible to be without actually having to clean the toilets. They'd passed each other in the corridor a few times and even shared a lift together, but without him so much as flicking a glance in her direction. At least, not as far as she was aware.

The man had a widely known reputation for what used to be called "having an eye for the ladies" but was nowadays more commonly referred to as being "a dirty old letch with wandering hands". Holly had heard from several of her female colleagues who'd had direct experience of Bendix's "accidental" bodily contact, but none of them had bothered to lodge a complaint. Given that they were all nearly as low-ranking as herself, who was going to believe their word against that of one of the Director General's inner circle? Besides, there was an unwritten understanding that allegations of sexual harassment were "not encouraged" within the close confines of the Service.

Holly was not affronted in the slightest that Bendix had not considered her worthy of even a fleeting appraisal of her feminine charms. Quite the reverse, in fact, and she was almost grateful for her unremarkable appearance. 'We should have called you Jane,' her mother had told her more than once when she'd been a young girl. 'Plain Jane.'

Over the years, however, she had gradually overcome this early battering to her self-esteem and had not only learned to live with her less-than-stunning looks but had even come to appreciate them. Her short mousey hair, dull grey eyes and almost sickly pale skin were – as if she cared – never going to win her any beauty contests. 'You don't make the best of yourself' had been one of her mother's other mantras as Holly had got older, but she'd always steadfastly refused to wear makeup of any kind. Apart from knowing that so much of that stuff was tested on animals, she had no intention of pandering to some idealised notion of how she should look.

As far as Holly was concerned, her lack of head-turning features could be positively advantageous. Besides avoiding any unwanted attention from the likes of Wyatt Bendix, her relative anonymity made her ideally suited to become a spy, which was one of a number of reasons why she'd decided to apply to join the Service in the first place.

Feeling the first tentative spots of rain on her face, she took the pathway on her left that led at right-angles away from the river and towards the monument. It was about thirty feet tall and twelve feet in diameter at the base, and the top half was shaped like the nose cone of a space rocket. Through one of the open arches at the base, Holly could see a man in a dark brown trilby hat gazing up at the underside of the pointed roof. Despite having his back to her, the man was instantly recognisable as Wyatt Bendix. Well above average height, he had the bearing of a guardsman on sentry duty and broad shoulders that barely sloped by more than an inch on either side.

'Miss Gilmartin, I presume,' he said without turning as she came up behind him. His voice was rich and plummy, similar to the upper-class accents of BBC newsreaders of old that Holly had seen on archive footage from the 1950s.

'Yes, sir,' she said, deciding against pointing out that she preferred "Ms" as a title.

Bendix pulled out a gold pocket watch from the waistcoat pocket of his three-piece charcoal grey suit. 'Spot on time, I see. Good for you. Been here before, have you?'

'No, sir.'

He spun round to face her with the glimmer of a thin, unconvincing smile on his lips. Behind the thick-rimmed glasses, however, his dense brown eyes told a different story, scrutinising her with a mixture of distaste and suspicion.

'Buxton Memorial Fountain. Splendid piece of architecture,' he said, spreading his arms wide like he'd designed and built the thing himself. 'Rather a fascinating history too. It was commissioned by an MP called Charles Buxton in 1865 to commemorate his father's involvement in getting slavery abolished in the British Empire. Originally stood in Parliament Square but moved here in 1957. Can't quite remember why now, but it created quite a hoo-ha at the time. No water from the fountain itself any more, of course. Pity really. So I expect you're wondering why I asked you to meet me.'

The sudden shift from the potted history of the Buxton Memorial Fountain caught Holly completely unawares, even though she'd been expecting him to get to the point eventually.

'Well, yes I—'

'Course you are. Course you are. Little job for you, that's all. Come along then.'

As he finished speaking, he swept out through one of the monument's arches, and Holly had to almost break

43

into a trot to keep up with him as he strode down the path to the embankment, twirling his rolled umbrella as if it was Charlie Chaplin's walking stick. When he reached the path that ran parallel to the river, he turned left and carried on for another thirty yards or so until he came to an abrupt halt by one of the wooden benches. He briefly scanned the surrounding area, then took a pristine white handkerchief from the top pocket of his suit jacket and carefully wiped the area where he was about to sit.

'This'll do nicely,' he said, and Holly sat down beside him, making sure that there was a gap of at least two feet between them and placing her black canvas shoulder bag on her lap.

'Can't be too careful in our line of work, eh?' he went on. 'Never know who might be listening in, even out here in the open, what with all the fancy technology there is nowadays. Should be safe enough here, though, I think. Didn't want to have our little chat back at HQ. Bunch of earwigging nosey parkers the lot of them. Still, that's their job, I suppose.'

Was that a chuckle of laughter or was he simply clearing his throat? Holly couldn't be sure.

Bendix banged the tip of his umbrella three times on the ground between his feet like he was bringing a meeting to order. 'So then, to business, and I'm sure I don't have to impress upon you that what I'm about to tell you is damn near as top secret as you're ever likely to hear. Understood?'

He tapped the side of his nose, which Holly noticed was riddled with a network of red and purple veins.

'Understood, sir, yes,' she said, then broke eye contact to gaze out across the murky waters of the Thames to the trees on the opposite bank.

The anxiety she'd experienced when she'd first received the memo instructing her to meet Bendix was as nothing compared to the ferocity with which the blood was now throbbing in her temples. She'd known fear on plenty of occasions before, and most especially during the often brutal periods of her training as an MI5 field officer, but Bendix was starting to scare the crap out of her. "Top secret as you're ever likely to hear"? What the hell was he going to get her to do?

7

I took hold of Oleg's arm and hustled him back through the swing doors into the restaurant dining area. Over my shoulder, I spotted the maybe-Russian woman jump up from her chair and barge her way through into the toilets.

Back at our table, the waitress was delivering three plates of omelette and chips. Scratch turned his head away as if even the smell of the food might set off an allergic reaction. Alan picked up his knife and fork with the gleeful exhilaration of a big game hunter who'd finally cornered his prey after days of stalking.

'We need to leave,' I said, keeping my voice as calm and measured as possible.

Alan's forkful of omelette froze half way between his plate and his mouth. 'Piss off, Max. I've only just—'

'As in we need to leave NOW!' Bugger calm and measured.

'Fine by me,' said Scratch.

Alan swallowed the chunk of omelette, rammed half a dozen chips into his gob and got to his feet, almost knocking over his chair in the process.

'How much do we owe you?' I said to the waitress.

'I don't know, *monsieur*,' she said, suddenly more bemused than grumpy. 'I will have to make up your bill.'

'Sorry, we don't have time for that.' I dug out a fifty-euro note from my wallet and thrust it at her. 'This cover it?'

The waitress screwed up her face. 'Well, the vodka is not cheap, of course, and then—'

I pulled out another fifty and tossed both notes onto the table. 'Nice little tip for you in there, I imagine.'

I still had Oleg by the arm, and I marched him towards the exit. Scratch followed with Alan lagging behind and clutching a fistful of omelette in one hand and a bunch of chips in the other.

'What's going on?' said Scratch as soon as we were out of the door and heading back to the hotel.

'Good question,' I said, 'and Oleg here has got a fuck of a lot of explaining to do.'

* * *

Not another word had been spoken between the four of us until we got back to the hotel. I was too bloody freaked out by what I'd just witnessed in the restaurant toilets and was wondering what the hell we'd got ourselves into. Oleg was probably working out what story he was going to give us, and Alan and Scratch were too busy munching on the omelette takeaway and a banana respectively to contribute anything more than the occasional grunt.

But now that we were back in my hotel room, I sat Oleg down on one of the beds while Alan, Scratch and I perched on the edge of the other, facing him like the grand inquisitors we were about to become.

'So then, Oleg,' I began. 'Do you want to start by telling us what all that was about back at the restaurant?'

Oleg shrugged and opened his mouth to speak, but Scratch butted in with, 'Hang on a sec. What "what" was all about?'

Desperate though I was to hear what Oleg had to say for himself, it was fair enough that I should first fill the others in on what had gone on in the restaurant toilets, but I stuck to the bare essentials. I told them that I'd thought that the maybe-Russian couple looked distinctly shifty, and when I saw the male one following Oleg when he went for a piss, I decided I ought to check that everything was all right. But the moment I stepped through the doors, I could see that everything was far from all right. The maybe-Russian guy was lying spark out on the floor with a small pool of blood by his head, and Oleg was standing over him with the broken end of a toilet cistern's porcelain lid in his hands.

'Jesus,' said Scratch and eyed Oleg with evident disbelief.

Oleg gave a chuckle and spread his palms wide. 'I wasn't always this shape, and in any case, you never forget your training.'

'Training?'

'KGB,' Oleg said, like it was the most natural thing in the world. 'Although it's not called that any more, of course.'

'Fuck me,' said Alan.

'Quite,' I said, 'but I think now's the time we get to hear exactly why we're supposed to be smuggling a bloody KGB spy into the UK?'

Oleg took a deep breath and launched into what I suspected was going to be a heavily edited version of the truth.

'Those two in the restaurant? They're not "maybe-Russians", they're very definitely Russian. They're either SVR or GRU agents, and they no doubt have orders to kill me,' Oleg went on. 'You noticed they had an umbrella with them? That's what the bastard tried to stab me with in the toilets. Probably had a tiny pellet of something like ricin in it. It's what's called a Bulgarian umbrella after one was used to assassinate Georgi Markov in London in the late seventies.'

'What, so the guy tried to stab you with his umbrella and missed?' said Scratch.

Oleg grinned. 'Smacking him over the head with a cistern lid rather spoiled his aim. Fortunately, I was ready for him, so as soon as he came through the door and I saw he had the umbrella— Bang! I'd had a pretty good idea of who the two of them might be anyway, and who the hell takes an umbrella into the toilet with them?'

'So you *knew* they were Russian agents?' I said.

'Not for certain, no, but it takes one to know one, as they say.'

'OK. So here's the sixty-four thousand dollar question. Exactly *why* were they trying to kill you?'

'It's their job.'

'That's not what I asked.'

'Very well,' said Oleg with a sigh that started from somewhere near his feet. 'But before I explain, is there any chance we could get a bottle of vodka from somewhere?'

'None whatsoever.'

There was a lengthy pause while Oleg considered his response, and when he spoke, it was in little above a whisper as if in fear that he might be overheard.

'As you now know, I am a Russian spy – or more accurately, *was* a Russian spy. As a young man, I was trained to be posted in Germany and Britain, which included many months of learning German and English so that I could speak both languages as close as possible to a native speaker. My most recent posting was in Berlin, and it was during my last few months there that I decided to defect. You don't need to know my reasons, and all I will say is that your British intelligence service has made me an offer which I found hard to refuse. Naturally, they would never have made such an offer if they didn't believe I had a great deal of information that they would find most invaluable. At the same time, of course, my Russian masters would be deeply unhappy if such information were to… fall into the wrong hands, which is why they are determined to stop me by whatever means possible.'

'Which is why all this cloak and dagger stuff having to smuggle you into the UK,' I said. 'And who we're actually working for is M-I-bloody-5?'

'Six, to be strictly correct.'

'Oh well, that makes all the difference, doesn't it?' said Alan, who stood up from the bed and began pacing what little area of the floor was available. 'I mean, here we are in a shithole of a hotel and a shithole of a town with a Russian spy who might as well have a sodding great target printed on his back. And tomorrow we're supposed to smuggle him across the Channel in a coffin while hopefully avoiding being caught in the crossfire when a couple of assassins try and waste him.'

'As a matter of fact, there could well be more than two of them,' said Oleg.

'Fucking great,' said Alan. 'That makes me feel a whole lot better.'

'I'm sorry, but that's the truth of it. And there's another reason for all this "cloak and dagger stuff", as you put it.'

All our eyes were pinned on Oleg as we waited for yet another hammer to fall.

'How do you think those agents knew where to find me? And why do you think my contact at MI6 hired the three of you to get me to the UK instead of using their own agents?'

Again we waited.

'Because my contact believes there's a very strong possibility that there's a mole within the British intelligence services, and he's no idea who he can trust and who it is that's feeding information to Moscow.'

8

It was a tight fit, but Antoine had done a pretty good job with Oleg's coffin, given the time available.

'I had to work most of ze night to get it ready for when you needed it,' he said.

The rest of us hadn't had much sleep either. After what Oleg had told us, we'd all stayed in the same room, eyes fixed on the door and ears pricked for any sound that might indicate the arrival of a pair of Russian assassins. Not that I had the slightest idea what we'd do if they did come crashing in with whatever death-dealing devices they'd armed themselves with. About the only weapons we had between us were Alan's nail scissors and Scratch's rolled-up copy of an *Allergy Monthly* magazine. Disappointingly, Oleg had none of those innocuous-looking 007 type gadgets that turned into a deadly weapon at the flick of a hidden switch. His wristwatch, for instance, was utterly incapable of emitting a laser beam that would cut a person in half just by rotating the bezel by a couple of degrees. According to Oleg, it didn't even keep particularly good time.

'This isn't very comfortable,' said Oleg.

He was lying flat on his back in the coffin with his hands clasped across his belly and less than an inch between each elbow and the sides of the coffin that Antoine had widened.

'It's not supposed to be comfortable,' said Alan. 'Coffins are generally made for *dead* people, and they're not gonna complain, are they?'

'To be fair, they *are* usually padded and lined with satin or something,' said Scratch.

This was true, of course, and Oleg's coffin was little more than a coffin-shaped wooden box. Any padding would have meant Antoine having to make the sides even wider, and besides, would have cost quite a bit more money.

'I've drilled some holes in ze sides so he can breathe,' said Antoine, and Alan muttered something that sounded like "That's a shame".

'That's great. Thanks, Antoine,' I said, 'but we really ought to get going, so if you could let us know what we owe you, we'll be on our way.'

Antoine pursed his lips and scratched his head. 'I don't know exactly. I'll have to work it out.'

He sauntered off into the office, and I followed, watching as he stooped over the desk and started tapping keys on an ancient adding machine that should probably have been in a museum. He clicked his tongue a few times and jotted some figures down on a scrap of paper.

'I'm sorry, but I cannot make it any cheaper,' he said, drawing two heavy lines under what was presumably the total and handing me the paper.

'*Bloody hell,*' said the voice in my head as I read the figure at the bottom of the page. '*Couldn't have made it any more expensive, he means.'*

Moments after I'd digested the amount with a faint gulp, I had a flash of inspiration.

'Listen, Antoine. You know the coffin we brought with us from England? Well, it seems we won't be needing it any more, so perhaps we could come to some sort of part exchange arrangement.'

'*Quoi?*'

'You keep our one and knock the price off what we owe you.'

Once again, there was a brief pause while Antoine pursed his lips and scratched his head. 'I'll need to look at it first and see what I zink it's worth.'

'Of course,' I said. 'It's right outside in the hearse.'

I turned to lead the way out of the office and almost came chest-to-chest with Alan, who was on his way in. His expression was one I'd very rarely seen on him before. Sheepish and even bordering on genuinely apologetic.

'Sorry, Max. Bit of a problem.'

'Oh Jesus. Now what?'

'I've looked everywhere, and I just can't find the bloody thing.'

'You wanna tell me what it is that you can't find?'

'His dick, probably,' said Scratch from over Alan's shoulder.

Alan ignored him. 'My sodding passport. I've gone through my bag, all of my pockets. Fucked if *I* know where it is.'

'Definitely fucked,' said Scratch. 'It means you'll just have to stay in France, I guess. Still, I'm sure there's a lot nicer places than Calais, and you'll get your wish to see Paris after all.'

'I'll clatter you in a minute if you don't shut up.'

Alan flicked him the finger but kept his back to him. 'Maybe I left it back at the hotel or dropped it in the restaurant.'

If Alan was thinking we could nip back to either of them to look for his missing passport, he was shit out of luck. Oleg's Russian pals had failed to kill him at their first attempt, but sure as hell they'd be having another pop whenever they got the chance, so no way was I going to waste any more time pratting about in Calais. The absolute number one priority right now was to get Oleg across the Channel and hand him over to Mr Mysterious or MI6 or whoever it was that wanted him. This was always assuming, of course, that they *did* still want him. I'd been trying the number Mr Mysterious had given me on and off for the best part of twenty-four hours now, but nobody had answered.

The question that remained, however, was how we were going to get Alan back to the UK without a bloody passport.

'I've got an idea that might work,' said Scratch.

Alan rounded on him, his fists clenched. 'I'm warning you, Scratch. If you don't stop with the—'

'No, I'm serious, unless you want to get stuck in France for the rest of your natural.'

* * *

Squeezing Oleg into Antoine's adapted coffin had been tricky enough, but getting two coffins to fit side by side in the back of the hearse was harder still. It was no great surprise that Alan had kicked up an almighty fuss about being shut inside a coffin till we got back to the UK, but he'd eventually been forced to admit that it was the only way of getting him there without a passport.

'In any case,' I'd told him, 'we'll be using the tunnel this time, so you won't be in there for much more than an hour, depending on how long it takes to get through all the customs stuff.'

I'd tried to sound as upbeat as possible, but truth be told, I was shitting myself at the prospect of getting caught smuggling what were effectively illegal immigrants into the country. Not just Oleg now, but *two* of them.

Half a mile from the Eurotunnel terminal, we pulled off the road into a lay-by. Oleg was already in his coffin as there was no room for all four of us up front. We'd left the lid off until now, and we'd allowed him half a bottle of vodka he'd insisted on to ease the discomfort. And now it was Alan's turn to play dead.

Scratch opened the tailgate of the hearse, and Alan stood gazing upwards, casting his eyes across the murky grey sky as if he was a condemned man that really was about to meet his maker.

'In you pop then, mate,' said Scratch, an encouraging hand on Alan's shoulder. 'Sooner you're in, the sooner it's over.'

'It's all right for you,' said Alan and began to clamber into the back of the hearse. 'You're not the one who's gonna be banged up in a bloody wooden box for Christ knows how long.'

'Yeah, well, it wasn't me that lost his passport, was it?'

Whatever Alan muttered in response was lost under Oleg's stentorian snoring.

'Jesus, he's asleep already,' he said, more audibly this time.

'Might not be a bad thing if he doesn't wake up till we get to Blighty,' said Scratch.

'As long as the customs lot don't hear him snoring.'

'Maybe the lid will muffle the noise a bit.'

Alan had bent almost double and had managed to climb over into his own coffin. Then he knelt down and reached over Oleg to take hold of the top end of the coffin lid that was propped up against the side window of the hearse. Scratch grabbed the bottom end, and together they lifted it into place. We all listened for a few seconds, and although the snoring could still be heard, it was a good deal quieter than before.

'It'll have to do,' I said, 'and we'll need to get a shift on or we'll miss our slot for the tunnel.'

With much grunting and groaning, Alan twisted himself round so that he was sitting in his coffin instead of kneeling. His own lid was leaning against the other side window of the hearse, and he grasped the two handles that Antoine had fitted to its underside.

'I hope he's drilled enough holes in this thing,' Alan said, and with another groan, lay back and pulled the lid down after him.

'See you on the other side,' said Scratch and slammed the tailgate shut.

9

The almost constant drizzling rain meant that Holly Gilmartin had to have the Mondeo's windscreen wipers switched on permanently. She'd found a lay-by off the main road from the Eurotunnel terminal which gave her a perfect view of all the traffic arriving from Calais, but she needed a clear windscreen to maintain visibility at all times.

According to Wyatt Bendix's "sources", her target was booked on the shuttle that was due to get to Folkestone at 15:55. This was her first real mission, though, so she'd found her spot and parked up nearly two hours earlier to make absolutely certain she didn't screw it up.

Bendix couldn't have been clearer about the purpose of the mission but somewhat vague about why it was so important.

'Oleg Radimov,' he'd said as they'd sat on the park bench overlooking the Thames. 'Russian spy who's decided to swap sides, and our chums at MI6 are wetting their pants over all the lovely intel he's likely to cough up. On the other hand, some of us MI5 bods are infinitely less enthusiastic about comrade Radimov's imminent arrival in England's green and pleasant land as we understand that he has certain *other* information that we cannot allow to be made public.'

Holly had asked what sort of other information he meant, but Bendix had been cryptic in his response.

'Let's just say it relates to a particular individual who has been a tad imprudent in their extracurricular activities,' he'd said and casually flapped a hand at the nearby Houses of Parliament, which was apparently as much of a clue as he was going to give her concerning the individual in question.

'But none of that need concern you, Miss Gilmartin,' he'd continued, edging uncomfortably close to her on the bench. 'The real crux of the matter is that Oleg Radimov has to be neutralised before he gets to blab his mouth off and before Six have him in their clutches.'

Holly took a cigarette from the packet on the dashboard and lit up. It was her third in the last half hour, but she was barely conscious of smoking any of them. She'd known precisely what Bendix had meant by neutralising Radimov, and she'd been trained in dozens of different methods and techniques, but she could never have imagined that she'd be ordered to take someone out on her very first mission. And to complicate matters, she was under strict instructions to: 'Make bloody sure it looks like an SVR or GRU hit. After all, the Russians will be pretty desperate to stop him spilling their precious beans, so their motive is a damn sight more obvious than ours.'

Holly took a deep draw on her cigarette and exhaled slowly through her teeth.

'Sorry, but do you mind if I open a window? It's getting to be a bit of a fug in here.'

'Be my guest if you don't mind getting wet,' said Holly without taking her eyes off the flow of traffic in front of her.

She heard a soft click and a whirring sound as the passenger window was fully opened.

Jonah Wilson was in his mid twenties and only a few months into his training as an MI5 field officer. From what Holly had heard, he hadn't been doing particularly well, so she was at a loss as to why Bendix had assigned such a rookie to her as her partner.

To be fair, Holly hadn't yet had any direct experience of how he was going to shape up if things got heavy, but it was definitely a mark in his favour that he was six feet tall with the physique of a heavyweight boxer. Not that she was expecting the job to involve anything quite so crude as down and dirty hand-to-hand combat, but it was best to be prepared for all eventualities.

On the downside, however, he was one of those people who couldn't bear silences that lasted for more than a few minutes.

'Shouldn't be hard to spot, I guess,' he said, less than sixty seconds after he'd asked to open the window. 'I mean, there can't be too many hearses using the Channel Tunnel.'

'Probably not.'

'Black one, is it?'

'Apparently.'

'Should be any time now, I reckon.'

'Uh-huh.'

'But what if they got pulled over and they found Rodikov?'

'Radimov.'

'Sorry?'

'Radimov. His name's Radimov.'

'Oh yes. Radimov. Anyway, they'll have him down as an illegal immigrant, so that'll be our mission well and truly buggered, won't it? It's not exactly going to be easy getting to him if they haul him off to one of those detention centre places.'

Holly exhaled a series of smoke rings towards the roof of the car. 'They've been told not to.'

'Eh?'

'Customs and border control have been instructed to wave them through without anything more than a quick once-over. From what I was told, the French authorities weren't very happy about it, but when Bendix had a word with his opposite number in France, orders were passed down the chain of command and the problem disappeared.'

'Oh, right. Well, that's a relief then, isn't it?'

'For Max Dempsey and his crew it will be, yes.'

'I expect they must have been bricking it.'

'Very probably.'

'Yeah, I know I would be. I dunno what the penalty for smuggling illegals is now, but I'm fairly sure that...'

Holly was aware that Jonah was still speaking but managed to tune him out by focusing all her attention on the whooshing sound of the wiper blades and continuing to stare through the windscreen at every approaching vehicle.

10

I could breathe again. We were out through the tunnel, and the customs people had barely given us a second glance. If they'd pulled us over, they were bound to have heard Oleg's snoring – muffled as it was – and would have carried out a thorough search. Well, not that thorough even. Less than half a minute to lift the lids of two coffins and find a living person in each one. I could have feigned ignorance, of course, and tried to con them into believing that the pair of them must have got in when Scratch and I were otherwise occupied. But even if they'd swallowed it, seeing Alan led away in handcuffs was never going to be an option. Oleg wasn't really my concern, and I was pretty sure that MI6 wouldn't have had any problem springing him from whatever hellhole he'd be banged up in. The real bummer with that, though, was it would probably have meant kissing goodbye to the second half of our fee for getting him here.

'Can I get out of this bloody thing yet?'

It was the third time Alan had asked the same question since I'd told him we were free and clear.

'There's a motorway services about three or four miles up ahead,' I said. 'Hang on a few more minutes, yeah?'

'Well, put yer foot down then. I'm dyin' of claustrophobia in 'ere.'

'You couldn't be in a better place if you do actually croak,' said Scratch, but Alan's response was a clear indication that he didn't appreciate the joke.

Minutes later, I took the exit ramp from the motorway and found as secluded a spot as I could in the services' car park. Even before I'd switched off the engine, Alan had the lid off his coffin and was already beginning to clamber out.

'Thank Christ for that,' he said as Scratch opened the hearse's tailgate and helped him out onto the tarmac.

I scanned the immediate area to make sure nobody was watching, although it was a bit late now that our very own Lazarus had apparently risen from the dead. None of the vehicles nearby were occupied apart from a dark grey Ford Mondeo, but neither the driver or the passenger were looking in our direction.

'Oleg's stopped snoring,' said Scratch. 'He's not gone and bloody died on us, has he?'

'One way to find out,' said Alan, and the two of them slid the lid off the adapted coffin.

There was an ominous silent pause before Oleg very slowly sat upright like a much shorter, fatter version of Bela Lugosi in one of those old Dracula films. He yawned, stretched and rubbed his eyes with the back of his fists.

'Have we arrived?'

'Welcome to England,' said Scratch, somewhat half-heartedly.

'Excellent timing. It seems I have run out of vodka,'

said Oleg and held up the empty half bottle as evidence.

'I could murder a drink meself after being cooped up in there all this time,' said Alan.

'Bit of grub wouldn't go amiss,' Scratch added.

'Sorry, guys, you'll have to wait,' I said. 'I want to get Oleg where he's supposed to be and out of our lives forever.'

'And where's that exactly?'

'Can't remember off the top of my head. It's on the sheet that Mr Mysterious gave me.'

'There's no way I'm going back in that coffin again. I tell you that right now,' said Alan.

'You won't have to. You can come up front with Scratch and me, but Oleg'll have to stay put till we get where we're going. In fact, why don't you two get him out of there so he can stretch his legs for a few minutes while I check out Mr M's instructions.'

As it turned out, this took considerably longer than a few minutes. The paper with all the details wasn't in the glovebox of the hearse where I thought I'd left it, nor in any of my pockets or my overnight bag. Eventually, I had to accept the awful truth that I'd somehow managed to lose the sodding thing altogether.

'What d'you mean you've lost it?' Alan snapped when he, Scratch and Oleg returned from their stroll around the car park and I made my confession.

'Says the man who lost his bloody passport.'

'Can't you remember what it said? An address or whatever?'

'No, Alan, I can't. Otherwise I wouldn't need the fucking paper, would I?'

'Maybe you could try phoning Mr Mysterious again?' said Scratch, speaking softly in his newly adopted role as peacemaker.

He'd also phrased it more like a question, so I didn't feel justified in jumping down his throat and reminding him how many times I'd tried calling the bastard but had never got an answer.

'Worth a go,' I said, failing miserably in my attempt to sound in the least bit positive, and my complete lack of optimism proved to be spot on. Nobody picked up.

'So now what do we do?' said Alan.

'What *you* do, Alan, is you shut the fuck up and let me think for a minute.'

I turned my back on the three of them and paced up and down beside the hearse while I scoured my brain cells for the faintest memory of where we were supposed to deliver Oleg. At one point, I even screwed my eyes shut and tried to conjure up a mental image of the sheet of paper in case the words on it might miraculously appear beneath my eyelids. They didn't.

'*There was a seven, wasn't there?*'

I'd been surprised that the voice in my head hadn't already popped up to give me a shitload of abuse for losing Mr M's paper, and now here it was and seemingly being helpful for a change.

'A seven?'

'*Part of the address, yeah.*'

'Oh, that's a great help, that is. So all we have to do now is find out which one of millions of addresses in the country that has the number seven in it is the one we want.'

'*Don't get pissy with me, pal. I'm not saying it's a street number. I'm saying the address included the word "seven", not the number.*'

'Seven?'

'*Seven.*'

'What, like in the name of a town or something?'

'*Yep.*'

The voice stayed quiet for a moment to allow me to think.

'Westbury-on-Severn, for instance?' I had an aunt who lived there, which is why it came to mind.

'*No. Severn's the river. It was definitely "seven" with no R in it. There was something about trees too.*'

'Seven trees?'

'*Not just trees. A particular type of tree.*'

'Birch? Elm? Pine? Oak? Fir?'

'*Oak! That was it.*'

'Seven Oaks?'

'*Sevenoaks, yeah.*'

I stopped pacing and made my gleeful announcement to Alan and Scratch that I'd remembered where we were supposed to take Oleg.

'And that's it, is it?' said Alan. 'Sevenoaks. It's a bloody big town, Max. So what do we do? Drop him off somewhere in the centre and leave it at that?'

'There were more specific details,' I said, 'but I can't remember them just now. Hopefully they'll come back to me, but at least we've got somewhere to aim for.'

Oleg protested vigorously about being crammed back in his coffin without having his supply of vodka replenished but eventually complied when I persuaded him that motorway services didn't sell alcohol and we'd stop at the nearest off licence or supermarket as soon as we found one.

As I drove the hearse out of the car park with Alan and Scratch beside me, I spotted that the man and the woman in the dark grey Mondeo still hadn't got out of their car but didn't seem to be paying us any attention. In any case, they obviously weren't the Russians from Calais, so I didn't give them a second thought.

11

I kept the hearse at a reasonably sedate pace as we headed north-west on the motorway, mainly to give myself a little extra time to think before we hit Sevenoaks. Scratch had googled it, and the town's population was about thirty thousand, so a very rough estimate meant something like ten thousand houses. If I couldn't remember the exact address that Mr Mysterious had given me, we were screwed.

On the bench seat beside me, Scratch and Alan weren't actually bickering for a change and were merrily chatting away with the occasional laugh thrown in. I was far too busy racking my brains to pay them any attention, although some of what they were saying must have filtered through the maelstrom inside my head, because something suddenly pinged.

'What did you just say, Scratch?'

'Eh?'

'Just now. What were you talking about?'

'I was telling Alan this joke I'd heard down the pub.'

'About?'

'Wheelie bins. You see, there was this guy who was

late putting out his bin for the dustcart, so when he heard it coming up the road – the dustcart, that is, and not the bin – he leapt out of bed and quickly wheeled the bin out onto the pavement. But because all he had on were his underpants, the—'

'That's it!' I said, not in the least interested in waiting for the punchline.

'What is?'

'I knew it wasn't just Sevenoaks. There was another word as well.'

'Oh yeah?'

'Weald.'

'Wheeled?' said Alan.

'W - E - A - L - D. Sevenoaks Weald.'

'So where's that then?'

'Somewhere near Sevenoaks would be my guess,' said Scratch and turned to his trusty Google again.

The speed with which some people could tap out whole messages with the tiny little letters on their smartphones had always amazed me, but Scratch was one of the exceptions. Apparently unable to use more than one finger at a time, and certainly neither of his thumbs, he was further handicapped by that finger being as thick as a Havana cigar. A variety of expletives accompanied the frequent punching of the delete key until he finally announced that Sevenoaks Weald was indeed only about three miles south of Sevenoaks town centre and was a village with a population of less than fifteen hundred. Approximately five hundred houses in that case. Not quite such a massive haystack to find our needle in, and I was sure there was another part of the address which I hoped might come back to me once we got to the village.

'Set the controls for the heart of Sevenoaks Weald,' I

said and floored the accelerator.

* * *

After we'd left the motorway, we still had about fifteen miles to get to the village, but the roads were mostly free of traffic, and we were making good progress. Something was beginning to bother me, though, and the voice in my head was equally rattled.

'Forgive me if I'm being a little paranoid here, but I reckon that black Skoda's been following us ever since we came off the motorway.'

The voice was right. The car had been keeping a distance of about thirty or forty yards between us, but if it *was* following us, the driver wasn't taking too much trouble to be discreet about it. In all the TV cop shows and movies I've seen – and there have been plenty – the golden rule when you're tailing somebody is to keep at least one vehicle between you and your target. The Skoda wasn't doing that. Perhaps the driver hadn't watched as many cop shows as I had, or maybe it was because of the dearth of other vehicles to hide behind. By far the preferable explanation, of course, was that it wasn't following us at all.

I decided to put my preferred theory to the test by using the time-honoured method of slowing down to little more than a crawl and then suddenly speeding up again. On each occasion, the Skoda maintained almost exactly the same distance behind us. Shit.

'I think we might be being followed,' I said.

Alan and Scratch twisted round in unison and looked through the back window of the hearse.

'You sure?' said Alan.

'Sure as I can be.'

'So who the hell is it?'

'Russians?'

'You think?'

'Dunno. They're too far behind to make out if they're the same ones that tried to bump Oleg off in Calais. And in any case, he told us it might not be just those two who are after him.'

'Looks like they're speeding up,' said Scratch as we hit a long, straight stretch of road.

I glanced in my wing mirror. The Skoda was now less than twenty yards behind, and the gap was closing rapidly. I put my foot down, but the hearse wasn't designed for racing and the next thing I knew, the Skoda was right alongside us.

'It's them!' Alan shouted. 'The same ones from Calais.'

Precisely *who* they were was utterly immaterial as my one and only concern at that particular moment was keeping the hearse on the road when the Skoda hit us with an almighty broadside. I fought with the steering wheel, wrenching it hard to the right with every ounce of my strength. It wasn't enough to keep the nearside wheels from mounting the grass verge, but enough to stop the hearse from smashing into the line of trees a couple of yards beyond.

The Skoda edged away to the side, and I managed to get all four wheels back onto the road before it slammed into us for a second attempt. The impact was marginally less, and this time I was ready for it and barely clipped the verge. Something else in our favour was that the hearse was a damn sight bigger and heavier than the Skoda, so as long as I kept doing what I was doing there was only a slim chance that we'd get forced off the road completely. The Russians were clearly determined to give it another go, however, but as they were creating an even wider gap than before – presumably to give themselves some extra momentum – an impressively large truck appeared round a shallow bend up ahead.

I was still braced for the next broadside, but the Russians must have hesitated, no doubt weighing up their chances of piling us off the road before being totally obliterated by a head-on smash with the lorry. Apparently, the truck's flashing headlights and blaring horn were instrumental in helping them to reach their decision, and the Skoda began to slip backwards. I have to admit that I was sorely tempted to keep pace with it so that the then inevitable and instant demise of the two Russian agents would get them out of our lives for good, but it took only a nano-second to consider the plight of the poor innocent truck driver, and I hit the accelerator hard.

'Bloody hell. That was close,' said Scratch.

I checked my wing mirror. The Skoda had resumed its original position of about thirty yards behind us. 'It's not over yet, though. They'll be having another crack at us as soon as there's another straight bit of road.'

'What's going on?' It was Oleg's muffled voice from inside his coffin. 'I've been rocking about all over the place. You trying to kill me or what?'

'*We're* not,' I said, 'but your two Russian pals are after us again.'

'They followed us from Calais?'

'Seems like it.'

'They must have fitted some kind of tracking device on our car. Probably when we were parked up outside the funeral place.'

'It's not a car. It's a hearse,' Alan muttered, but Oleg either didn't hear him or chose to ignore him.

'We need to find it and get rid of it.'

'Yeah,' I said, 'but not right now. No way we can stop till we've shaken them off.'

'How about this?' said Scratch. 'The next time they come alongside us, we smash into them before they can do it to us. Force *them* off the road.'

It was a possibility, but I wasn't entirely confident of the outcome. Still, it was the only plan we had, and I took a solid grip of the steering wheel as we rounded a bend and saw that the road ahead was straight for more than a mile and completely free of traffic.

'Hang on a sec. I've got a better idea,' said Alan and began to clamber over the back of the seat into the back of the hearse.

'What the fuck you doing?' said Scratch.

Alan didn't answer but crawled on his belly over the top of Oleg's coffin and fumbled with the latch on the tailgate for a few seconds before flinging it wide open. Not only could I see in the wing mirror that the Skoda had already started its run-up, but I could also now hear the increasing volume of its engine.

With uncharacteristic agility, Alan scrambled back onto the front seat, then swivelled round and took hold of the top end of the empty coffin. He waited a moment, watching as the Skoda quickly gained on us, and with a cry of 'Bombs away!', launched the coffin out of the open tailgate.

I was paying almost no attention to the road ahead as I stared at the mirror to see the coffin crash to the ground less than a dozen feet in front of the onrushing Skoda. Taken by surprise, the driver swerved sharply to the right, shot diagonally across the road, over the grass verge, and piled headlong into the trunk of a massive oak tree.

'Jesus, Alan, you're not as stupid as you look,' said Scratch.

Alan beamed back at him. 'Coming from you, that's quite a compliment, although I have to confess I had half a mind to use Oleg's coffin instead. Kill two birds with one stone, kinda thing.'

'What was that?' Oleg shouted.

'Just kidding,' Alan shouted back, although I wasn't entirely sure he was.

12

Holly Gilmartin swerved to avoid the coffin and dropped down a gear as she cruised slowly past the Skoda with its front end embedded into the base of an old oak tree, steam gushing from its mangled bonnet.

'D'you think we ought to stop and make sure they're OK?' Jonah asked.

'No, I don't,' said Holly and sped up again.

'Seems rather—'

'Seems rather what? They're almost certainly Russian agents, for Christ's sake.'

'How do you know that?'

Holly snorted. 'Did you or did you not just witness how they were repeatedly trying to force the hearse off the road, and do you remember me telling you that the Russians have their own reasons for wanting to stop Radimov?'

'Yes, but—'

'And would you not also agree that our number one priority right now is to make bloody sure we don't lose sight of the target we happen to be following?'

Jonah fell silent, which Holly counted as a

significant blessing. She needed some peace and quiet to be able to think.

She'd been surprised at the motorway services when two men had climbed out of the coffins in the back of the hearse and wondered if they were *both* Russian defectors. Maybe Bendix had got it wrong, but whether he had or not, his orders had been perfectly clear, so whoever the second guy was, he wasn't her concern. Oleg Radimov had been easy enough to identify from the photographs Bendix had given her and also from his description: 'Dead ringer for Danny DeVito if you ask me. Should have been called Danny DeVitov.' He'd laughed at his own joke, and Holly had forced a smile in response.

It was a pity the Russians hadn't been better at their job or her mission would have been successfully completed without having to kill anyone herself. Neutralise Radimov and do whatever you can to make it look like the SVR or GRU took him out. That's what Bendix had told her, so it would have been the perfect solution, but it wasn't to be.

Bloody amateurs. For a start, they'd failed to follow the golden rule of keeping at least one vehicle between you and the car you're tailing, and simply slamming into the side of the hearse was hardly ever going to work, given how much bigger and heavier it was than the Skoda. If they'd been properly trained, they'd have known that the most effective technique would have been to ping the hearse on its offside rear corner and force it into a spin.

Holly momentarily considered using the same method right now but quickly dismissed the idea. If Bendix had allocated her a pool car, then maybe she would have done, but the Mondeo was her own car and only a few months old. Even the slightest scratch would have seriously pissed her off.

The phone rang. Holly checked the screen on the dashboard. Bendix.

'Hello?' she answered.

'Sit rep?'

Straight to the point, eh? From the sound of background chatter and clinking of glasses, Holly guessed he was in a pub or restaurant, or very likely the bar at his golf club.

'Situation report?' Holly knew very well what he meant, but she hated the way they used so many abbreviations in the Service. Did a couple or so more syllables involve that much more effort?

'Correct.'

Holly briefly explained how she'd followed the hearse from the Folkestone Eurotunnel terminal but had no idea yet where it was heading. She also told him how she'd just witnessed another car trying to force it off the road.

'Russian agents?' said Bendix.

'Almost certainly.'

'Damn shame they bungled it then. Would have done our job for us.'

'My thoughts exactly.'

'Maybe you should keep after the hearse but sit tight in case the Russkies have another pop. But don't leave it too long, eh? If Six manages to get its grubby little mitts on Radimov, we're buggered.'

'Yes, sir.'

'And incidentally, I really don't give a rat's arse how you get it done as long as you achieve the objective.'

'Sir?'

Bendix sighed heavily. 'Collateral damage, Miss

Gilmartin. If there has to be collateral damage, then so be it.'

Then he hung up.

'What's he mean by that?' said Jonah.

'Collateral damage?'

'No, I know what that is. But what does he mean in this particular situation?'

'Basically that he doesn't give a shit how many people have to die as long as one of them is Radimov.'

'Like the three others in the hearse?'

Holly shrugged. 'Maybe, but who knows? Perhaps there'll be others.'

'Jesus,' said Jonah. 'But those guys are just a bunch of undertakers.'

'So they'll know all about death then, won't they?'

Jonah exhaled loudly, sat back in his seat and stared out of the side window.

He was clearly shocked by her callousness, which was precisely what she'd intended. It seemed to her that if her rookie sidekick was to have any future in the Security Service, he needed to wake up to the reality of the job sooner rather than later. Not that she had the least intention of getting any innocent people killed on this mission or any future one, and she sincerely hoped that the Radimov job didn't develop in such a way that it became unavoidable.

She eased off the accelerator to let a Range Rover overtake her, and at the same moment realised that the hearse was pulling off the road and onto a lay-by. Damn it. The lay-by was long enough that she might be able to stop at a decent distance behind it without attracting any attention, but she didn't dare run the risk. She was desperate to keep the hearse in sight at all times, but she had no other option than to keep driving.

Jonah was of a different opinion. 'What are you doing? Why didn't we just stop and kill the guy now? It's the perfect opportunity.'

'And I thought you were the one who was getting squeamish about collateral damage a minute ago.'

'So?'

'So we could have just left the other three alive to tell their tales, could we? And besides,' Holly added. 'You heard what Bendix said. Keep following the hearse and hope the Russians have another go at Radimov.'

'Bit tricky with their car wrapped round a tree.'

'Then we'll just have to be patient, won't we?'

'Yeah, I s'pose.'

What Holly had omitted to say was that killing the other three other men would have been well within Bendix's definition of collateral damage, so she was surprised, as well as greatly relieved, that he hadn't given the order right then and there. Blaming Radimov's death on the Russians was obviously a big deal as far as he was concerned.

Half a mile up ahead, she found a narrow farm track on the left and reversed into it. All she could do now was to sit and wait and hope to hell that the hearse had only stopped because somebody needed a pee break and it would pass by at any minute.

13

Alan said that if we didn't stop so he could have a pee in the next two minutes, he was going to wet himself, and Oleg was desperate to find the tracking device he insisted the Russians had fixed to the hearse, so I pulled over into the next lay-by.

While Alan trotted off to find a convenient tree, Scratch and I helped Oleg out of his coffin.

'Probably somewhere underneath,' he said and waved vaguely towards the underside of the hearse in case we didn't understand what he meant.

When he got no response from either of us, he used both index fingers to point to an area somewhere around his midriff. 'Well, I can't get under there, can I?'

This was undeniably true, so I turned to Scratch, who made much the same gesture as Oleg. He certainly wasn't fat, but his muscular proportions rendered him equally incapable of wriggling himself between the bottom of the hearse and the ground.

'So that'll be me then, yeah?' I said, grateful that I was only wearing T- shirt and jeans rather than my full undertaker's regalia.

I sunk to my knees, then twisted over onto my back with the side of my head on the tarmac and stared into the semi gloom. 'You want to tell me exactly what I'm looking for?'

'A tracking device,' said Oleg unhelpfully.

'Christ, Oleg, I think I'm aware of that, but perhaps you could be a bit more specific.'

'Anything that seems like it shouldn't be there.'

'I'm not a bloody mechanic, for fuck's sake. How am I supposed to know what—' That's when I spotted a black plastic box about the size of a cigarette packet attached to the chassis about a foot in from the edge. I took hold of it and pulled. It came away easily, only a magnet on the base of the device holding it in place.

Back on my knees, I held it out for Oleg's inspection. 'This what you're looking for?'

He took it from me but didn't answer straight away. Instead, he turned it over and over in his hand, carefully examining it from every angle, before dropping it to the ground and stomping on it a dozen or so times until it was utterly demolished.

'I'll take that as a yes then,' I said and pushed myself upright.

'They must have planted it when we were parked outside Antoine's and picking up Oleg's coffin,' said Scratch.

Alan returned from his "comfort break", zipping up his fly. 'What's with Oleg? Doing a little happy dance to celebrate his safe arrival in England?'

Scratch indicated the shattered remains of the black plastic box with the toe of his boot. 'Tracking device.'

'Shit. So that's how they managed to keep tabs on us.'

Scratch raised his eyes heavenwards. 'The man's a bloody genius, I tell you. A bloody genius.'

'Piss off, Scratch.'

'Right then,' I said, partly to pre-empt another prolonged bickering session, but mainly recognising the need to get Oleg dropped off and out of our hair as soon as possible. 'Now that we've shaken the Russians off, we'd better be on our way.'

'You don't think we ought to nip back and pick up the coffin?' said Scratch. 'It might not be too badly damaged, and it's worth quite a few quid.'

'And whose fault is that?' said Alan. 'Of all the coffins we had in stock, you had to go and pick a Highgrove Deluxe. It's about the most expensive one we've got.'

'Because I actually thought we'd be bringing it back with us, until you decided to lob it out the back of the hearse and very possibly trash the thing.'

'Whilst saving all our lives, you mean.'

On this occasion, I didn't have to intervene myself. The interruption came instead from the arrival of a marked police car, which rolled to a halt a few feet behind the hearse. Two uniforms stepped out. A woman with sergeant's stripes and a tall lanky guy who didn't look more than school age. They sauntered over to us. Both unsmiling.

'This yours?' said the sergeant to none of us in particular and with a cursory nod at the hearse.

'Yes,' I said, deciding to take it upon myself to act as spokesperson and partly to jump in before Alan or Scratch could say something stupid like: 'No, we fucking nicked it. What do you think?'

'And the coffin in the road back there. That yours too, is it?'

'No.'

'No?'

'No. In fact, we had to swerve to avoid it. Quite dangerous whoever left it in the road like that. Could have caused a nasty accident.'

'You didn't see it then?'

'See what?'

'The accident. Car left the road and slammed into a tree.'

'Oh dear. No, sergeant. It must have happened after we'd passed. We stopped off here a few minutes ago so that... Well, call of nature if you know what I mean. Were either of them badly hurt?'

The sergeant raised an eyebrow. '*Either* of them? Didn't you just tell me you didn't see the accident?'

'*I can't believe you said that*,' said the voice in my head, and quite frankly, nor could I.

'Er...'

'The car or the tree,' said Scratch. 'Were either of them badly hurt?'

The sergeant raised her other eyebrow to join its twin and aimed both at Scratch.

'You'll have to excuse my friend,' said Alan, reaching up to lay a gentle hand on Scratch's shoulder. 'I'm afraid he had quite a bad bump on the head recently, and he's not been entirely with it since.'

'Is that so?' said the sergeant.

'How about the people – or person – in the car?' I asked in the hope she'd move on from the total nonsense of the last few seconds. 'Are they – or he or she – OK?'

She hesitated ominously before answering. 'They were both very lucky, considering. If it hadn't been for the airbags, they might have been your newest customers. I take it you *are* undertakers.'

'Oh, yes indeed. Or funeral directors, as we're sometimes known.'

The sergeant grunted, then pointed at the lidless empty coffin in the back of the hearse. 'Off to pick up a body, are we?'

'Absolutely.'

'Needs all four of you, does it?'

'The deceased is an especially heavy one.'

'Well, we shan't detain you any longer in that case. Can't keep the dead waiting, can we?'

Was that the flicker of a smile? No, probably just a nervous twitch. Either way, she retraced her steps to the car with her partner ambling along behind, and we watched as they made a U-turn and presumably headed back to the scene of the accident.

'Jesus, Scratch. Were the tree or the car badly hurt?' Alan scoffed.

'I was only trying to dig Max out of the hole he'd dug,' said Scratch.

'Yeah, but if—'

'Never mind that now,' I interrupted. 'We need to get the hell out of here sharpish.'

14

The trees, hedges and fields on either side of the road that led to the village of Sevenoaks Weald soon turned into a mixture of traditional English cottages and the more utilitarian modern houses. I still hadn't been able to remember any more of the address Mr Mysterious had given me other than the name of the village, and according to my rough calculations, there were about five hundred houses to choose from. However, I did have a vague idea – a very vague idea – that it didn't include a street number and may have involved the word "cottage", but that probably wouldn't narrow the field much in a place like this.

I drove on, ignoring any side roads, until the houses began to peter out at what was the far end of the village. I parked the hearse next to a surprisingly large village green and switched off the engine.

'So now what?' said Alan.

'I need to think,' I said, already predicting what Alan's response would be.

He'd been annoyingly pissy ever since he'd claimed that being jolted about in a coffin had reactivated his old weightlifting injury, and he'd made everyone constantly aware of it by resorting to the padded neck brace which he always carried with him.

'You've had bloody ages to think,' he snapped, 'and you're still no nearer to knowing where we're supposed to dump Oleg. We might as well start knocking on doors and asking, "Excuse me, but is this the MI6 safe house and are you expecting delivery of a Russian spy?".'

'Or you could try phoning Mr Mysterious again,' said Scratch.

Based on several recent experiences, I knew it was pointless but called him anyway just to buy myself a few more seconds. Again, no answer.

'How about giving MI6 headquarters a go then?'

'In your contacts list, are they?' said Alan.

'No, but they must have a number for reporting suspicious goings-on or whatever. Imminent terrorist attacks? That sort of thing.'

Alan grunted, and Scratch took out his phone and started stabbing at the screen.

'Do you think I could get out of here now? My legs are dying.'

I glanced at the rear-view mirror. Oleg was sitting up in his coffin, his head twisted towards the front seat.

By the time Alan and I had gone round to the back of the hearse and helped Oleg out onto the road, Scratch had found what he was looking for.

'Doesn't seem to be a direct number for MI6,' he said, waving his phone at us, and then read from the screen. '"If you are living within the UK and you have information that relates to an imminent threat to life or property, please contact the police on 999 or the police Anti-Terrorist Hotline on 0800 789 321".'

'I'm not sure there's an imminent threat to life or property,' I said, although throttling Alan for being a pain in the arse was becoming a distinct possibility.

'What about the Russians trying to kill Oleg? That wasn't even just a threat.'

Scratch had a point, but it still wouldn't put us in touch with MI6 directly. Anyway, it was worth bearing in mind if push came to shove.

'There's a pub over there,' said Alan, somewhat irrelevantly in the circumstances.

We all turned to look, and there was indeed a rather fine country pub on the corner of the village green about thirty yards from where we were standing. I was about to say that this was no time for sinking a few beers and we needed to get on with finding the safe house when I realised that Oleg was scuttling towards the pub as fast as his little legs would carry him.

'OK, one pint and that's your lot,' I said, having to raise my voice at the backs of Alan and Scratch as they were already following hot on Oleg's heels.

I closed the hearse's tailgate and was locking up when a young woman with long auburn hair and wheeling a sleeping toddler in a pushchair tapped me on the shoulder.

'If you're looking for Mr Stebbings, you've missed the turning.'

'Pardon?'

'Mr Stebbings. Can't remember which house, but it's definitely Mount Pleasant Road. If you turn round and head back towards the main road, it's the second on your right after the pub.'

'Stebbings?'

'Yes. I mean, I knew he was on his last legs, but I hadn't heard he'd actually snuffed it.'

'Er, yes. Tragic really, but I suppose he'd had a good innings, as they say.'

The woman squinted at me and fingered the gold stud in her nose. 'I'm not sure I'd call mid fifties a good innings. Not these days anyway. Back in the Middle Ages maybe but not in this day and age.'

'No, of course, although—'

'Still, I'd best get on before Oliver wakes up and starts screaming his head off.'

With that, she was away, wheeling the pushchair along the edge of the village green, calling back over her shoulder the repeated instructions of where to find where Mr Stebbings lived – or didn't.

'*You should have asked her if there was an MI6 safe house in the village,*' said the voice in my head, but I ignored it.

I waited until I decided it was unlikely she was going to look back and see that I wasn't turning the hearse round and then crossed the road to the pub.

The interior was as promising as its quaintly traditional exterior with thick bundles of dried hops hanging above the bar and some of the tables consisting of old wooden beer barrels. Oleg, Alan and Scratch were sitting at one of the more conventional rectangular tables in the far corner, Oleg necking the last mouthful of what had presumably been a large vodka and the other two supping pints of bitter.

'Perfect timing,' said Oleg and held out his empty glass.

I took it from him, more as an automatic reaction than any great desire to buy him another drink, but I could do with one myself, so I went up to the bar.

It was early evening, so there was only a handful of other customers in the pub, and the barman or landlord was waiting for me with his palms spread wide and planted firmly on the top of the counter. Pushing sixty, he had longish, greying hair and a matching enormous moustache that was stained a brownish yellow in the middle. Heavy smoker, I guessed.

'And what can I get you, sir?' he asked with a beaming smile.

Definitely the landlord.

'Pint of bitter, please.'

'Any particular one? As you can see, we have an excellent range of some of the finest ales available.'

He wafted a hand over the half dozen hand pumps, each displaying a large colourful badge with names I'd never even heard of.

I jabbed a finger at the pump with the least garish badge. 'Pint of that, please.'

'Excellent choice, sir. Not too hoppy but just enough to get the old tastebuds tingling.'

As I watched him pour the pint with loving expertise, I wondered if the landlord of what appeared to be the only pub in the village would be the best person to ask. Surely he'd know everything about everyone's business and quite possibly about the existence of an MI6 safe house. The main problem, however, was how to broach the subject as subtly as I could without coming across as a complete nutter.

I started uncontroversially enough with, 'Nice pub. Good to know there are still some places that haven't been turned into bistros or gastro-pubs.'

'We've won awards, you know.'

'I'm not surprised.'

He finished pulling the pint and placed it in front of me. A deep red with the perfect amount of a firm white head. 'Come far, have you?'

'Not really, no. We're actually funeral directors.'

'Undertakers?'

'That's the one, yeah.'

'I s'pose you're here to pick up Jack Stebbings then.'

'Er, yes. That's right.'

'It was common knowledge he hadn't got long, of course, but I hadn't heard he'd finally shuffled off his mortal coil. Shame. Not that I knew him that well. Used to pop in here every now and again when he was still able. Nice chap. Always polite. Quiet spoken. Solicitor, I think.'

'I believe so, yes.'

'You always dress like that when you go to pick up a body? Save all the formal black stuff for the actual funeral, yeah?'

It immediately dawned on me that apart from Oleg in a dishevelled-looking suit, the rest of us were all still in T-shirts and jeans. 'Er, no. Just having a quick break, and we'll obviously get changed before we go and collect Mr um... the deceased.'

'Anything else?'

'Sorry?'

The landlord tapped the rim of Oleg's empty glass on the bar. 'Large vodka, is it?'

'Make it a single. Can't afford to have him pissed on the job.'

'Fair enough,' he said and took a fresh glass from under the counter. 'Russian, is he?'

'Uh-huh,' I said and saw a glimmer of a chance to find out what I really needed to know. Well, if there was an MI6 safe house in the village, there was a reasonable possibility it had been used for harbouring Russian defectors before now. 'Don't suppose you get many of his kind in here – or in the village generally.'

'Danny DeVito lookalikes?' he chuckled as he held the glass up to a vodka optic behind him.

I forced a faint chuckle myself. 'Russians.'

He set the glass down on the bar and added ice and a slice of lemon. 'Not that I recall, and I've had this pub for nigh on fifteen years now. Mind you, we do get a fair smattering of foreigners wanting to try out a "genuine English pub", but I can't usually tell whether they're Russian, Dutch or from Timbuktu.'

'*You're gonna have to be a bit more direct,*' said the voice in my head.

'Um… I don't suppose you know of any British intelligence people who spend time in the village?'

'*Intelligent* people?' I think he may have pursed his lips while he considered the question, but it was hard to be sure as they were mostly hidden under the thick moustache. 'Well, there's a university professor of economics or something, although I think he might be German. Then there's Sally whatshername who once made it to the finals of *Mastermind*, so they must be pretty intelligent. Who else? Oh yes, there's a—'

'Sorry, no,' I cut in. 'I meant British *intelligence*. Like MI6 kind of thing.'

'MI6?'

'Yes.'

'Oh, you mean Evans the Spy at Ivy Cottage.'

I could scarcely contain my euphoria at this unexpected breakthrough, but my elation lasted no more than about six seconds, which was when the landlord's deadpan expression suddenly collapsed, and he guffawed with laughter.

'Evans the Spy?' he chortled. 'Had you going for a moment there, didn't I?'

'Yes, you certainly did,' I said, unable to crack even

a hint of a smile at his hilarious joke.

'Odd thing for an undertaker to ask, though.'

I shrugged. 'Call it idle curiosity.' And before he could follow up with any difficult questions – as was virtually inevitable – I quickly added, 'How much do I owe you?'

I settled up and went back to join the others, handing Oleg his vodka and taking a large gulp of my pint. 'Drink up. We're leaving.'

15

The wooden bench was close to the road and faced inwards across the village green, but by turning her head through thirty degrees to the left, Holly Gilmartin had a clear view of the pub and an even better one of the hearse. Jonah Wilson was walking back from it now and smiling to himself.

'Job's a good'un,' he said as he slumped down next to her on the bench.

'You checked it's working?'

'Of course.' To prove it, he fished his phone out of his pocket and angled the screen at her so that she could see the zoomed-in map of their present location and the blinking red dot in the centre. 'No chance of losing them now, eh?'

Holly didn't answer. What was the point in encouraging him when she knew full well that he'd rabbit on regardless? On this occasion, fifteen seconds of silence was over the limit of what he could bear.

'Instead of a tracker, maybe we should have put a bomb under the hearse. Then as soon as they got back in – *boom*!'

'I thought you were against collateral damage.'

'I didn't say that. Not exactly.'

'So, all of a sudden, you're quite happy to blow three innocent people to kingdom come.'

'Not *happy*, no. Certainly not, but—'

'And you happen to have the appropriate explosives with you, do you?' Holly's gaze had remained fixed on the entrance to the pub, but her peripheral vision caught Jonah dropping his chin a fraction towards his chest like a scolded child. She almost felt sorry for him. Almost, but not quite.

'Also, if you happen to have forgotten, this operation is supposed to be *discreet*, and I don't know about you, but I would have thought that a bloody great bomb going off in an otherwise quiet country village is hardly going to fit that particular description.' Jonah's chin was still drooping, but she carried on anyway. 'And as I've already told you, it's rather important that we try our damnedest to make it look like it's the Russians who've taken out the target and not us. You see any Russians round here – apart from Radimov himself, of course?'

The silence this time lasted a lot longer than fifteen seconds and getting on for a full minute. Must be nearly a record, Holly thought.

'Poet roads,' Jonah said at last.

Holly fleetingly switched her attention from the pub to the half smile on Jonah's face. 'What?'

'Poet roads. It was in this DVD I was watching the other night. TV series from the 1980s or so called *Boon*. Really quite good in fact. Anyway, there's this scene in it where a young family's being evicted from their house, and there's two bailiffs sitting in a car to make sure they do actually leave. Then one of the bailiffs – the older, more experienced of the two – says something like, "Poet roads. I bloody hate poet roads. Always problems whenever I do a poet road." You see, the road they're in is called Byron Close, and he mentions various others like Tennyson Drive, Wordsworth Avenue and so on.'

Holly waited for some kind of punchline, but apparently there wasn't one. 'And this is relevant here because…?'

'Well, it's just that us doing surveillance like this just happened to remind me of it.'

'Not that we're in a "poet road" then?'

'No. Long Barn Road, I think the sign said.'

Jesus, thought Holly, the sooner we get this job done, the better, and I can forget I ever even met this idiot. And as if in answer to her unspoken prayer, the pub door opened and out came Oleg Radimov, who seemed to be needing a certain amount of coercion from the other three men.

16

It was almost a relief to be back at the funeral parlour – not the Calais one, but our own one. Having failed to find an MI6 safe house in Sevenoaks Weald, and therefore still being unable to offload our Russian defector, we'd decided to head for home and give ourselves some breathing space to decide what to do next. Besides, we had a business to run, and even though customers had been few and far between of late, we couldn't expect the skeleton staff we'd left behind to cope if there happened to be a sudden rush of corpses. As an undertaker, skeleton staff is probably not the most appropriate term to use, but that's essentially what they were. Sanjeev and Alice. Just the two of them.

The decision to keep Alice on as our mortuary assistant after we took over the business from Danny Bishop had been a no-brainer. In her mid twenties and with enough facial piercings to throw an airport metal detector into a hissy fit, she was surly to the point of downright belligerent and a veritable pain in the arse. She was, however, bloody good at her job at prettifying cadavers, often making them look better in death than they had been in life.

Sanjeev, on the other hand, had been a different matter altogether. After all, why the hell would we want to employ a guy who'd been about to help Danny murder us on top of a Scottish hill before Fate had intervened in the form of Scratch and a rifle, killing Danny and seriously wounding Sanjeev himself? Less than an hour after being released from hospital, he'd come to us and pleaded to have his old job back as an assistant funeral director. Perhaps not surprisingly, our immediate response was to tell him to fuck off, which was when he'd sunk to his knees with his hands clasped in front of him and his eyes flooding with tears.

'I wasn't going to shoot any of you,' he'd wailed. 'If it hadn't been for Scratch turning up when he did, I was planning to turn my gun on Danny and stop him. I didn't even want to be there at all, but Danny made me, along with all the other shit he got me to do.'

He'd then explained the hold that Danny had had over him and why he could also get away with paying him less than the minimum wage. Not only was Sanjeev in Britain illegally, but so too were his parents, a brother and two sisters, and Danny had exploited this knowledge to the full, threatening to report them all to the immigration authorities if Sanjeev didn't do *exactly* what he was told, whenever he told him to do it. In effect, Sanjeev had been Danny Bishop's personal slave.

By the time he'd finished pouring his heart out, the poor bloke was in bits, the tears beginning to drip from his chin, so I helped him up off his knees and said that we'd need to think about it and he should come back the next day to hear our decision.

In fact, he could have come back half an hour later because that's about as long as it took to make up our minds. It would have been a lot less than that, except Alan had some serious reservations, which he expressed at some length, and he became extremely loud and vociferous when Scratch accused him of being a racist. And what swung Alan over to our side in the end? Well, that was when I said, 'All in all though, Alan, he does make a bloody good cup of tea.'

And so it was that when we walked in through the door of "Max Dempsey and Partners: Funeral Directors", Sanjeev was busily polishing one of the display coffins and humming softly to himself.

'Oh, hi, guys. Welcome back,' he said, dropping his polishing cloth onto the top of the coffin and hurrying towards us. 'How'd it go?'

'Not without a few hiccups,' I said.

'You got what you went for, though, yeah? Do you need a hand bringing the body in?'

'No thanks, Sanjeev. That won't be necessary.'

'Oh?'

'Because he's right here.'

I jabbed a thumb over my shoulder at Oleg, and Sanjeev gulped.

'But he's…'

'Yes, we know. He's still alive.'

'I don't understand.'

'It's rather a long story,' I said, already wondering how much of it I was going to tell him, but none of it just yet. 'Been busy since we left?'

'Just the one. Alice is working on him down below?'

'Down below?' said Alan with the hint of a snigger.

Sanjeev didn't really do innuendo. 'Downstairs. In the mortuary.'

'There haven't been any… unusual visitors dropping in, have there?' I asked.

'Unusual?'

'Sort of… mysterious. Anyone, for instance, with black, greased-back hair and a pencil moustache? Light-coloured trenchcoat and heavy on the aftershave?'

'Nobody like that, no. I would have remembered.'

'OK. No worries.'

'"*OK. No worries*?"' said the voice in my head. '*Who the fuck are you kidding*?'

'Still,' said Sanjeev chirpily, 'I expect you're all gagging for a cup of tea. Anyone fancy a cuppa?'

We all told him this was an excellent idea. All except Oleg, who said he'd prefer vodka. Sanjeev took my advice and ignored him, then disappeared off into the storeroom near the front of the parlour, which was also laughingly described as a staff restroom.

'So what do we do with Oleg?' said Scratch.

I honestly didn't know, but it was getting late in the day, and I was too knackered to do much more in the way of thinking. 'He'll have to stay here tonight. You never know, Mr Mysterious would be expecting us back by now, and maybe he'll turn up and take him off our hands.'

Given that he hadn't picked up any of my calls since he'd first come to the funeral parlour and given us the job, I considered this to be a tad unlikely, but where there's desperation, there's always hope.

When Carla and I had divorced and sold our house, I'd moved in to the flat above the parlour, which the estate agent's blurb had described as a "spacious and elegantly furnished apartment". It was nothing of the kind, of course, but good enough for my needs. There was only the one bedroom, so Oleg would have to make do with the settee, which was at least going to be a hell of a lot more comfortable than being crammed inside a coffin.

'You want us to stay as well?' said Scratch. 'You know, in case the Russkies show up again?'

This wasn't a possibility that had occurred to me until now, and I rather wished that it hadn't. The two Russian agents who we'd forced off the road were probably in no fit state to come after us again for a while, although Oleg had mentioned that there may well be others. He'd also told us that there was probably a mole in the British intelligence services, which was how the Russians knew where to find Oleg in Calais. But even so, we'd had zero contact with anyone at MI6, MI5 or any of the other spook organisations, so the mole would have nothing to pass on about our current whereabouts. Sure, Mr Mysterious would know, but why would he drop us in it when it was him who'd hired us to collect Oleg from France in the first place?

'Thanks for the offer, Scratch,' I said, 'but we'll be fine. Why don't you and Alan head off home and get some kip? But make sure you're back here first thing tomorrow.'

'Don't tell me I've gone to all this trouble and you're gonna bugger off without drinking it,' said Sanjeev, appearing with a tray of steaming mugs of tea and setting it down on top of the nearest coffin.

17

That I hadn't slept well was a major understatement. Although I'd tried to convince myself that we were in no danger from Russian assassins for now, I'd still been worried shitless. Every unusual sound had sent my pulse rate soaring, and whenever I'd heard a vehicle pull up in the street outside, I was up out of bed and at the window in seconds. Oleg's now familiar cacophonous snoring hadn't helped either. Even though I'd closed the door to my bedroom and used a rolled-up towel to seal the crack at the bottom, the din still managed to find its way through and render any chance of sleep virtually impossible.

The fact that Oleg had had an infinitely better night than me was perfectly evident the next morning when I sat him down on the settee that he'd been sleeping on and fed him toast and coffee. His round, pink face was positively brimming with health and vitality, despite having knocked back a nightcap of half a bottle of vodka.

'No eggs?' he said cheerily as he slathered a generous layer of butter onto his third slice of toast.

'Sorry, no,' I said. 'If I'd known I was going to have a guest staying, I'd have done a proper shop.'

'Maybe next time then.'

He clearly hadn't picked up on the sarcasm in my tone, and as for "maybe next time", there ain't ever gonna be a next time, pal. During my sleep-deprived hours, I'd put together a plan of sorts which I hoped would get Oleg safely out of our lives forever. I wasn't at all certain it would work, but it had been the best my aching brain could come up with. If Alan or Scratch had a better idea, then I looked forward to hearing it, although I wasn't exactly holding my breath on that score.

'Do we have to have that on so loud?' I said, pointing at the television in the corner of the room that was blaring out some inane breakfast show.

Oleg waved the remote at the TV, but the volume remained much the same, so I carried on quietly sipping my coffee and staring blankly at the screen.

A man with a beard and a chestnut-haired woman in spectacles were sitting on a semi-circular red sofa and apparently having a good old laugh with some young bloke in a yellow T-shirt with "STAY WEIRD" printed on it. A minute later, the image on the screen switched to a woman in green wellies standing in the middle of a field and flapping her arms about like she was directing traffic in Piccadilly Circus during the rush hour. I couldn't be arsed to find out what it was she was quite so enthused about, so I got up to put the kettle on. If I was to get through the day with any functioning brain cells, a plentiful intake of caffeine was absolutely essential.

While the kettle was boiling, I went into the tiny bathroom to grab a quick shower, setting the temperature as cold as I dared. It didn't help me feel any more awake, and I'd just finished towelling myself dry when I heard Oleg's voice from the living room. I couldn't make out what he'd said over the racket from the telly, so I wrapped the towel round my waist and opened the bathroom door.

'What you say?'

Oleg was sitting forward on the settee and jabbing a half eaten piece of toast at the TV screen.

'It's him,' he said with the exhilaration of someone who'd just made some momentous scientific discovery.

'Him who?'

'The man I know things about.'

'What *things*? What are you talking about?'

The beardy guy and the chestnut-haired woman were still sitting in their same positions on the red sofa, but the young bloke in the yellow T-shirt had been replaced by a man in his mid fifties, immaculately dressed in a dark suit and blue tie. Dark hair greying at the temples and a razor sharp parting, rimless spectacles and a smugly supercilious grin. The caption on a red banner across the bottom of the screen read: "Peter Hayes-Edlington MP".

'I have evidence,' said Oleg.

'Evidence of what?'

He turned to me with a beaming smile. 'Big fucking scandal evidence, that's what.'

'You want to be a bit more specific?'

And he was.

According to Oleg, Peter Hayes-Edlington MP had been having a longstanding extramarital affair with a young woman who was less than half his age. This in itself was no big deal, of course, since there were any number of MPs who seemed to consider this sort of thing as one of the perks of the job. What *was* a big deal, however, was that his mistress was not only Russian but also the daughter of one of Vladimir Putin's best mates, and the Dishonourable Member had been pillow-talking some juicy snippets of top secret information. Although Oleg had no specific proof of this, what he did have was photographic and video evidence of the MP and Natalia Makarova in what he called "compromising situations". As far as he was aware, the British authorities had no idea about the affair, but if it were to be made public, the repercussions would be explosively catastrophic for the government and the intelligence services.

'Bloody hell,' I said when Oleg had finished. 'So is that what you intend to do? Make it public, I mean?'

Oleg gave me another beaming smile and paused briefly before he answered. 'Not necessarily, no.'

'I don't understand.'

He shrugged, and the smile drooped a little. 'As you're aware, your MI6 is very keen to hear what I have to tell them about my country's own state secrets, and they have promised me certain… rewards in return. But if I tell them I also have evidence of a potentially serious threat to *British* national security, perhaps they will decide to be a little more generous with their offer.'

'Or otherwise you'll sell your story to the media.'

'Hopefully it won't come to that, but blackmail is by no means uncommon in my line of work.'

'I'm sure it isn't, although I very much doubt that MI6 will let you get anywhere near the media before they put a bullet in your head.'

'This is true, but as I say, it's very unlikely to come to that. They'll be far too interested in finding out who it is that might be passing secrets to the Russians.'

'But what if—?'

I didn't get to finish the question because at that moment there was a knock on the apartment door and in walked Alan and Scratch.

'Is that toast I can smell?' said Alan. 'I overslept and didn't have time for any breakfast.'

18

I hadn't fancied another sleepless night terrified that the Russian agents might launch an attack at any moment, and Alan and Scratch had agreed that it was only a matter of time before they'd track Oleg down to the funeral parlour. I was beginning to quite like the guy, and I'd no wish to see him come to any harm, but equally I had no desire to get caught in the crossfire of a shootout. As far as I was concerned, the only solution was to hand him over to the police so at least he'd be safe, and they'd be in a much better position to pass him on to the security services than I was.

I bloody hate police stations, so I'd wanted to send Oleg with Alan and Scratch, but they'd insisted that I went as well since it was mostly my fault we were having to do this in the first place. Rather unfair, I thought, considering they were both going to get equal shares of the dosh we were being paid to bring Oleg over from France. Whether we'd ever get paid the second half of the fee was another matter altogether as we'd still been unable to get hold of Mr Mysterious or anyone at MI6, which was precisely why the four of us had piled into my battered old VW Polo and were now stepping through the door of the local cop shop as a last resort.

The uniformed officer behind the reception desk was tapping away at a computer keyboard as we approached and seemed totally oblivious to our presence.

'Excuse me,' I said after waiting patiently for well over a minute.

The officer raised a palm to silence me without taking her eyes off her computer screen, then carried on tapping. Her fingers were long and thin like a pianist's, and she wore a plain gold wedding ring. At a guess, she was in her mid forties, although the dark brown hair tied back in a tight bun made her look older.

Another long minute passed until she finally deigned to acknowledge us.

'Yes?' she said with a sigh that clearly indicated her annoyance at having to deal with members of the public when she had important keyboard tapping to do.

'Good morning,' I said brightly in the hope that my cheery greeting would go at least some way towards melting the icy stare she fixed me with. It didn't, so I carried on while trying to avoid eye contact as much as possible. 'It's about this man here.'

I thumbed at Oleg over my shoulder, and Scratch gave him a gentle nudge forward.

'What's he done?' said the officer, her gaze travelling the brief distance up and down Oleg's diminutive stature.

'Sorry?'

'Has he committed a crime or what?'

Well, technically he was an illegal immigrant, of course, but I wasn't going to tell *her* that without incriminating ourselves as people smugglers.

106

'Er, he's a Russian spy,' I said.

'A what?'

'A spy. Russian. A Russian spy.'

There was the faintest suggestion of a smirk on the officer's face. 'You're shitting me.'

Hardly a remark I would have expected from an officer of our great British police force, but I then told her a whole bunch of lies about how we'd found him wandering in the street and that he urgently needed to contact MI6 about matters of national security.

'Why doesn't he do that then?'

'He doesn't seem to be able to get hold of his contact, so we thought you'd be able to give MI6 a call and sort him out.'

'Me?'

'Well, not you specifically, but I thought the police had some sort of hotline to the security services.'

'I don't know about a hotline but—' She broke off as a door at the far end of the reception area swung open, and a tall thin man in plain clothes strode through on his way to the exit. 'Excuse me, Inspector.'

The man stopped in his tracks and turned to the officer behind the reception desk. 'What is it, Maitland? I'm due in court in half an hour, and I'm gonna be late if I don't get a shift on.'

'Sorry, sir, it's just that they claim that this man is a Russian spy and he urgently needs to get in touch with MI6.'

She nodded at Oleg, and the inspector gave him the same disdainful once-over as the officer had done a few minutes earlier.

'The Danny DeVito lookalike?'

'Uh-huh.'

The inspector checked his watch, then headed for the

exit as he spoke. 'I dunno. I don't have time for this right now. Get someone to interview him, and if his story checks out, give MI6 a bell.' He paused momentarily when he reached the glass door that led out onto the street. 'And whatever happens, don't let him out of here until you're bloody sure he's not carrying any of that Novichok shit. We don't want another Salisbury on our hands.'

With that, he was out of the door and gone.

* * *

The interview room was cramped and windowless and furnished with a cheap table and four plastic chairs, two on each side of the table. Oleg and I were sitting side by side, and after the best part of two hours, my arse was complaining bitterly.

First of all, we'd been ushered into the interview room while Alan and Scratch had been instructed to remain outside in the reception area, and we were then kept waiting for thirty minutes or more before another plain clothes cop entered and introduced herself as Detective Inspector Pickering. Another half hour passed as she questioned us with what appeared to be little genuine interest, or more importantly, *belief* in what we were telling her.

'Very well,' she'd said, gathering up her notepad on which she'd written Oleg's name and not a lot else. 'I'll need to make a couple of calls.'

That had been an hour ago, and when she finally came back into the room, she wasn't looking best pleased.

'So, I've been in touch with MI6 HQ, and nobody there has ever even heard of an…' She checked her notepad. 'Oleg Radimov.'

Oleg began to object, but the inspector shouted him down. 'Shut up or I'll be charging you with wasting police time! Now piss off out of here and go and play out your little James Bond fantasies somewhere else.'

She held the door of the interview room open as Oleg and I shuffled back out into the reception area like a couple of schoolboys who'd just been given a severe roasting by the principal.

We collected Alan and Scratch on our way out of the police station, and they were already firing questions at us as we stepped out onto the street. I had a question or two of my own that I wanted to ask Oleg, but first I was in dire need of a drink, and I led the way to the nearest pub.

19

Holly watched as Jonah Wilson made his way back from the ancient-looking VW Polo, grinning like the idiot he was. And not just walking either but walking… jauntily.

Christ almighty, she thought, could this guy do *anything* that didn't draw attention to himself? Any minute now and he'll start swinging round a lamp post like he's Gene Kelly in *Singin' in the Rain*. The word "covert" was clearly not in his vocabulary.

He flung open the door of Holly's Mondeo and flopped down onto the passenger seat. 'Hey, I'm getting good at this.'

Holly took a last drag on her cigarette and flicked it out of the open window. 'At what exactly?'

'Fixing tracking devices,' said Jonah as if this was another major triumph he deserved a medal for.

'Yeah, that's definitely one for the CV.'

Holly looked past his stupidly grinning face and resumed her surveillance of the main entrance to the police station on the opposite side of the street.

There was silence for almost twenty seconds before

Jonah spoke again. 'Not really what I signed up for, this isn't.'

'Oh yeah?' She had no wish to encourage him with a response but was fully aware that he'd carry on blathering whether she answered him or not.

'All this sitting around. All this watching and waiting. Bit bloody boring, isn't it?'

'It's called surveillance, and in case nobody mentioned it before, it's pretty much what the intelligence agencies do for most of the time.'

'Yes, I know but—'

'So what, may I ask, *did* you sign up for? The fast cars? The all expenses paid jaunts to distant lands? The getting laid by stunningly beautiful women every other night?'

'Course not. All I'm saying is that I thought there might be a little more... action involved. And that's another thing. It might help a bit if I knew a little more about why we're after this Radimov bloke in the first place. So far, you've told me diddly squat about who he is or why we have to kill him or why the Russians also want him dead.'

'You ever hear the phrase "need to know basis"? I'll tell you what you need to know if and when you need to know it.'

'Can't you even tell me what—'

This time, Jonah was interrupted by Holly's phone ringing. She checked the screen on her dashboard. Bendix wanting another "sit rep", she assumed.

'Bendix here. Any news?'

Oh, not an actual "sit rep" then.

'Still surveilling the target. He's currently inside a police station with the men from the funeral parlour.'

'What the fuck is he doing in a police station? Not

been arrested, has he?'

'Not as far as I know. Seemed to go in voluntarily with the others.'

'Why the hell would he do that? He's a bloody illegal immigrant, for Christ's sake.'

'Don't know, sir, but I very much doubt he's turning himself in as an illegal.'

'Oh, you do, do you?'

There wasn't much Holly could say to that, so she sat through a lengthy pause while she mentally pictured Bendix's face glowing gammon red and the strong possibility of steam coming out of his ears.

'Are you alone?' he said at last.

'I'm in the car with Wilson.'

'Well, tell him to take a hike. I need to speak to you in private.'

Holly turned to Jonah and nodded towards the passenger door. He returned her gaze momentarily, then got out of the car, muttering, 'Oh great. Here we go again', before slamming the door so hard that the Mondeo rocked slightly on its suspension.

'Jesus!' said Bendix. 'Does he always slam doors like that? Damn near deafened me.'

'Only when he's in a mood, sir.'

'In a mood? What's he got to be in a mood about?'

'It's because I've hardly told him anything about why we're after Radimov.'

'Good. Make sure you keep it that way.'

Once again, Holly decided this remark didn't require a response, and she didn't have to wait long before Bendix carried on with, 'I've got an update for you based on new information that has only just come to light. What it boils down to is that Radimov is very likely to be in possession of physical evidence against the person whose sorry arse we're trying to protect. If that's so, he's either got it on him or he's stashed it somewhere safe. It is therefore *essential* – and I cannot stress the word strongly enough – that you recover this evidence *before* neutralising the bastard. Do I make myself clear?'

'Yes, sir. Perfectly clear,' said Holly, already wondering how she was going to find this evidence – which may or may not exist – when it had so far proved next to impossible to take Radimov out cleanly as originally instructed. 'Any idea what *sort* of evidence I'm looking for?'

'Kompromat, Miss Gilmartin. Compromising material. Photos? Videos? Anything that constitutes hard evidence of our naughty Member of Parliament *in flagrante delicto* with his Russian floozy.' Bendix chuckled. '"Hard" evidence, eh? Rather an apposite choice of words, wouldn't you say?'

Holly wouldn't, but said 'Quite' anyway.

'So keep me updated as soon as there are any developments, yes?'

'Certainly, sir.'

'There's a good girl.'

The line went dead.

'Prick,' said Holly, but at least she'd gleaned a bit more detail about her assignment. Until now, Bendix hadn't let on whether it was an MP or a member of the House of Lords who she was supposed to be protecting from Radimov. Nor had he specifically mentioned an affair and that the woman involved was Russian.

Pondering the possible implications of this new information, she took a cigarette from the packet on top of the dashboard and slotted it between her lips. But before she had a chance to light it, she saw the door of the police station open and Radimov and his undertaker pals spill out onto the pavement.

One of them – Dempsey – seemed to be in quite a hurry, leaving the other three men in his wake as he legged it up the street. But instead of stopping at their car, he carried straight on and then came to a halt at a scruffy looking pub on the corner. Moments later, all four of them had disappeared inside.

Holly got out of the Mondeo and spotted Jonah leaning with his back against a nearby wall, his arms folded across his chest and staring sullenly at the ground between his feet.

'When you've quite finished feeling sorry for yourself, perhaps you could get back to doing your job and keep an eye on the pub.'

'Pub?' Jonah looked up and down the street. 'The one on the corner, you mean?'

'Correct. And if you'd been paying the slightest bit of attention, you'd know that Radimov and his escort have just gone inside.'

'Oh, OK.'

'And call me if anything happens.'

'Like?'

'Like them coming out again?'

'So where will you be?'

This was turning out to be her day for not answering stupid questions, thought Holly, as she was already half way across the street and very obviously making for the police station.

The uniformed officer behind the reception desk was busily tapping away on her computer keyboard, and her only response to Holly's 'Excuse me' was to raise a do-not-disturb palm at her. Holly was in no mood for waiting, so she pulled out her Security Service warrant card and thrust it in front of the officer's eyes, obscuring her view of the computer monitor.

Having briefly examined the warrant card, the officer's fingers froze on the keyboard, and she eyeballed Holly with undisguised irritation. 'Yes?'

'The four men that just left,' said Holly. 'What did they want?'

'Claimed that one of them was a Russian spy. The short, fat one. Wanted us to hand him over to MI6.'

'And?'

'Apparently, they'd never heard of him.'

'MI6?'

'Yes.'

'You sure about that?'

The officer shrugged. 'So I was told.'

'By?'

'What?'

Holly's patience was already hanging by a thread. 'Who was it that told you MI6 hadn't heard of him?'

'The inspector who interviewed him. DI Pickering.'

'OK, I'll need to talk to them. Now.'

The officer picked up the receiver of one of the three telephones on the reception desk. 'I'll see if she's available.'

'She's got ten seconds to *make* herself available.'

Holly didn't have time to even start trying to figure out what the hell was going on, and in particular, why Six had denied all knowledge of Radimov, because her mobile rang just as her brain began the unscrambling process.

'Hello. It's Jonah. Can you hear me? Over.'

'Yes, I can hear you, and this is a mobile phone, not a fucking walkie-talkie.'

'Shit. Yes, course it is. Sorry about that.'

'You have something important to tell me or is this a social call?'

'Radimov and the other three have come back out of the pub.'

'Already?'

'Now they're getting into their car. You think I should follow them?'

'Stay where you are. You put a tracker on it, remember?'

'Sure.'

Holly's conversation with DI Pickering took less than two minutes. That was as long as it took for the detective inspector to confirm that she'd contacted MI6 and that they had no knowledge of anyone by the name of Radimov, and nor were they expecting a defecting Russian spy any time soon.

Whoever the DI had spoken to might well have been lying, of course. It wouldn't have been the first time that the intelligence services had withheld information from the plods, and especially in cases as hush-hush as this one clearly was. But even so, Bendix had been adamant that MI6 were champing at the bit to get their hands on Radimov, so why had they still not picked him up?

Holly had already pulled out her phone to call him as she left the police station, but Jonah was in her face as soon as she stepped out onto the pavement.

'You know I told you about them coming out of the pub and getting in their car?' he said. 'Well, I reckon they might have been being followed.'

It wasn't often that Holly had to wait for him to carry on with his prattling, so she raised an eyebrow at him until he did.

'Two people on a motorbike. Tore off after them as

soon as they left.'

'Coincidence?'

'Could be, although I'd noticed them hanging around earlier not far from the car when I went to fit the tracker.'

Holly asked him if he'd got the registration number of the bike, but he said that it had only occurred to him after it had disappeared round the corner.

What a surprise, she thought, but if Jonah was right, then it was a fair bet it was the Russians again. But the goalposts had shifted now. No longer could she hope that they would do her job for her and eliminate Radimov. First, she had to make sure that any incriminating evidence he might have didn't fall into the wrong hands. She also needed to contact Bendix and find out what the hell MI6 were playing at. Right now, though, the priority was to get after the motorbike and stop Radimov having his brains blown out.

20

I'd changed my mind about getting a drink at the
nearest pub after we left the cop shop. The place was a
complete horror show. I mean, I've downed a few pints
in some pretty grim dives in my time, but even I have
my limits. Christ, we'd have needed hazmat suits if
we'd stayed a minute longer than we did. The pub stank
like a long neglected public toilet with the added
aromas of stale sweat, rotting fish and, rather bizarrely,
burning rubber. Most of the furniture looked as if it had
been recently retrieved from a skip, and the walls and
ceiling were as nicotine-stained as my chain-smoking
granddad's fingers. And was that really a patch of dried
blood over in the corner or where somebody had once
smashed a glass of tomato juice?

As for the clientele, every one of them fell abruptly
silent, and fifteen or so pairs of eyes swung in our
direction, not unlike a scene in one of those Western
movies when a tall dark stranger walks into a saloon
with a pearl-handled pistol on each hip. Apart from a
couple of old guys sitting near to the door, the rest of
the customers were variously dressed in Ben Sherman

shirts and Crombie coats, and most wore the legs of their jeans rolled up to better display their lovingly polished Doc Marten's boots. And as if their clothing wasn't enough of a clue, their closely shaven heads and the occasionally visible swastika tattoo absolutely nailed it.

'*Fucking skinheads*!' yelled the voice in my head. '*This isn't so much a pub as the AGM of the British fucking National Party.*'

Time to leave, I agreed. The only trouble was that Oleg probably had no idea what a skinhead was and didn't seem to give a toss that the place was a potential health hazard as long as he got his vodka levels topped up. Accordingly, he was already setting off towards the bar when I grabbed him by the arm and frogmarched him out of the door.

On the way back to the car, I had every intention of finding another pub that didn't cause havoc with my osmophobia and just as importantly, if not more so, wasn't stuffed full of fascist scumbags. By the time we'd driven off, however, it appeared that I'd lost my urgent need for alcohol so decided to knock the pub plan on the head altogether. After what we'd been told at the police station, I was determined to get some answers out of Oleg while he was at least relatively sober.

I was driving, and I pulled over at the earliest opportunity so I could swap with Alan and sit next to Oleg in the back of the car. I wanted to be able to look into his eyes to get a better idea of whether he was bullshitting me or not.

'So then, Oleg, what's the story?' I said as Alan rejoined the steady flow of traffic.

'Story?'

'The one about MI6 never having heard of you, your so-called defection and all the top secret shit you're supposed to pass on to them.'

'Clearly, they must be lying.'

'Oh, really? And why would they do that?'

'I've no idea, except that this is all so top secret that they don't want anyone else to know, including your splendid British police force.'

It was certainly plausible, but I needed to know for sure that Oleg was really who he said he was if we were to keep putting our own lives on the line to keep him safe.

'*You could always take him back to the basement at the funeral parlour and torture the bugger till he coughs up the truth,*' said the voice in my head, but there was no way that was going to happen.

'Bloody bikers,' said Alan, scowling into his wing mirror. 'Tryin' to get the jump on us when the lights change, I s'pose.'

He'd brought the car to a halt at a set of traffic lights, and I shifted my focus from Oleg's eyes to look past him at the motorcycle that had pulled up close to us on our right. The bike was large and black, and both riders were dressed identically in black leather jackets and black full-face helmets fitted with black tinted visors.

'I wouldn't fancy our chances if we tried to burn 'em off,' I said and was about to ask Oleg my next question when I realised that the pillion passenger was staring straight into the back of our car and was unzipping their jacket.

Call it intuition or simply a growing sense of paranoia based on recent experiences, but I had a very bad feeling indeed about what might be coming next.

'Get down!' I shouted and forced Oleg down in his

seat so his head was below the window. Then I flung myself backwards with the top half of my body as flat as possible on the back seat.

Even from this position, I could see the gun in the pillion passenger's hand and that they were using their other hand to open the car door.

Before the gap was more than an inch, I launched the soles of both my feet at the door, ramming it open as far as it would go. Judging by the muffled cry of pain from beneath the passenger's helmet, it must have caught them a jarring whack to the leg – or possibly the knee – and judging by the "*phut!*" sound, the silenced weapon had fired a round harmlessly into the air.

Seemingly undeterred, the biker tried again but with the same result, except without the gunshot this time. At the third attempt, a gloved hand took hold of the edge of the door and held it open while the business end of the pistol made its appearance.

I heard Scratch shout, 'Floor it, Alan!', and the car shot forward and then made an immediate ninety degree turn to the left. Thrown around as I was on the back seat, it was undeniably preferable to having a bullet in my head.

Once the car had straightened up again, I checked on Oleg. He was fine apart from being partly wedged between the front and back seats.

'It seems that they left something behind,' he said and retrieved a silenced semi-automatic from somewhere in his groin area. 'Grach MP 443. Russian standard issue. The doorframe must have knocked it out of the shooter's hand when Alan took off.'

'Christ, Oleg. Watch where you're pointing it,' I said when he gave me a too-close-for-comfort view of the muzzle. 'And make sure the bloody safety catch is on.'

'OK, OK, but help me back onto the seat, will you? I appear to be rather stuck.'

'I should stay where you are if I were you,' said Alan, his eyes on the rear-view mirror.

I twisted round to look through the back window. For an old banger, the Polo still had plenty of poke in it but nowhere near enough to outpace the bike, which was gaining on us fast. Still, what were they planning to do now that they'd lost their gun? Run us off the road? Hardly.

Scratch must have read my mind. 'I guess we can't assume that they've only got the one weapon on them.'

Thanks for that, Scratch.

21

The old VW Polo was the first to stop at the traffic lights, and Holly edged her Mondeo a little to the right to get a better view. There were four other cars between her and the Polo – four cars and a motorcycle with two black-clad riders on board and directly behind it. Not that it stayed there for long. Seconds later, the bike pulled alongside the Polo and the pillion passenger took out a gun and began to open the back door. As they did so, the door flew outwards and smashed into the passenger's leg. They tried again with the same result, but on the third attempt they managed to hold the door open and thrust the gun inside.

Holly flipped open the glove compartment and reached for her own weapon, but at the same moment the traffic lights had barely changed from red to red and amber when the Polo shot forward and hung a left. The bike followed, but the vehicles in front of her waited obediently for the lights to go green. All of them went straight on, so she had a clear run after the Polo and the bike.

The Mondeo wasn't great on acceleration, but the

oncoming traffic prevented the motorcycle from pulling alongside the Polo, so she soon caught up with it. Without dropping her speed, she rear-ended the bike and sent it slithering on its side diagonally across the road towards the pavement. Both riders followed suit.

'What the hell you do that for?' Jonah shrieked as Holly slammed on the brakes and hit the switch for the hazard lights. 'They were gonna kill Radimov.'

'New information. We need him alive for now. That's all you need to know.'

Holly was already out of the car when Jonah started his now familiar bleating about being kept in the dark, and she sauntered over to the unseated riders. One was sitting up and massaging their knee, and the other was on their side and slowly raising themself up onto their elbow.

'Sorry about that,' said Holly, looking down at them with a fixed smile. 'I was on the phone and didn't see you till it was too late. You OK?'

The biker who was sitting took off their helmet and shook loose their shoulder-length dyed blonde hair. A woman in her mid to late thirties with prominent cheekbones and pencilled-in eyebrows. 'Stupid bitch. You could haff killed us.'

Holly had assumed that they must be Russians, and the accent went a long way to confirm it.

'Weapons, please,' she said and pointed her semi-automatic at the woman's chest, making sure that the gun was out of sight of any passing rubberneckers.

'I haff no weapon.'

'So how about you?' said Holly.

There was a grunt of pain as the other biker forced themself up into a sitting position on the kerb and removed their helmet. Of a similar age to the woman, he had close-cropped dark hair with a neatly trimmed goatee beard. His unusually high forehead featured a three-inch cut held together by a series of butterfly stitches, and there was a band aid over the bridge of his nose.

'My, haven't you been in the wars,' said Holly. 'Car smash, was it?'

The man muttered something in a language which she instantly identified as Russian and also as being extremely impolite. She repeated her request to hand over his weapon – in Russian this time – and he slowly unzipped his leather jacket. Following Holly's instructions, he used only his forefinger and thumb to pull out a semi-automatic and toss it towards her feet.

'Who the fuck are you?' he said and winced again as he shifted his position.

Holly stooped to pick up his gun and slipped it into her shoulder bag. 'Oh, if I told you that, I really would have to kill you.' She paused for a beat, then beamed a grin at him. 'Ha ha. Just kidding. British Security Service. MI5. And you are?'

'Vot?' said the woman.

'SVR? GRU?'

'Vot?'

'Russian spies?'

'Vot?'

Holly was reminded of the scene in *Pulp Fiction* where Samuel L. Jackson's character, Jules, is interrogating a guy who keeps saying "What?" in answer to his questions until Jules loses patience and shoots him in the arm. Tempting though it was, she held back and instead told them to get into her car – one in the driver's seat and one in the passenger's seat. That way, she could sit in the back with her gun on them while she had a little chat.

She had no intention of letting Jonah hear any of it, though, and once the Russians were inside the car, she turned to him and told him to pick up the bike and move it off the road and onto the pavement. But no sooner had Jonah begun to spout his inevitable protestations than she heard a car engine firing up behind her, and she knew exactly whose car it was.

She spun round as the Mondeo leapt forward.

"Fuuuuccckkk!' she yelled and instinctively aimed her gun at the rapidly retreating car before another, more materialistic, impulse took over. Shit, this was her own car and only a few months old without so much as a scratch on it. She swore again, a little more quietly, and lowered her weapon.

'Why didn't you shoot?' said Jonah.

'What? Out here on a busy public highway? Are you fucking serious?'

'Still, bit embarrassing, eh? Left the keys in, did you?'

Holly resisted the almost overwhelming urge to punch the annoying prick very hard in the face. She didn't need *him* of all people to reinforce the utter humiliation she felt at having made such a rookie mistake, but when it came down to it, the fuckup was entirely her fault and not his. 'How bad's the bike?'

Jonah stood the motorbike upright and checked it over. 'OK, I think. Nasty scrape on the side of the fuel tank, a smashed mirror and a couple of busted indicator lights. Gear lever hasn't been bent or snapped off, so I guess it's still a runner.'

'You know how to ride one?'

'Sure.'

Finally, he had his uses.

'Good. Grab a helmet and let's get going.'

22

Maybe it was an accident, but it certainly hadn't seemed like that to me. I'd been getting my feet in position to smack open the back door of the Polo, waiting for the bike to come alongside again, when I looked out of the rear window to see a dark grey Mondeo slam into the back of it and send the bike and its riders scattering across the road. But accident or not, whoever'd been driving the Mondeo had very probably saved our arses.

'Shit, that was a close one,' said Scratch. 'How the hell did they find us this time?'

'Maybe they ran a trace on the car's plates, then followed us from the funeral parlour,' said Alan.

'So how'd they run a trace?'

'Dunno. Contact in the police perhaps?'

'They don't need one,' said Oleg, struggling to unwedge himself from between the front and back seats. 'This is the Russian secret service we're talking about here. They can hack into whatever system they want, anywhere in the world.'

I helped him up onto the seat beside me while I

listened to the voice in my head: '*I don't know about you, but I'm getting pretty sick of these "close ones", as Scratch calls them. The next time – and you can be bloody sure there will be a next time – we might not be quite so lucky.*'

There was no denying it. Oleg was becoming a dangerous liability. No, not *becoming*. He'd been a liability ever since we'd first clapped eyes on him in Calais, or even more accurately, ever since I'd accepted the damn job from the now disappeared Mr Mysterious. Enough was enough. After what we'd been told at the police station, I'd been hell bent on getting the truth out of Oleg and particularly whether he really was a defecting Russian spy or just full of shit. And if it was the latter, why were these Russian agents still so intent on killing him? After this latest incident, though, I could hardly have cared less. All I did care about was dumping him somewhere out of harm's way while Alan, Scratch and I tried to come up with a less temporary plan for what to do with him.

It obviously wasn't safe to keep him at the funeral parlour any more, but alternative options were seriously limited. In fact, the more I thought about it, the more I came to realise that there was really only one possibility, and even that was a long shot that nobody in their right mind would have put money on.

* * *

'Of course, darling. We'd love to have a Russian spy staying here for a day or two, even though there's some bad people who want him dead, and there's every possibility that we might all get killed when they find out where he is.'

129

OK, it was hardly the response I'd been expecting, and it wasn't the response I got either. Instead, what I got was: 'Are you shitting me? Absolutely not. No.'

Carla and I hadn't exactly been on the best of terms since the divorce, but then again, the same also applied to the last year or so of our marriage. The only reason we were still in touch at all was because she had custody of our teenage kids, Emma and Brad, who I saw a lot of and had a far better relationship with now than I ever did when Carla and I were together. This was perhaps partly because they both thought that their new "dad" was a complete and utter dickwad, and that I'd grown in their estimation by comparison.

The dickwad in question – one Dimitri Spiropoulos – was the half-her-age Greek toyboy that Carla had been having an affair with while she and I were still married, and she'd moved in with him after the divorce. Dimitri had become the not so proud owner of the Acropolis Restaurant by default rather than by choice, the default part being the sudden and violent death of the previous owner, his uncle Nikos. By rights, the restaurant should have passed into the hands of Nikos's three sons, but since two were in prison and the other had avoided the same fate by fleeing the country, Dimitri had been next in line to take over the family business.

He was here now, in the dimly lit room at the back of the restaurant that served as a storeroom-cum-office. It was cluttered with surplus furniture from the restaurant, a few broken chairs, several towers of bottle crates and a whole load of cardboard boxes. He was sitting on a swivel chair behind an impressively large desk that looked totally out of place amidst all the crap. No longer expensively dressed like a Tommy Hilfiger model, Dimitri was wearing an off-white T-shirt under a grubby-looking dark blue apron. Ever since his cousin Vasilis had done a runner with almost all of the restaurant's liquid assets, Dimitri had been forced to run the business with a drastically trimmed-down staff of himself, Carla and a couple of part-timers. Not that he'd needed any more than that to keep the dwindling flow of customers satisfied, although satisfaction was in short supply, judging by most of the online reviews I'd read.

Carla didn't look too happy with her new role in life either. Working her butt off as head cook and bottle washer clearly wasn't anywhere close to what she'd dreamt of when she'd shacked up with the swarthy young Greek. When we were together, she used to spend a fortune at the hairdresser's, whereas now her long blonde hair looked as if she'd washed it in cooking fat. Her unmade-up face was showing signs of lines that I'd never seen before, and they certainly weren't laugh lines.

We were sitting facing each other on the opposite side of the desk to Dimitri while Oleg was mooching around amongst the bottle crates, presumably in the hope of finding vodka. I'd dropped Alan and Scratch off at the funeral parlour before heading to the Acropolis for my unwelcome and ill-fated visit and taking extreme care that I wasn't being followed.

Naturally, I'd left out some of the details about Oleg when I'd told Carla why I needed a place where he could stay for a day or two, but being stupidly honest, decided that I had to at least come clean that there might – just *might* – be a wee bit of danger involved. Stupidly honest, yes, but how else was I going to impress upon her how vital it was to keep Oleg out of sight for however long he was there?

'I don't even know if he really is a spy,' I'd said as if this would make the slightest difference to her decision.

It didn't.

'All I care about is there's people trying to kill him,' she'd said, 'which is bound to put me and the kids' lives at risk, so I don't give a damn whether he's a spy or the president of Timbuktu.'

My pointing out that Timbuktu is actually a city and wouldn't therefore have a president was admittedly ill-advised and didn't help my case one bit. It did amuse me, though, that she hadn't included Dimitri among the list of lives she gave a shit about.

I knew Carla well enough to know that once she'd made her mind up about something, there was no shifting her, so I was about to get up and leave when Dimitri delivered his one and only contribution to the conversation so far: 'How much?'

'What?'

'How much you gonna pay us if we keep the Russkie here?'

Before I could answer, Carla cut in with: 'Have you not been listening to a word I said? Like the word "no", for instance?'

Dimitri's head sank into his shoulders like a frightened turtle retreating into its shell.

'And what are you still doing here?' she added. 'You think those dishes are going to wash themselves?'

Despite the question being very obviously a rhetorical one, Dimitri felt the need to answer it by mumbling '*Gamiméni skýla*', which I assumed didn't translate as a term of endearment.

Soon after he had slouched out of the storeroom-cum-office, Oleg and I made our way through the empty restaurant and out onto the street. As we walked towards the car, I noticed a dark grey Mondeo pull out from its parking space on the opposite side of the road. Coincidence probably. After all, there must be hundreds, if not thousands, of dark grey Mondeos in the UK, so no need to get paranoid.

When it passed us, however, I caught sight of the driver, and there was something oddly familiar about the unusually high forehead and the little goatee beard.

23

As new experiences went, this was by far one of the most terrifying that Holly had ever endured. She'd never been on a motorcycle even once in her life, and her fear of the two-wheeled projectiles was now a nausea-inducing reality. Jonah was making full use of the bike's seemingly infinite reserves of power and frequently overtaking when there was scarcely more than inches to spare between the vehicle in front and the oncoming traffic. Not that she had any cause for complaint, of course. It was her own idiotic fault that Jonah was having to dice with both their deaths in an attempt to salvage what remained of her grievously wounded pride.

In the desperate hope that her torment would soon be brought to an end, she slid open one eye and peered past Jonah's helmet at the road ahead. And there at last was her Mondeo, little more than a hundred yards in front and with a clear run between it and the bike.

'Gotcha, you bastards!' she yelled, but it was highly unlikely anyone would have heard her through her helmet and over the roar of the bike's engine.

Her eyes wide open now, she began to release her grip around Jonah's waist, unaware until that moment that she had been clutching on to him quite so tightly. Hopefully, he would have been concentrating so hard on what he'd been doing with the bike that he may not even have noticed.

Right now, that was the least of her concerns, though. Right now, the Mondeo was less than fifty yards ahead of them and—

So why the hell was Jonah slowing down all of a sudden?

She leant forward so that their helmets were almost touching and was about to ask him this exact question when she heard the two-tone siren immediately behind her. She had no need to turn and see where the sound was coming from, and as Jonah steered the bike close to the kerb and brought it to a halt, she changed her original question to: 'Christ's sake, Jonah, what are you stopping for?'

'It's the police,' he said and pointed at the remaining unbroken mirror on the handlebars as if she might want to confirm it for herself.

'Yes, I do realise that, thank you, but we're MI-fucking-5 in case you'd forgotten.'

Even if Jonah had had an answer to that, he had no time to respond since a uniformed police officer was now standing beside them and instructing them to remove their helmets.

'In a hurry, are we?' he said, specifically addressing Jonah.

'We are, yes,' said Holly before Jonah could open his mouth.

'Well, at least that's honest. Quite refreshing really. More often than not, I get some guff about—'

'Yeah, I'm sure that's all very interesting, officer, but my car's just been stolen by two Russian agents, and it's rather urgent that—'

It was the cop's turn to interrupt. 'Whoa there a minute. Russian agents, you say? What sort of Russian agents?'

'The secret service type of Russian agents?'

'Like spies, sort of thing?'

'Uh-huh.'

'Bit of a hurry, were they, Charlie?' said the officer's partner, who appeared beside him, brushing imaginary dust from the sergeant's stripes on the sleeve of his jacket, possibly to establish his superior status for Holly and Jonah's benefit.

'Apparently so, sarge. Chasing after a couple of Russian spies, they reckon.'

'Is that so? And who've we got here then? James Bond and er... Ooh, what's her name? You know. Ursula whatsherface. The one who comes out of the sea wearing nothing more than a skimpy white bikini and a bloody great knife.'

'Honey something-or-other, I think.'

The sergeant clicked his fingers. 'That's it, yes. *Thunderball*, wasn't it?'

'*Dr No* actually,' said Jonah helpfully.

'Well, you should know, I guess... Mr Bond.'

Charlie spoke the name as if he was supposed to be Blofeld or some other Bond villain, and he and the sergeant had a good chuckle until Holly brought it to an abrupt end with: 'Look, I know how proud you cops are of your well deserved reputation for sarcasm, which I can see you find incredibly amusing, but we've got a job to do, and it's a matter of national security.'

The sergeant and his partner exchanged a brief

glance before the senior officer turned his icy attention to Jonah. 'Licence and registration… please.'

Jonah fished inside his jacket pocket and produced a leather wallet, from which he extracted his driving licence. His hand was trembling as he passed it to the sergeant, and after checking the details on the front of the plastic card, he flipped it over and raised an eyebrow.

'According to this, you're not actually qualified to ride a motorcycle.'

'Er, no, but I have had a lot of experience.'

'Have you indeed?'

Holly stayed silent even though she dearly wanted to scream at him for driving like a maniac and putting her life in danger when he wasn't bloody qualified. That would have to wait till later, but she'd make damn sure his ears would be bleeding by the time she'd finished with him.

'OK,' said the sergeant. 'So far, we've got riding a motorcycle without a licence, speeding and very possibly reckless or dangerous driving.'

'Not to mention a pair of busted indicators,' Charlie added.

'Good point. How about registration for the bike?'

Before Jonah could tell them that they didn't own the bike and add vehicle theft to the list of charges, Holly decided it was high time to put an end to all this nonsense by flashing her Security Service warrant card. 'Listen, we're MI5 officers, and if you want proof, I can show you my ID.'

But as she opened the flap of her shoulder bag to retrieve it, the sergeant took a step back and jabbed a finger at the bag. 'Jesus! Is that a… gun?'

Holly looked into the bag as if to check for herself.

The butt of the Grach she'd taken off the Russians was clearly visible. 'That's none of your business, but what I've been trying to tell you is—'

'Hold it right there!' the sergeant shouted when Holly continued to hunt for her warrant card. 'Hands on your heads! Both of you! Now!'

'Oh for—' Holly began but broke off when the sergeant produced a taser and Charlie wielded an extended steel baton. 'You're gonna regret this. You know that, don't you?'

'So are you if you don't do what I say.'

He adjusted his grip on the taser, and Holly slowly raised her hands and clasped them behind her head. Jonah had already beaten her to it.

The sergeant shuffled his feet until they were about a yard apart and aimed the taser at Holly's chest. 'Now hand over the bag.'

'With my hands behind my head?'

'OK, smartarse. Charlie, get the bag off her.'

'What?'

'Go on. I've got you covered.'

With evident reluctance, Charlie tucked his baton under his arm and took hold of the bag as gingerly as if he expected it to explode in his face at any moment. But since Holly was wearing the strap over her left shoulder, it very quickly became apparent that there was no way to take the bag from her while her hands were behind her head.

'You'll have to put your arms up straight,' he said, and when Holly duly obliged, he eased the bag upwards, taking several seconds before it was fully liberated.

Then he gently set it down on the pavement, and the sergeant borrowed his baton to have a cautious poke around inside.

'While you're in there,' Holly said, 'you might like to dig out the warrant card I was telling you about.'

Neither cop interrupted their inspection of the bag's contents – other than both of them telling her to 'Shut it' – and since they were so absorbed in their task, she seized the opportunity to whisper in Jonah's ear and ask him if he had his own warrant card on him.

He had.

'Here,' he called out, brandishing the ID at the two officers. 'If you can't find hers, perhaps mine will do instead.'

Charlie and the sergeant turned towards him, then straightened up from their stooping positions. There was a lengthy pause before either of them spoke.

'Stay where you are and toss it over here,' the sergeant barked.

'It could be fake,' said Charlie after they'd finished their minute examination of the warrant card.

'Of course it's not bloody fake,' said Holly. 'And if you'd stop pratting about and have a look at mine, you'll see that it's also not a fake, and you'll let us go so we can get on with doing our fucking job.'

'Ooh, I think *Mrs* Bond's getting a bit antsy, wouldn't you say, Charlie?'

'I would indeed, sarge. I would indeed.'

'Maybe we should put in a call and run a few checks. Make sure these people really are who they claim to be.' ·

'Good idea. I'll do that right now.'

'Such a pity it always seems to take forever for anyone to call back, though,' said the sergeant, and Holly easily caught the exaggerated wink he gave his partner before he strolled back towards the police car.

24

Alan wasn't known for his mind-reading skills, but nor did he have to be. The expression on my face was clear enough to tell its own story when Oleg and I walked in through the door of the funeral parlour.

'No joy with Carla then?' he said.

'Nope.'

Sanjeev apparently *was* a mind-reader, however. 'Tea?'

I nodded and slumped down onto the leather-upholstered chair behind the reception desk.

As for Oleg, he turned down the offer of tea and said he was off upstairs to the apartment for a lie down, claiming to be exhausted after all the excitement – whatever he thought that might have been. My guess? He was on the hunt for vodka, and quite frankly, I couldn't give a shit whether he found the bottle I'd stashed away and drank himself senseless.

Alan sat on one of the two chairs on the customer side of the desk. 'So now what do we do? He can't stay here, that's for sure.'

'You think?'

'Yeah, I know. Preaching to the choir. It's just that Carla was our last shot, so if we're not gonna end up dead ourselves, our only option is to dump him somewhere and let him fend for himself. After all, from what the cops told you, he's probably not even a Russian spy, and Christ knows what other bullshit he's been feeding us.'

It was a fair point, of course, but somehow it didn't feel right to simply feed Oleg to the wolves like that, which was pretty much what we'd be doing. It was a guaranteed death sentence.

'What's up?' said Scratch and pulled up the chair next to Alan's. 'I take it Carla wasn't keen.'

'We need to dump him,' Alan repeated.

'Oh yeah? And get him killed, basically.'

'You got a better idea, genius.'

'I might well have, as it happens. See, I've been giving it a lot of thought, and I think I may have the perfect solution. Well, maybe not perfect, but it's the best I can come up with.'

Like Scratch said, it didn't sound like the perfect solution to our problem, but it was a straw worth clutching at, and ten minutes later, he and I bundled Oleg into the Polo while Alan stayed behind to give Sanjeev a hand in the unlikely event of a sudden rush of customers.

* * *

We were standing on a stone footbridge overlooking a straight stretch of tree-lined canal and checking out the dozen or so narrowboats that were moored end-to-end on the right-hand side. None of them were exactly the same, but most looked in immaculate condition. There were three that were bright red with a dark green stripe above the hull, two with the opposite colour scheme, and others of varying shades of blue. Some had round porthole style windows and some had larger rectangular ones. Some had names painted on their sides and some sported elaborate floral designs or both. The only thing they had in common was that they were all about seven feet wide, but their lengths were anything between thirty and fifty feet.

'Which one's hers?' I asked.

Scratch pointed to a boat half way along the row. 'That one. The one behind the pale blue one with the yellow stripe.'

Assuming he was right – and why wouldn't he be? – it was by far the shabbiest and least cared-for boat of all. By *far*. Where once it must have been a dazzling bright red with a green trim, the colours had now faded to a kind of muddy brown, and the gold lettering on the side was so washed out as to make any words utterly illegible. There were also several large patches of rust on the black hull that were clearly visible above the waterline.

'And she lives in *that*?'

'Has done for years,' said Scratch. 'Never goes anywhere in it, though. Engine's buggered.'

'Why am I not surprised? I'm amazed it hasn't sunk, looking at all that rust. God knows what it must be like under the water.'

'Well, I told you it wasn't gonna be ideal. You wanna meet her or not?'

'*Fuck it*,' said the voice in my head. '*Carla was your last hope, so unless you want to take Alan's advice and have Oleg's inevitable death on your conscience, you don't have a lot of choice. Or maybe you want to ask*

142

Oleg which he'd prefer. A few days on a shitty old rustbucket or a bullet in the back of the head.'

No way was that going to happen, so I set off down the cobbled ramp that led down from the footbridge and onto the towpath.

'You'd better let me go first,' said Scratch as we closed in on the boat. 'She can sometimes be a bit funny with people she doesn't know.'

'Funny?'

'Er, like with a gun.'

'What? You saying she shoots people?'

'No, not really.'

'Jesus, Scratch. What do you mean "not really"?'

'Well, it was just the one time, far as I know. Only winged them, though. Not much more than a flesh wound. She said they were trying to nick something from her boat.'

Oh, terrific. This just gets better and better.

There was a small platform at the back of the boat and a pair of narrow doors, one of which was partially open, mainly because it had almost parted company with its hinges.

Scratch stepped onto the platform and lowered his head to call through the opening. 'Hello? Anyone home? It's me. Michael.'

Apparently, Scratch's Aunt Betty didn't use his nickname.

Scratch waited for a response, but when none came, he tried again a little louder. 'Aunty? Are you there?'

'Who's there? I've got a gun, you know.'

The voice from somewhere inside the narrowboat was gruff but verging on posh, and was followed by a protracted bout of lung-dredging coughing.

'It's me. Michael.'

'Who?'

'She's a bit on the mutton side,' Scratch said, turning to me and Oleg and tapping his ear. Then he seriously upped the decibels to yell through the open doorway. 'It's Michael! Your nephew!'

'Well, bugger me sideways. Can't even remember the last time I saw my little Mikey.'

My little Mikey? I couldn't resist a quick snigger, and Scratch flicked me the finger.

His aunt's voice had grown louder as she approached, and Scratch stepped back onto the towpath to give her room to come out through the doorway and stand facing us on the platform.

She was probably in her early seventies but could have been older – or younger. It was hard to tell from what little I could see of her face. She was wearing a rainbow-coloured knitted hat pulled down low over her forehead and covering her ears, and if the conspicuous split on the side was anything to go by, it had originally been intended as a tea cosy. Although it was a warm day, she had on an old army greatcoat that must have dated from the First World War, and it was buttoned to the neck with the collar turned up. Beneath the coat, the bottom few inches of a faded paisley skirt reached down to a pair of heavily scuffed ankle boots.

'Come here, you big lump,' she said, 'and give your old aunty a hug.'

Back on the boat, Scratch had to bend almost double to embrace his aunt, who was well over a foot shorter.

She gave him a peck on the cheek, then looked past him to where Oleg and I were loitering on the towpath. 'So aren't you going to introduce me to your two chums?'

Introductions over, Aunt Betty invited us all to

'Come aboard for a cuppa or something stronger if you prefer.'

I'd never been inside a narrowboat before, but everything was much as I would have expected. Wooden floor with paler wood cladding on the ceiling, and a highly imaginative use of the long, narrow space. A range of fitted cupboards on the left, and on the right, a cooker and sink. Beyond these, a small table with two chairs, and further on, a pair of armchairs either side of a wood-burning stove. At the forward – for'ard? – end, a door in a wooden partition that presumably separated the sleeping area and probably some kind of bathroom from the rest of the interior.

What struck me straight away was that the inside of the boat was in complete contrast to its shabby exterior and, to be brutally honest, the boat's owner herself. Everything was neat, tidy and, as far as I could tell, spotlessly clean. The downside? The combined stink of paraffin, engine oil and diesel was likely to bring on the osmophobia headache and nausea at any moment, and to cap it all, the air was thick with tobacco smoke and more than a hint of ganja.

'You'd better take one of the armchairs, Michael,' Aunt Betty said when she spotted Scratch having to stoop to avoid whacking his head on the ceiling. 'And you two grab those dining chairs and bring them over.'

Once the three of us were settled around the unlit wood-burner, she rubbed her hands together, or more specifically, the fingerless woollen gloves she was wearing – one red and one blue – and asked who wanted tea.

'Did you say you had something stronger?' Oleg asked with an expression of bright anticipation. 'Vodka perhaps?'

'He's fine with tea,' I said before Aunt Betty could answer.

25

The Hidden Gem Café was far from being hidden, since it was slap bang in the middle of a moderately busy high street, and it was certainly no gem. The state of the cutlery alone was what the term "greasy spoon café" was coined for. There was scarcely room enough for the ten Formica-topped tables, each with a pair of black plastic chairs on either side, and every piece of furniture was securely bolted to the ground as if the café owner was afraid they'd be nicked. The bottom three-quarters of the front window was obscured by a red and white gingham curtain, which was quite possibly intended to prevent browsers checking out the interior and deciding to go somewhere else.

'Beggars can't be choosers,' Jonah had said when he and Holly had stepped inside and realised that the place shouldn't simply have been hidden, it should have been blasted into oblivion.

When he'd also added 'Any port in a storm', Holly had been forced to agree, although not out loud.

Not only were neither of them dressed for the sudden downpour of rain that was bouncing off the pavement in front of the café, but they were also desperate to find anywhere with a plug socket so that Jonah could recharge his phone's dead battery.

As expected, Sergeant Dumb and Constable Dumber had taken their own sweet time to confirm that Holly and Jonah really were who they said they were and finally allowed them to be on their way, even having to withdraw their threat of confiscating the gun in Holly's shoulder bag. What they did have to leave behind, however, was the motorbike, which didn't come as a big surprise given that, MI5 officers or not, they'd still be riding it illegally. Jonah hadn't let on that they had in effect stolen the bike and claimed instead that they'd borrowed it from a friend, so the cops informed him that the bike would be impounded until the friend came to collect it – 'Assuming that he or she has actually passed their test, that is.'

Now that Holly and Jonah were lacking any form of motorised transport, Jonah had politely asked the cops if they could give them a lift somewhere and had got the kind of response that Holly predicted.

'Sorry, mate,' the sergeant had said with a theatrically fake expression of regret. 'We'd love to help, of course, but the thing is, the constable and I will have to wait here until they send somebody from the pound to come and pick up the bike.'

And so it was that Holly and Jonah had had to walk the mile and a half to the Hidden Gem Café and drink coffee that tasted as if it had been brewing for at least a week while Jonah chomped his way through a doorstep of a bacon sandwich that he'd slathered with obscene amounts of tomato ketchup.

'Well?' said Holly, averting her gaze as Jonah took a massive bite out of his sandwich and a thick stream of ketchup oozed down his chin.

'Eh?'

'Your phone. Has it charged up enough yet?'

Chewing noisily, Jonah bent down from his chair to check his phone, which was on the floor and connected to a low level power point with the short charger lead that Holly always carried with her in her bag.

'Getting there,' he said and sat back up again.

Holly swore softly to herself. This whole assignment had turned into a complete bloody disaster. As soon as they'd got clear of Dumb and Dumber, she'd asked Jonah to fire up the tracking app on his phone so they could at least find out where the hell the Polo was. Nothing doing. 'Oops. Looks like the battery's died.'

Fucking "oops"? How in the name of Christ could he have let his battery die? Because he's a total and utter prick, that's why.

And what were they going to do when they did track down the Polo? *Run* after it?

Her Mondeo could be miles away by now as well, and the cops were hardly likely to pull out all the stops to recover it. Sergeant Dumb had been unsurprisingly pessimistic and was still refusing to accept that it had been stolen by Russian agents.

'Well now,' he'd said with a slight tilt of the head and a slow intake of breath. 'It'll be joyriders if you ask me. It'll probably turn up on some wasteland somewhere, and they'll have torched it to destroy any evidence... or maybe just for kicks.'

Holly raised the chipped white mug of tepid coffee to her lips, then changed her mind and set it back down on the table.

'I'm going outside for a smoke,' she said and got to her feet.

Despite the all-pervading stench of fried food in the café, which may well have been a health hazard in itself, the law decreed that she couldn't light up inside as this could be detrimental to the health of other customers. Yeah, well, the amount of crap that most of the dozen punters were shovelling down their necks was far more likely to kill them than a few whiffs of fag smoke.

Mercifully, the rain had stopped, although a stiff breeze made the process of lighting her cigarette an irritating challenge. Once she'd got it going, however, she inhaled deeply and already felt the soothing effect on her severely jangled nerves. Not that her craving for a nicotine hit had been her only reason for stepping outside the café. It was also a ruse to enable her to phone Bendix out of Jonah's hearing.

He answered on the third ring. 'Miss Gilmartin. How lovely to hear from you. I trust you are the bearer of good news?'

'If you don't mind, sir. I have a question for you first.'

There was a pause, during which Holly could hear only silence in the background. For once, he didn't appear to be carousing in some bar or other.

'Fire away,' Bendix said after he'd no doubt been weighing up whether to allow this audacity from such a low level operative. His voice sounded distinctly wary. 'What do you want to know?'

'It's about Radimov.'

There was an audible sigh from Bendix. 'And who else would it be about?'

'Well, I'll spare you the details, but—'

'Oh, please do.'

'It seems that Six don't know anything about him

defecting. In fact, they say they've never even *heard* the name Oleg Radimov.'

The pause this time was considerably longer, and Holly had several drags on her cigarette before Bendix spoke again. 'And you got this information how exactly?'

'The police contacted Six and asked if Radimov was—'

Bendix's howl of laughter was more than enough to prevent her finishing the sentence.

'The police? Seriously?' he said when he'd managed to regain his composure. 'You honestly believe that the Secret Intelligence Service would share that kind of information with the plods? Good God almighty, Miss Gilmartin, the defection of a Russian agent is as top bloody secret as it gets.'

'Yes, I understand that, sir, but all the same I—'

'All the same, nothing. Even if it turns out that Radimov *isn't* a defecting Russian agent – which I sincerely doubt – it doesn't have a damn thing to do with your current assignment, so I'd suggest that you stop listening to idle rumours and get the hell on with what I asked you to do. Do I make myself clear, Miss Gilmartin?'

By the time Bendix finished speaking, he was almost yelling, and Holly had to hold her phone away from her ear for fear of being deafened.

'Perfectly clear, sir.'

'In any event,' Bendix said, returning to a more normal volume, 'if what you've heard does happen to be true, it would make your job a whole lot easier.'

'Oh? How's that?'

'Well, think about it. Since your mission is to nobble Radimov before Six get their hooks into him, then that's one less thing you have to worry about. A rather large thing, in fact. Every cloud has a silver lining, eh?'

It was an adage that Holly had never subscribed to, and she wondered how many more clichés she was going to have to hear that day. Her cigarette had burned down almost to the filter, and she ground it into the pavement with her heel.

'Of course,' Bendix went on, 'none of this means you should take your foot off the throttle, Miss Gilmartin. Not for one moment. I want Radimov dealt with and the sooner the better for all concerned.'

'Yes, sir.'

'Anything else?'

Holly had no intention of telling him about the latest string of disasters, so she told him there was nothing new to report.

'Make sure you keep me updated then,' he said and ended the call.

'Pompous overbearing twat,' Holly said when she was certain that Bendix could no longer hear her.

She was about to go back inside the hellhole of a café when her phone rang. Fully expecting that it was the pompous overbearing twat calling back to give her another ear-bashing, she answered without checking the screen. And miracle of miracles, it was the police informing her that her stolen Mondeo had been found and would be towed away if it wasn't collected within the next two hours.

'Blimey, that was quick,' said Jonah when she told him the good news.

'Yes,' Holly said, 'but I'd lay odds that Dumb and Dumber had bugger all to do with it.'

26

Scratch's Aunt Betty hadn't taken too much persuading to keep Oleg on her narrowboat for a few days. She'd said that she'd be glad of the company and had become particularly enthusiastic when she'd discovered that they had a mutual passion for the game of chess.

We'd been totally up front with her about the threat to Oleg's life and that this might put her in danger too, but she'd shrugged it off, saying, 'I always keep my gun loaded and handy, and I'm not afraid to use it.' Then with a wink at Oleg, she'd added, 'And *you'd* better not trying any funny business with me either, or I'll put a hole in your head.'

As Scratch and I had said our goodbyes and started up the short flight of three wooden steps onto the platform at the back of the boat, I noticed Aunt Betty on her hands and knees in front of one of the fitted cupboards. The telltale clink of bottles was evidence enough that chess wasn't the only thing that she and Oleg had in common.

It was a huge relief to get Oleg off our hands, of course, even if only for a few days, and a bonus that it seemed he might actually enjoy his time with Aunt Betty and vice versa. I was still worried, though, and I said as much to Scratch as we made our way back along the towpath.

'I know your aunt was serious about her gun and all that, but I doubt she'd be much of a match for any Russian agents that happen to drop by.'

'Not gonna happen, Max,' said Scratch. 'We were more careful than ever to make certain we weren't being followed, so how are they gonna know where Oleg is? And in any case, Aunt Betty isn't the only one who's armed. Oleg still has that gun the Russians dropped in the car, remember?'

I did my best to feel reassured but couldn't quite get there. Oleg was well aware of what he was up against, but if anything happened to Aunt Betty, I didn't know how I'd be able to forgive myself.

I took several deep breaths of fresh air. The fug inside the narrowboat had become almost unbearable by the time we left, mainly due to the extraordinary number of roll-ups she'd smoked in such a short period. She had, however, refrained from skinning up a spliff. Very probably, she'd be getting on to that as soon as Scratch and I had left. Maybe she thought her nephew wouldn't approve.

'How'd it go?' Alan asked when Scratch and I walked through the door back at the funeral parlour. He was sitting behind the reception desk and looking decidedly glum.

'What's up with you?' said Scratch before I could answer.

Alan grimaced and fingered the flesh-coloured padded neck brace he was wearing. 'Did my neck in, didn't I?'

'Again?'

'Yes, *again.*'

'Christ, Alan, you do your neck in more often than you take a shit.'

'How did it happen?' I said, pre-empting Alan's inevitable retaliation about Scratch's innumerable allergies.

'I was helping Sanjeev shift a couple of coffins and all of a sudden, bang! Hurt like bloody hell, it did. Still does, as a matter of fact.'

'Gets you out of shifting any more coffins for the foreseeable future, though, eh?' said Scratch with a wry smirk.

'Yeah, thanks for the sympathy. So are either of you gonna tell me how it went with Oleg or what?'

'Aunt Betty can't keep him there forever, though,' Scratch said when we'd finished taking it in turns to fill him in on the details. 'We need to work out how to get him out of our hair for good so we don't have to be looking over our shoulders for Russian assassins all the time.'

I fully expected Alan to make some snide remark about Scratch's own hair being almost non-existent but, to my amazement, all he said was: 'Sounds good to me.'

I glanced at my watch. 'I don't know about you guys, but I'm knackered. Maybe we should all sleep on it and see what we can come up with in the morning.'

'Sounds good to me,' Alan said again, and when he and Scratch had left, I locked up and headed upstairs to the apartment. I wasn't at all convinced that any of us would be able to concoct some brilliant plan overnight as to how to solve the Oleg problem, and I definitely included myself in that. I was far too tired to do any more than pour myself a large Jameson and flop down on the settee in front of the telly for a couple of hours till it was time for bed. I was in dire need of some "me time", and I had no intention of giving the Oleg problem so much as a single thought until my alarm clock shattered my well-earned peace the following morning.

They say that God laughs when people make plans, however, and no sooner had I taken my first sip of whiskey than my phone rang. The caller was unidentified, and I was sorely tempted not to answer, but curiosity got the better of me. What if it was Scratch's aunt screaming that her boat was under attack by Russian agents?

'Hello?'

Several seconds passed before the caller spoke. 'Ees zat Mix Dimpsey?'

The accent was strong. Eastern European? Russian maybe? Or was it Spanish? Hard to tell since the voice was also muffled as if the caller had a scarf or something over their mouth.

'This is Max Dempsey, yes. Who is this?'

'You do not know me, bat I am knowing you, Mr Dimpsey.'

'OK, I don't know you, so do you have a name?'

'Yes.'

'Which is?'

There was an abrupt chuckle at the other end of the line. 'Ha ha. You think you can kitch me out so easy, eh?'

I was about to tell whoever it was to fuck off and hang up when an irritating thought occurred to me. 'Look, if this is Alan or Scratch, I'm not in the mood for any of your pissing about.'

'Zis no pissing about, Mr Dimpsey. Zis is you eff sumsing I want, and I eff sumsing you want.'

'Come again?'

'Olaf Radaboff.'

'Oleg Radimov, you mean?'

'Er… Yes. Zat ees correct.'

'What about him?'

'We vant him.'

'We want him?'

'Correct.'

'So who's "we"?'

'We are KBG.'

'Kaby Gee?'

'No. K - B - G.'

'You mean KGB?'

'Er, yes. KGB. My Eenglish ees not so good.'

'I thought the KGB didn't exist any more.'

'Well, it fucking does, OK?'

The sudden lack of accent floored me for a moment, and I waited for the caller to speak again.

'Ees you still zair?'

The accent was back again.

'Yes, I'm still here. So you wanna tell me why I should give you Radimov?'

'Who?'

'Oleg Radimov.'

'Him, yes. You giff him to us and we giff you beck your nephew Toby.'

'Toby? What are you talking about?'

'We heff him kidnepped.'

'Kidnapped?'

'Correct. And eef you do not pay twenty thousand of your Eenglish pounds, you will neffer see him again.'

I felt the veins in my temples begin to throb wildly,

157

and my hands shook so that I very nearly dropped the phone. Toby was a great kid, and I was extremely fond of him. He often called in at the funeral parlour after school for a chat and to help out occasionally, and I probably saw as much of him as I did my own kids. There was something about the KGB guy's threat that didn't sit right, though.

'Hang on. You're saying you want twenty thousand pounds, but I thought the whole point of this was that you wanted Radimov.'

'Er, yes. Ze cash and him too. I will contact you again in twenty-four hours to arrange ze details.'

I started to yell at the bastard and tell him what I'd do to him if he so much as *looked* at Toby the wrong way, but the line had gone dead.

I drained the rest of my whiskey in one gulp and slumped back on the settee.

Jesus wept. This was all I needed.

27

The Mondeo had been abandoned in a back street about eight miles from the Hidden Gem Café, and after hailing a cab, Holly Gilmartin was relieved to find that there was no additional damage to the Mondeo and only a barely noticeable dent in the front bumper where she'd slammed into the motorbike. The interior, however, smelt like a chip shop, and there were two empty polystyrene takeaway containers and a couple of empty beer cans lying on the back seat.

She told Jonah to gather them up and chuck them in the nearest bin so they didn't stink the car out any more than they had done already. 'And get a move on, will you? We need to get to this canal.'

When Jonah's phone had charged up enough to be able to use the tracking app and check on the Polo's location, he'd said that it was somewhere near a canal about twenty minutes away.

Holly dug the spare Mondeo key out of her shoulder bag and fired up the engine, not waiting for Jonah to fully close the passenger door before setting off with a screech of tyres.

'Hang on a sec,' Jonah said, his eyes fixed on the tracking app. 'Looks like they're on the move.'

'OK, make sure you make a note of exactly where they were. I expect we'll need it later, but for now we'll get after them and see where they're going.'

After ten minutes of silence, Jonah looked up from his phone. 'I reckon they might be on their way back to the funeral parlour.'

'You reckon?'

'Well, I can't be sure, of course, but—'

'And do you also reckon we can get there before them?'

'I'd say so, yes, but you might have to break a few speed limits.'

'Fine by me,' said Holly, dropping down a gear and accelerating past a dawdling Honda Civic.

Getting pulled over by the cops again was not an option, so she told Jonah to keep her updated on the Polo's progress and the distance she still had to cover, so she could adjust her speed accordingly.

They made it with only seconds to spare and parked up in a side alley with a clear view of the funeral parlour, watching as Dempsey and one of his mates got out of their car and went inside.

'Radimov's not with them,' said Jonah.

Holly lit a cigarette. 'Well spotted, that man.'

'Maybe they dropped him off here before they went to the canal.'

'That's certainly a possibility. Perhaps you'd like to pop in and find out.'

'In the undertaker's?'

'Yeah.'

'But surely that would—'

'Joke,' said Holly and took in a deep lungful of

smoke before exhaling slowly through her teeth. 'Not much point hanging around here. May as well find out if there's anything interesting at this canal. Possibly even the man himself.'

'Radimov?'

'Uh-huh.'

'You think they might have taken him there to chuck him in? Drown him, like?'

'No, Jonah, that's not what I think at all.'

* * *

There was nothing of interest in the small car park which is where Jonah was adamant the Polo had been parked, so Holly led the way up over a stone footbridge and down a cobbled ramp onto the canal towpath.

They walked slowly as if they were out for a late afternoon stroll, but there wasn't a soul in sight to take any notice. She glanced in through the windows of every narrowboat they passed, assuming that any inhabitants would consider this to be irritating but perfectly normal behaviour from curious landlubbers.

Once they reached the last of the boats in the row, they carried on until they rounded a bend in the towpath. Satisfied that they couldn't be seen if anyone happened to come out on deck, Holly stopped and turned to Jonah.

'Spot anything useful?'

'Er, not really, no.'

'What about the really shitty boat? The one that looks like it's about to sink at any minute.'

Jonah shook his head. 'Not apart from it stood out a mile from all the other boats. Did you see something then?'

'Well, I can't be a hundred per cent certain because the windows were filthy and I only caught a glimpse of the back of his head, but there's a very slim chance it was Oleg Radimov. I don't want to make a move till we're sure, and I also need to know – if it *is* Radimov – whether he's on his own or not. So, we'll make a second pass and try and get a better look. Just don't make it obvious, OK?'

They set off back along the towpath, and when they got to the narrowboat, Jonah stopped and made a pretence of tying up his shoelaces even though he was wearing slip-ons. Holly stopped too and feigned impatience with him as if they were running late for an appointment or somesuch.

'Anything I can help you with?'

The voice came from the back of the boat, and Holly and Jonah looked round to see a woman in her seventies wearing a rainbow-coloured woollen hat and an old army greatcoat standing on the small platform next to the tiller.

'No, we're fine, thanks,' said Holly.

Jonah pulled himself upright from his crouching position. 'I was just doing up my er…' He switched his gaze from the woman down to his feet and left the rest of the sentence hanging as if suddenly remembering that he'd only been miming.

'Can't be too careful,' said the woman. 'I'm all on my own here, you see, and you get all sorts traipsing up and down the towpath at any time of the day or night. Most of them are just gawpers, of course, and that's to be expected, I suppose, but you never know, do you?'

'You don't, no,' said Holly with an ingratiating smile. 'Too many crazy people around these days, I'm afraid.'

'You're not wrong there, dear. I can hardly open a newspaper nowadays without reading some horrific story about elderly pensioners being murdered in their own homes.'

Holly was about to agree with an expression of concerned sympathy when Jonah gave a slight nod at the boat and cut in with: 'So you've got no internet on here then?'

'Excuse me?'

'World Wide Web.' Jonah spoke the words slowly like he was talking to an imbecile, and Holly refrained from kicking him. 'You said you read newspapers.'

The woman chuckled. 'Don't even have a computer, dear. Invention of the devil if you ask me.'

'Anyway,' said Holly before Jonah could spout any more nonsense, 'we'd better be going, and I don't want to take up any more of your time.'

'No problem. It's nice to have a bit of company now and again. In fact, I'd invite you in for a cup of tea except it's all rather topsy-turvy inside at the moment.'

'Another time perhaps.' Holly beamed at her and took Jonah by the arm. 'Come along, Adrian. We're going to be terribly late as it is.'

She waited until they'd started up the cobbled ramp to the footbridge and then: 'Excellent work, Jonah. Highlighting the fact that you were only pretending to fix your shoelaces when you didn't actually have any was a masterstroke. Pure fucking genius. And what was all that shit about her not having the internet?'

Jonah shrugged. 'Just making conversation, I guess. Thought it would give us a bit more time to look through the windows and see if it really was Radimov.'

'And?'

'Same as you. All I could see was the back of the

163

guy's head, so I couldn't tell one way or the other.'

'On the other hand,' said Holly, her tone marginally less abrasive, 'the woman seemed a little too keen to stress how all on her own she was.'

'Yeah, I clocked that too. Definitely suspicious. So what do we do now? Grab him or what? I doubt the woman's gonna be able to put up much of a fight, and even if Radimov's tooled up, we've got the element of surprise on our side as well as a couple of guns.'

Holly pondered for several seconds, weighing up the risks involved and the chance of getting Radimov out alive if it ended up as a shootout.

'We can't know for sure that it's only the two of them on the boat,' she said at last. 'Maybe he's got minders with him, and I also don't want to go storming in and find that the guy is just some bloke who happens to have a head that looks a lot like Radimov's. No, for now, we wait and watch. See if he comes out so we can identify him properly. And if there's anyone else on board, they might make an appearance as well.'

While they'd been talking, they'd made their way back to the car park, and Holly unlocked the Mondeo and opened the driver's door. 'You take the first shift, and I'll relieve you in an hour. If you get yourself up into those woods where you can't be seen, you should have a perfectly clear view of the boat.'

'Oh, goody. More bloody surveillance,' Jonah muttered as he slouched off up a steep pathway that led from the car park to a heavily wooded area overlooking the canal.

28

The kidnapper's phone call had left me in such a state of shock that it took several minutes before I could think straight, and it took about the same amount of time for my hands to stop trembling enough to be able to pour myself another large whiskey. I left the cap off the bottle and tried to remember as much as I could of what the kidnapper had said. And not just *what* he'd said but the *way* he'd said it.

The accent had been one of the weirdest I'd ever heard and seemed to slip to a different part of the world even within the middle of a sentence. Admittedly, I don't have a great ear for accents, and I hadn't come across too many English-speaking Russians other than Oleg, but I was doubtful that the caller was genuinely Russian. For one brief moment, the accent had gone altogether, but the voice was muffled, and although I had a vague feeling that it was a voice I'd heard before, I was damned if I could place it. I was certain as I could be that it wasn't Alan or Scratch pissing about, so who the hell else could it be?

Weird accent or not, maybe I simply had to accept

that the caller really was one of the Russian agents that was after Oleg and that's just how they spoke.

'*You know what I'd do*?' said the voice in my head.

'No, what's that?'

'*Call him back. The number's registered on your phone.*'

'And how's that gonna help?'

'*Worth a shot, isn't it? You never know, they might be stupid enough to answer, and if you're right about the voice sounding familiar, you might actually strike lucky and get a better idea who it is.*'

I wasn't convinced, and in any case, it made far more sense to make another call first.

Toby's phone was either switched off or out of signal range, so I tried his mum's phone and got the same result.

'Hi there. It's me,' I said when I finally got a result with the third number I called.

'What do you want?' Carla snapped. 'If this is about your Russian bloke again, you can go take a—'

'No, no, no,' I interrupted quickly. 'It's not about him at all.'

I was attempting to sound as if I didn't have a care in the world and probably failing miserably, but there was no way I was going to let on to Carla that Toby had been kidnapped.

'So what is it then? I'm on a dash to the supermarket because Dimitri forgot we'd run out of half the veg we need for the restaurant tonight.'

This was rather more information than I needed, but it appeared that Carla wanted to vent at someone about her toyboy's shortcomings, so it may as well be me.

'OK, I'll make it quick,' I said. 'It's only that I've been trying to get hold of Toby and can't get any answer.'

'Probably because he's on holiday in Corfu.'

'On his own?'

'With his mum.'

'Melanie?'

'That *is* her name last time I checked, yes.'

'You're absolutely sure they're both in Corfu?'

'What the hell *is* this, Simon?' She never called me Max. 'You think I don't know where my own sister and nephew are, for God's sake? They rang me from the hotel less than an hour ago.'

'On one of their mobiles?'

'No, the hotel landline. Too worried about global roaming charges to use their own phones.'

'Yes, of course. Perhaps you could text me the number of the hotel then.'

The sigh at the other end of the line was long and heavy. 'When I get round to it, but like I say, I'm a bit bloody busy right now.'

Then she hung up.

It was reassuring that Toby's apparent kidnapping was evidently a hoax, of course, but I wouldn't be entirely satisfied until I'd spoken to the lad himself. If she bothered at all, it could easily be an hour or more before Carla sent me the hotel number, and I couldn't bear to wait that long.

'*May as well try Plan A then,*' said the voice in my head. '*Ring the bastard back.*'

As I'd anticipated, nobody picked up, and I was about to give up when: 'Hello?'

Even from that one word I had no trouble recognising the voice. The clattering of pots and pans in the background gave me an additional clue. It was the unmistakable sound of a busy restaurant kitchen.

167

'Hello, Dimitri,' I said with as much composure as I could muster. 'It's Max here.'

If it hadn't been for the racket in the background, the silence would have been deafening.

'Dimitri? You there?'

'Er, yeah. Hi, Max. Bit busy right now.'

'It's OK. This won't take long.'

'What won't?'

'Kidnapped anybody lately, have you?' Again, Dimitri stayed quiet, so I carried on. 'You know what you are, Dimitri? Apart from being a complete fucking idiot, that is. I mean, I've met plenty of utter wankers in my time, but you get the gold fucking medal. What you just did was—'

'Shit, Max. Look, I'm really sorry. Honest I am. It was a stupid thing to do, I know, but the thing is I'm totally on my uppers here and desperate for cash. The restaurant is hardly breaking even, and any money we do have, that wife of yours pisses it up the wall on all kinds of crap that—'

'*Ex*-wife,' I corrected.

'OK. *Ex*-wife. But when I heard you talking about this Russian guy, I kinda couldn't help myself.'

'Course you couldn't. It's what anybody with shit for brains would have done in your position. And merely as a matter of interest, what was the next part of your cunning plan gonna be? You know. The part where you were supposed to call me back with the details of the handover or whatever, and what the hell were you gonna do with Oleg anyway?'

'Who?'

'Oleg Radimov. The guy you were so keen to get your hands on that you kidnapped a kid to trade for him.'

'Oh yeah, him. Well, it was really about the twenty grand. I couldn't give a toss about the Russkie.'

'Well, there's a surprise. So, come on then, Dimitri. Enlighten me. What was the rest of the plan?'

'Er, I dunno actually. I hadn't quite got that far. When I rang you, it was more of a spur of the moment kinda thing.'

'Stands back in amazement. There's another fucking surprise. But if you want my advice – and I sincerely hope you're listening very very carefully – I'd suggest that you *never* try anything on like this again or I won't have the slightest hesitation in cutting off both your balls and serving them up on a fucking souvlaki skewer. Clear?'

I didn't wait to find out if he was clear or not and ended the call. I was almost hoarse from yelling at him by the end, and I needed another whiskey to ease my throat. I reached for the Jameson bottle on the coffee table in front of me, but before I could lay a hand on it, my phone rang.

Jesus, if that's Dimitri again, I swear to God I'll... Unidentified caller. Oh, for fuck's sake.

I swiped the screen but only got as far as: 'Listen to me, you dozy twat' when I was interrupted by a voice saying, 'Iss diss Meester Dempsey?'

The accent was certainly strong but nothing like Dimitri's rubbish attempt, and besides, it was definitely a woman.

'Yes?' I said it more as a question than a statement.

'Vee haff your vife.'

Christ on a bike. Seriously?

29

Yet another night with little or no sleep wasn't helping my already addled brain cells, and just when I needed them to be firing on all cylinders. Unlike Dimitri's pathetically obvious attempt to extort money out of me, I was convinced that Carla's kidnapping was genuine. As far as I could tell, the caller's Russian accent had been authentic – or at least consistent – and this time there'd been no mention of any ransom money. All they'd wanted was Oleg, and if I ever wanted to see my wife alive again, I'd follow their instructions to the letter.

I'd momentarily considered pointing out that Carla was no longer my wife and that they should contact Dimitri instead, but I quickly dismissed the notion for a number of reasons. Firstly, Dimitri hadn't the least idea of where Oleg was. Secondly, he was a moronic prick who would totally screw everything up. And thirdly, even though Carla and I were divorced and there was little love lost between us, it would have been the epitome of callousness to shirk what was clearly my responsibility.

As soon as the Russian woman had ended the call, I'd tried phoning Carla several times but her mobile must have been switched off. I'd laid off the whiskey and switched to coffee, which had a lot to do with my lack of sleep, but I really needed to think. What the hell was I supposed to do? I honestly couldn't bear the thought of any harm coming to Carla, yet simply handing over Oleg and condemning him to his inevitable fate after we'd bent over backwards to keep him safe seemed almost equally unpalatable.

By the time Alan and Scratch turned up at the funeral parlour the following morning, any kind of solution was still well beyond my grasp.

'So what do I do?' I said after I'd told them about the threat to Carla's life.

'Jesus, Max, I dunno,' said Scratch. 'I guess Carla's gotta be the priority, though.'

'You mean we just give Oleg to the Russians and let them do what they want with him?'

'Kill him, I expect.'

'Oh yeah? You think?' Scratch's chin dropped a couple of inches towards his chest, and I instantly regretted speaking to him like the idiot he most certainly wasn't. 'Sorry, Scratch. This whole thing's doing my head in, so you'll have to forgive me if I'm a bit on the grouchy side.'

'It's OK, mate. It was a stupid thing to say anyway.'

Alan checked his watch. 'I make it a quarter past nine, which gives us… nearly ten hours before we have to hand Oleg over to the Russians. Should be enough time to come up with a plan of some sort.'

'Well, I'd be more than happy to hear any suggestions,' I said, 'but I've been up all night trying to think of a way out of this godawful mess and ended up with precisely zilch. And if you've got some kind of rescue in mind, we don't have the faintest idea where they're keeping her.'

Round and round we went for the best part of an hour, each of us failing miserably to think of any way we could avoid giving Oleg up while somehow also making sure that Carla didn't come to any harm. Eventually, however, we were all forced to agree that there was really only one choice open to us, and it was a choice that none of us wanted to make.

* * *

Scratch's Aunt Betty was sitting on an upturned plastic beer crate on the platform at the back of the narrowboat, smoking a joint and with an ancient-looking rifle across her lap.

'Hey, Aunty. How's things?' said Scratch when we were close enough for her to hear us, which in her case was little more than ten feet.

She took a deep draw on her joint and held it for several seconds before exhaling. 'Could be worse. Could be better.'

Scratch nodded at the rifle. 'Expecting trouble?'

'Not any more.'

I had a fleeting image of Oleg lying inside the boat with a bullet hole in his chest after Aunt Betty had caught him cheating at chess.

'Oleg inside, is he?' I asked, not entirely certain that the image was wrong.

''Fraid not, no.'

'Shit. Don't tell me he's gone for a walk or something. We told him to stay put and not show his face outside the boat.'

Her heavily glazed eyes flitted between me, Scratch and Alan, then back to Scratch again. 'I'm so sorry, Michael. I really am, but I honestly did the best I could.'

Scratch stepped from the towpath onto the boat and placed a hand on his aunt's shoulder. 'What do you mean? What's happened?'

'I managed to get one shot off, but then the bloody thing jammed,' she said, tapping the rifle on her lap. 'Serves me right for not maintaining it properly, I suppose.'

'Sorry, Aunty, but you're really not making a lot of sense.'

'Yes, I guess the dope isn't helping much, is it?' She took a last drag on the spliff and tossed the butt overboard. 'I'm afraid I've been rather overindulging since it happened. Only way to calm my nerves, you know. Anyone fancy a cup of tea?'

None of us did. All we did want was to hear what she had to tell us about Oleg and not waste any more time while she brewed up. My image of him with a hole in his chest was starting to feel all too real.

'Well,' she said and took a deep breath of fresh air. 'It was in the early hours, and Oleg and I were fast asleep. Separately, of course. I'm not that bloody easy. But that's not to say we hadn't hit it off from the start, by the way, because we did. Got along famously, in fact. Shared a bottle or so of vodka and played a couple of games of chess. We won a game each – although I'm fairly sure he let me win the second one – and we were setting up the board for the decider when we both realised we were far too pissed to play and thought we'd better be sensible and call it a night.'

Jesus. The suspense was killing me. Was she ever

going to stop waffling and get to the point?

'Anyway,' she went on, 'it must have been in the early hours, as I said – two or three in the morning probably – when a strange noise woke me. And I say "strange" because when you live on a boat like this, you get used to all sorts of sounds. The creaking of the woodwork, the ropes straining against their moorings, water slapping against the hull. All those kinds of things. But this was something different, and I couldn't place it at first, very likely because I'm a little hard of hearing, and whatever the noise was, it was coming from towards the back of the boat and I sleep in the bow. Well, I was quite startled, as you can imagine – especially after what you'd told me about those Russian agents – so I sat up in bed and was about to call out to Oleg when I heard a voice. Not Oleg's, but a woman's.

'Wide awake by now, I grabbed my rifle and threw open my bedroom door. Oleg was sitting on the sofa bed, and a woman and a man were standing over him, both pointing their guns at him. "Who the hell are you?" I shouted. "None of your business," said the woman. "I suggest you go back to bed if you don't want anyone to get hurt." "None of my business? You're on my damn boat, for God's sake." She turned her pistol on me, and I had my rifle levelled at her, aiming from the hip. I didn't mean to fire – not yet anyway – but I had my finger on the trigger and I suppose my hands must have been shaking from the shock of it all.'

'You shot her?' I said.

'No. The man with her must have been ready for it because, quick as a flash, he shoved her to the side, and I hit him instead. I don't think it was serious, though. Just nicked him in the arm as far as I could see.'

'Christ, Aunty. Are you OK?' said Scratch,

174

crouching down in front of her and looking into her eyes.

'I'm fine, Michael. Badly shaken, of course, which was why I needed a spliff.'

'So, what happened next?' I asked, even though I had a pretty good idea what the upshot was.

'Well, the man was down on the floor, clutching his arm, and the woman came towards me, yelling at me to put the gun down or she'd shoot. I honestly believed she was going to kill me whatever I did, so I pulled the trigger – deliberately this time – but the damn thing jammed, like I told you. Then she lunged at me and snatched the rifle out of my hands before forcing me back into my bedroom at gunpoint and shutting the door. "And you'll stay in there till we're gone if you know what's good for you" is what she said, and I didn't think it was an idle threat, so I stayed where I was until I could be sure the coast was clear.'

'And by then this man and woman had gone,' I said. 'Taking Oleg with them.'

Aunt Betty nodded slowly. 'I'm so sorry I didn't do more. Poor Oleg. I was really getting to like the chap. I do hope nothing bad happens to him.'

Two armed intruders coming on to the boat in the middle of the night and taking Oleg away at gunpoint sounded like something bad was very possibly going to happen to him, but I didn't say so. Instead, I asked her if she thought they might have been Russians.

'Definitely English,' she said, 'unless they had impeccable accents.'

She gave us a physical description of the man and the woman, but neither meant anything to us. In any case, if the Russians already had Oleg, why would they still need to keep hold of Carla, and if they weren't

175

Russians, who the hell were they? And more to the point, how were we going to hand over Oleg in exchange for Carla before the deadline in eight hours from now when we hadn't got even a sniff of a clue where he might be?

30

The MI5 safe house wasn't ideal, but it was the nearest available, and Holly needed to get Radimov somewhere out of sight and in a hurry. It was an old stone cottage that was seriously lacking in TLC, and judging by the overpowering smell of damp and thick layers of dust, it hadn't been used for months if not years, but at least it was remote.

What irked Holly even more than its semi-decrepit state was the absence of a basement. She'd always believed that interrogations were best carried out below ground level in a space that was as dingy and austere as possible since this considerably enhanced the subject's feeling of helplessness and therefore gave the interrogator a little more of an edge. On the other hand, this was her first real interrogation as her only previous experiences had been role-plays during her training, so any advantage to be gained from subterranean interrogations was probably based more on TV shows and movies than on any concrete evidence.

And with no basement available, Holly had had to make do with what she'd got, which was why Oleg

Radimov was now duct-taped to an upright wooden chair in one of the two poky bedrooms, while she sat opposite him on a similar chair and so close that their knees were almost touching. She'd already spent close to an hour grilling him about the evidence he had, but this was no easy task since she had such minimal information to work with. All that she'd been able to glean from Bendix was that the man they were supposed to be protecting was an MP who was having an affair with a woman who was Russian. Radimov, however, had repeatedly denied any knowledge of a British politician having intimate relations with a Russian woman, so had no idea what video or photographic evidence she was talking about. His stubborn refusal to cooperate was as infuriating as it was unsurprising, but what pissed Holly off nearly as much was the constant smirk on his absurdly round pink face as if he was actually enjoying himself.

Time for a break, she decided, and went to join Jonah in what served as an open plan living room and kitchen, ignoring Radimov's cheery request for a large vodka. She'd let the bastard stew for a while, and after she'd fortified herself with some strong coffee and a cig or two, she'd get back in there with a different approach and see how long it took to wipe the stupid smirk off his face.

'Any joy?' Jonah asked as she flopped down into a battered armchair and picked up the packet of cigarettes from the low table in front of her.

'Brick wall. So far, anyway. Any chance of a coffee?'

While Jonah busied himself in the kitchen area, Holly cast her mind back to the events on the narrowboat the night before. It had been soon after she'd taken over from Jonah to watch the boat that Oleg Radimov had come out on deck, presumably for a few breaths of fresh air. He didn't stay out for more than five minutes, and even though she'd now positively identified the target, she decided to wait before making her move. For one thing, she wanted to see if anybody else was going to show themselves so she could be as sure as she could be that Radimov and the woman were alone on the boat, and for another, the element of surprise would be that much greater once the pair of them were well and truly asleep.

Half an hour after all the lights had gone out on the narrowboat, she went to fetch Jonah from the Mondeo. But snatching Radimov hadn't gone as smoothly as she'd expected, mainly because Jonah couldn't have been more wrong about the woman not putting up much of a fight. Radimov had a gun but was way too sluggish to do anything with it, but the crazy cow went berserk and shot at them with a rifle that looked like it had last been used at the Battle of the Somme. It was still able to fire, though – once anyway – and Holly was well aware that she might have been badly wounded, if not killed, if it hadn't been for Jonah's lighting reactions in pushing her out of the way.

After they'd managed to bundle Radimov into the boot of the Mondeo and set off for the safe house, she'd thanked him and asked if he needed to get to a hospital, but he'd said he was fine and the bullet hadn't done any real damage. 'Bit more than a graze but nothing serious.'

'How's the arm now?' Holly said as Jonah handed her a mug of coffee.

He glanced down at the bandage that was just visible below the sleeve of his T-shirt. 'Twinges a bit but otherwise OK.'

She considered thanking him again but bit back the words before they entered her mouth. She was grateful, sure, but didn't want to make too big a thing of it. Didn't want the guy to get above himself, after all.

'Glad to hear it,' she said. 'You wouldn't be much use to me if you spent God knows how many hours hanging around in some A and E department.'

Jonah sat down in an equally battered armchair at right-angles to her own. 'To be honest, I can't see I've been that much use to you anyway.'

Holly half closed her eyes. Oh, spare me the little-boy-lost self pity, she thought. I could do without that sort of shit just now, but if he was fishing for compliments, how about this?

'So saving my life doesn't count?'

'Maybe the bullet wouldn't have hit you at all.' He shifted uncomfortably in his chair. 'It's just that you're in there interrogating Radimov, and I have absolutely no idea what you're trying to get out of him, especially as the original plan was simply to kill him and blame it on the Russians.'

Here we go again. Whingeing on about not telling him anything.

'It's like I told you before. You don't need to know what you don't need to know.'

'Look, you've made it perfectly clear that you never wanted me along on this operation and you think I'm as much use as a chocolate teapot, but if you're getting nowhere with Radimov, then perhaps – *perhaps* – there may be the tiniest of possibilities that I might be able to help in some way. At least as a kind of sounding board you could bounce ideas off and come up with a different strategy for how to break him. But I'll have to carry on being a chocolate teapot unless you give me a bit more information about what it is you're trying to find out.'

Holly was certainly struggling, it was true, and maybe there was something to be said for two heads being better than one, even though the second head happened to be Jonah's.

Shit, why not? What have I got to lose apart from a massive kick to my self-esteem if he outdoes me with some brilliant plan or other? Unlikely, of course, but it was still a risk.

'OK,' she said and stubbed her cigarette out in the grubby glass ashtray next to her coffee mug, 'although I have to say that Bendix has been less than forthcoming with the details, so I'm almost as much in the dark as you are.'

It took next to no time to fill him in on what little she knew, and she finished by telling him how adamant Bendix had been that it was vital to get the evidence of the affair from Radimov before killing him.

'Bloody hell,' said Jonah and sat forward on the edge of his chair. 'All this just to prevent some MP having their under-the-duvet shenanigans being made public?'

Holly took a sip of her coffee. 'So it would appear, yes, but I imagine there's a lot more to it than that.'

'Oh?'

'Think about it. Since this "naughty boy", as Bendix referred to him, is in government, it's not an unreasonable assumption that he may well have access to some rather sensitive information.'

'And Five are shitting themselves that he might be passing on secret intel to his Russian mistress.'

'That would be my guess.'

'But from what you've told me, it sounds like

Bendix is a lot less interested in stopping this MP guy passing on state secrets than he is about protecting his reputation.'

Holly shrugged and lit another cigarette. 'The thought had occurred to me, but perhaps someone else is dealing with that side of things.'

'Well, I certainly hope so. Otherwise, all we're doing is trying to stop anyone finding out that some MP has trouble keeping his dick in his pants.'

'Nicely put,' said Holly and was about to point out that, whatever the rights and wrongs, that was their assignment and they'd better be getting on with it when there was a knock at the front door.

Instantly, they both froze.

'Who the fuck is that?' said Jonah in a stage whisper.

Holly put her finger to her lips to silence him and picked up her gun from the table. She motioned to Jonah to take out his own weapon before slowly covering the short distance to the door. Taking hold of the handle, she glanced over her shoulder to check that Jonah was ready, then pulled the door open in one swift movement.

31

I was all out of ideas. With Oleg missing and presumed impossible to find, I hadn't got a scooby how to get Carla out of the clutches of the Russian agents, and I had less than six hours to figure something out.

Hardly a word passed between Alan, Scratch and me as we left Aunt Betty's narrowboat and drove back to the funeral parlour. I didn't know what the others were thinking, but in the absence of any practical solutions, all I could do was pointlessly run through a series of "if onlys" in my head – with the help of its resident voice, of course.

'If only Mr Mysterious hadn't vanished off the face of the Earth, you'd have been able to hand Oleg over to him or MI6 or whoever as soon as you'd got back from France.'

'If only the cops had taken him in when you took him to the police station.'

'If only these Russian agents hadn't been so hell bent on killing him or if we'd managed to give them the slip.'

'If only they'd kidnapped Dimitri instead of Carla, you wouldn't need to give a shit.'

And so on, and so on, culminating with: 'If only I hadn't taken the job of collecting Oleg from France in the first place, none of this fucking nightmare would ever have happened.'

'You're not wrong there, mate,' said Scratch, 'but we all agreed, so you don't have to take *all* the blame yourself.'

'What?' I hadn't realised I'd spoken the last "if only" out loud so hadn't expected a response.

'You were saying how we wouldn't be in this fucking nightmare if—'

'Oh, right. Yes. Sorry, I—'

'Anyway, we'll be back at Stiff City in two shakes. Get one of Sanjeev's brews inside yer, and it'll do yer the power o' good.'

'Yeah,' Alan snorted. ''Cos a nice cuppa tea is gonna solve all our problems, isn't it?'

'Fuck off, Alan.'

But I never did get Sanjeev to brew up because no sooner had we stepped through the door of the funeral parlour than he rushed up to us, arms flailing and babbling like a half-crazed crack addict.

I put what was intended to be a reassuring hand on his shoulder. 'You wanna calm down and tell us what you're so het up about?'

'There's a… There's a…' He was hyperventilating like he'd just finished a marathon and could barely get the words out.

'Maybe I should slap him,' said Alan. 'Looks hysterical to me.'

I ignored him. 'There's a what, Sanjeev? A what?'

'There's a… There's a…' Once again, this was as far as he got, so I told him to take a few deep breaths, which seemed to help.

'There's a body. A dead one. A man. Downstairs. In the… mortuary.'

'Yeah, well, in case it may have escaped your notice,' Alan said, 'this is in fact a funeral parlour, so a dead body in the mortuary isn't something particularly out of the ordinary. In fact, I'd go so far as to say it's perfectly bloody normal.'

'No, no. You don't understand,' Sanjeev gasped. 'I found him right outside. On the pavement. Slashed wrists. Suicide, I guess.'

Jesus. This was certainly not an everyday occurrence. 'You mean he killed himself right on our doorstep?'

'Must've done.'

'Can't see any sign of blood,' said Scratch, who was still standing in the open doorway and was inspecting the pavement behind him. 'You clean it up or something?'

'Fuck, no.'

'So what do we have here then?' said Alan. 'The curious case of the guy who topped himself somewhere else and then miraculously managed to get himself to our place even though he'd already croaked?'

'Somebody must have dumped him,' I said.

Alan clicked his fingers. 'Of course! I knew I could rely on you to solve the puzzle, Holmes.'

I'd known Alan for so long that ignoring a lot of the crap he came out with had become almost second nature. 'We'd better take a look for ourselves, I s'pose.'

I headed for the basement steps with Alan and Sanjeev tagging along behind. Scratch declined to accompany us on the grounds that somebody ought to stay behind and mind the shop. We all knew the real reason, however, which was his extreme phobia about anything to do with death and dying. Never having to go down into the mortuary had been one of his deal-breaking conditions for agreeing to become a partner in the business.

To be fair, I wasn't too keen on visiting the place myself. Nothing to do with death or corpses, it was the appalling stink that made me avoid it as much as possible because it was guaranteed to set off my osmophobia and the inevitable pounding headaches. It was way too cold down there to be the stench of rotting bodies, and anyway, the less recently deceased were kept in refrigerated drawers. No, the smell was more sort of "chemically" with more than a whiff of formaldehyde and chlorine in amongst it.

The mortuary also held the distinctly unpleasant memory of being strapped to one of the four stainless steel cadaver tables (as they're called in the trade) while Danny Bishop, the previous owner of the funeral parlour, threatened to cut off at least one of my fingers for failing to repay the money I owed him.

I tried not to breathe too deeply as I reached the bottom of the steps and made a mental note to get the leather straps removed from the table in question.

Our mortuary assistant, Alice, was sitting on a high stool at a workbench at the far end of the room, examining her fingernails and smoking a cigarette. This was strictly forbidden, of course – the smoking, that is, and not the fingernail inspection – but Alice wasn't a great one for following rules and became scarily belligerent if you tried to enforce them.

She was wearing her usual white lab coat, and her normally dyed blonde hair was now a highly unnatural shade of bright red.

I called out to her with a cheery 'Hi, Alice. How's it

going?', and she very slowly turned her gaze in my direction, the glare of the overhead fluorescent strip-lights glinting off her impressive array of facial piercings.

'All right,' she said, although it was more of a grunt than anything, so I couldn't be sure of the exact words.

I ploughed on regardless. 'I hear we have a new customer.'

'Uh-huh.'

'That one, is it?' I said, pointing to the cadaver table nearest to her.

She answered by tilting her head back and blowing a couple of smoke rings into the air. Understandable really, since all of the other tables were unoccupied, and this was very obviously the only one with the shape of a body on it, concealed beneath a pale green sheet.

Alan, Sanjeev and I approached it with caution as if we were uninvited visitors encroaching on Alice's domain. Our trepidation proved to be justified when she stubbed out her cigarette, slipped off her stool and stood beside the cadaver table like a vixen protecting her cubs.

'I've not done anything with him yet apart from removing the clothes,' she said, uttering her first recognisable sentence.

'Oh?'

'Not much point till we know who's gonna pay, is there?'

It was a perfectly valid assessment of the situation, for sure, but before Alice even considered setting to work on prettifying the corpse, there was a mystery we needed to get to the bottom of.

'Mind if we take a look?' I said.

Alice pondered the question for a moment while she

took the piece of gum she'd been chewing from her mouth and stuck it to the underside of the table. This was another habit of hers that I dearly wished she'd break but kept my mouth shut when I called to mind the first time I'd raised it as an issue.

'Suit yourself,' she said at last and began to gradually peel back the sheet to expose the head and shoulders.

As soon as the face was fully revealed, I grabbed hold of the edge of the table to steady myself. 'Holy shit.'

32

'Hello, Miss Gilmartin. Sorry to drop in unannounced, but I've been simply *dying* to know. Has he cracked yet?'

The imposing figure of Wyatt Bendix stood framed in the doorway of the safe house with a thin and unconvincing smile on his lips. He was wearing a dark brown trilby hat and an expensive camel hair overcoat.

Holly lowered her gun.

'Er, no, not yet,' she said, faltering slightly over the words as she fought to overcome her shock at her boss's unexpected appearance.

Bendix looked past her to where Jonah still had his semi-automatic pointing straight at him. 'Perhaps you might inform your chum that I am *not* the enemy here, Miss Gilmartin.'

Jonah returned his weapon to his shoulder holster. 'Sorry, sir, I—'

'"Sir", eh? Know who I am, do you?'

'Well, sir, I assumed that—'

Bendix cut him off again with a wag of his finger. 'Never assume, lad. Never assume. Want to know why? Because "assume" makes an ass of u and me. Expect you've heard that before but very true nevertheless. Especially in our line of business, wouldn't you say, Miss Gilmartin?'

Holly didn't feel the need to respond with anything more than a barely perceptible nod as Bendix marched into the room and took off his hat.

He held it out to Jonah. 'Hands clean, are they?'

'Sir?'

'Are they *clean*? Don't want your grubby little mitts all over it if you've just been for a Number Two and failed to do the necessary.'

Jonah's mouth formed an O shape as if he was about to speak but remained silent.

Bendix's laugh was as unconvincing as his smile. 'Ha ha. Only joshing, lad. Only joshing. Here. Look after it for me, will you? There's a good fellow.' Jonah took the hat from him and Bendix spun round to face Holly. 'Apologies for the intrusion, as I was saying, Miss Gilmartin, although since I hadn't had a sit rep from you since yesterday, I was somewhat anxious to learn if you'd made any progress. And if you're wondering how I found you, the chaps at HQ tipped me off that you'd requested a safe house, so I put two and two together and here we are. I take it that you have indeed nabbed the blighter, yes?'

'In the next room, sir.'

'Jolly well done, Miss Gilmartin. Jolly well done. But do I gather that Comrade Radimov has so far refused to spill the beans *vis-à-vis* the evidence we are seeking?'

'Not as yet, but I'm sure that—'

'*Nil desperandum*, my dear. *Nil desperandum*. Rather new to this sort of thing, eh? Perhaps you'd allow an old hand like myself to have a pop at him and see what falls out when I give his tree a bit of a shake.'

He didn't need Holly's permission, of course, so she simply watched as he produced a pair of lightweight black leather gloves from his overcoat pocket and took his time putting them on as if he was a surgeon preparing for a delicate operation.

'Wish me luck,' he said and disappeared into the bedroom that Holly had indicated, closing the door behind him.

'What an absolute bellend,' said Jonah quietly after Bendix had closed the bedroom door behind him. 'Who the hell does he think he is?'

Holly sat back down in her armchair and sipped at her coffee. 'Just be grateful you're not a woman.'

'Eh?'

Since Jonah was still a trainee and had only joined the Service a few months ago, he probably hadn't heard about their boss's reputation as a serial groper, but Holly decided this was neither the time nor the place to enlighten him. Instead, they sat in silence, which must have been a strain for Jonah, but they were both listening intently for anything they could glean from what was happening inside the bedroom. To begin with, they heard nothing at all, but then there was the unmistakable sound of someone being repeatedly punched in the face, each blow followed by a grunt of pain.

Out of the corner of her eye, Holly was aware that Jonah was staring at her with an expression of stunned disbelief. She studiously avoided making eye contact. Although she might have expected this kind of brutality from Bendix and was powerless to stop him, she saw no reason to let Jonah see quite how shocked and disgusted she was herself.

But no more than a minute or so later, the beating appeared to stop, and all that could be heard was an unintelligible murmur of voices. Soon afterwards, the bedroom door opened and out stepped Bendix, noticeably breathing more heavily than before he'd begun his interrogation of Radimov.

'It's all about technique,' he said, catching Holly's eye and delivering the words with a self-satisfied grin. 'You'll learn eventually, I'm sure.'

She watched as he slowly removed his black leather gloves, and it wasn't lost on her that he didn't return them to the pocket of his expensive overcoat.

'Anyhoo,' he went on, 'our portly and vertically challenged Russian friend has been kind enough to confide in me the whereabouts of the distastefully prurient images which we have been hunting for so diligently. He alleges – and may the good Lord help him if he's lying – that these are to be found on a thumb drive— Is that the correct term or is it a flash drive? I never quite know, but no matter. Comrade Radimov claims that he secreted it in the lining of a coffin at a certain funeral director's by the name of Max Dempsey and Partners. I believe you may have knowledge of this establishment, Miss Gilmartin?'

'Yes, sir.'

'Excellent. Might I suggest, therefore, that you accompany our guest there *tout de suite* and retrieve the blessed thing before carrying out the second phase of your assignment?'

'Yes, sir.'

'Splendid. But it is, however, with the deepest regret that I shall not be able to join you on this occasion as I have a prior and pressing engagement. Nevertheless, I have every faith in you to complete this mission cleanly and efficiently and come through with flying colours. Hat?'

This last word was the only one he'd addressed to Jonah since he'd left the bedroom, and it was spoken with hardly a beat separating it from the previous sentence.

Jonah stayed sitting in his armchair and picked up the trilby from the low and rather dusty table in front of him. He held it out to Bendix, who took it from him with a venomous scowl and gave it a cursory brush with the back of his hand.

'Very well then,' he said, clearly having to force his features into the faintest of smiles, 'I shall bid you farewell and *bonne chance*. And don't forget to keep me posted, Miss Gilmartin. I shall be awaiting your call with unsurpassed anticipation.'

He opened the front door of the safe house and was about to close it behind him when he turned back into the room. 'Oh, and incidentally. When you do retrieve this thumb drive thing, you are not on any account to view its contents but deliver it directly to me. Is that understood?'

'Yes, sir,' said Holly and took another cigarette from her almost empty packet.

33

To say I was in shock would be a gross understatement. Not that I was about to faint or anything like that, but my knees definitely went a bit wobbly for a moment. Even so, I couldn't take my eyes off the body on the mortuary table and the deathly grey pallor of the face with its pencil moustache and the black greased-back hair that was understandably a lot less neatly groomed than the last time I'd seen him. There was also the unmistakable scent of the overdone aftershave that I remembered from before, although it had now turned stale and a little less pungent.

'What's up, Max?' said Alan. 'Looks like you've seen a ghost. You know 'im or what?'

'I don't *know* him, but I'm pretty certain I recognise him. Mr bloody Mysterious. The guy who hired us to fetch Oleg over from France. The guy who we haven't been able to get in touch with ever since.'

Alan exhaled slowly through his teeth. 'Jeez. So how come he's turned up here then? It's hardly gonna be a coincidence, is it?'

'Perhaps whoever found him realised he was dead

and brought him here because this was the nearest funeral parlour,' said Sanjeev.

Alan told him he didn't know what he was talking about and to keep his trap shut unless he had anything sensible to say.

I shifted my gaze from the dead man's face and asked Alice if she had any idea how long he might have been dead.

'I dunno. I'm not a bleedin' pathologist.'

'Yeah, but with all your experience of dealing with—'

'Three or four days, I guess.'

I did a quick mental calculation. 'So that probably explains why we haven't been able to get hold of him. Sounds like he must have died while we were still in France and before I tried to call him for the first time.'

'OK,' said Alan, 'but why top himself so soon after he'd given us the job and before we'd delivered the goods? Unless…'

'Unless what?'

'Unless he didn't actually top himself. After all the shit that's happened lately, I wouldn't be at all surprised if someone did the job for him.'

'But his wrists were slashed,' said Sanjeev, and Alan told him to shut up.

Alice wouldn't normally do anything without a specific request, but she pulled the sheet further down the body so that we could check out the wrists for ourselves. Sure enough, there was a distinct gash across each wrist and a good deal of dried blood. Other than that, I didn't really know what I was looking at, so it was impossible to tell whether the injuries were self-inflicted or not.

'Been in the wars a bit by the look of 'im,' said Alan,

pointing to a roughly circular scar below the man's left shoulder and a similar one on the right side of the torso. 'Bullet wounds, I'd say, but fairly old. My granddad had one he picked up in the Second World War. Showed it to me when I was a kid.'

'There's something else,' said Alice. 'Couldn't help noticing when I was taking his clothes off. He's got three fingers missing from his right hand, and there's still dried blood on the stumps.'

I don't know why the rest of us hadn't spotted the missing digits, and we all leaned forward to take a closer look. She was right, of course, but the sight once again brought back the terrifying image of Danny Bishop standing over me with a pair of surgical secateurs and threatening to deprive me of one or more of *my* fingers.

'Seems like he was tortured then,' I said.

'Yeah? Or maybe he cut off his own fingers before slashing his wrists,' said Alan. 'Would have made holding a knife or a razor blade rather tricky.'

'And another thing,' said Alice. 'See all the dried blood that came from the wrists? It's all up the inside of the forearms. So unless I've totally misunderstood everything I thought I knew about how gravity works, this guy apparently cut his wrists with his hands above his head or at least raised upwards. Unlikely, I reckon.'

I'd never known Alice to be quite so garrulous, but perhaps she was feeling pleased with herself for solving the mystery – or one of them anyway. There wasn't a chance in hell that this could have been a suicide. From what she'd pointed out, it was very probable that Mr Mysterious had been tortured and then murdered by someone who'd failed miserably to make his death look like a genuine suicide. But who was that "someone" and why would they want to torture and kill Mr Mysterious? We didn't even have any real idea who the guy was.

I asked Alice if she'd found any ID on the body, but she hadn't bothered to look for any.

'His stuff's all over there if you want to go through it yourself,' she said and indicated a pile of neatly folded clothes on a nearby workbench.

On the top was the light-coloured trenchcoat that Mr Mysterious had been wearing when he'd shown up at the funeral parlour and asked us to collect "a body" from France. There was nothing in the pockets, so I tried the dark grey suit jacket that was underneath the coat. In one of the inside pockets was a phone, which I handed to Alan while I searched through the rest of the clothes.

'No ID that I can find,' I said. 'Anything useful on the phone?'

Alan was repeatedly swiping and tapping the screen of the smartphone. 'Nothing so far. No call log, no messages, no contacts, no— Oh, hang on. What's this?'

'Video clip, isn't it?' said Sanjeev, who was peering intently over Alan's shoulder.

Alan prodded the screen.

'*My name is Michael Edward Connelly, and I am an agent with the CIA. If you're watching this video, I am already dead.*'

34

I shouted at Alan to stop the video till I could get a look for myself, and with Sanjeev, me and even Alice crowded round him, he restarted the clip from the beginning.

The face was unquestionably that of Mr Mysterious, although nearly as grey as it was in death. He was staring almost directly into the camera and speaking in a flat monotone.

'*My name is Michael Edward Connelly, and I am an agent with the CIA. If you're watching this video, I am already dead. I managed to track down the two Russian agents who plan to liquidate Oleg Radimov, and I intended to kill them before they could do so. However, they easily got the better of me, and I have therefore failed in my mission to protect Mr Radimov. Consequently, I have decided that I am unable to live with the shame of this failure, and taking my own life is the only honourable course of action open to me.*'

Two seconds later, the screen went blank, and there was a lengthy pause before Alan broke the silence.

'Jesus. Only time I've ever seen anything like that

was on the telly when some terrorist group has got a hostage to spout whatever bullshit they forced them to.'

'Fairly obvious he was reading what they'd written for him,' I said. 'Load of crap as well since there's no way he went ahead and topped himself.'

'Must be bloody stupid, these Russians, if they thought anybody'd fall for the suicide thing. Screwed that one up big time.'

'But why bother even *trying* to make it look like suicide? They're paid assassins, for God's sake. Killing people is what they do, and they don't exactly make a secret of it, do they? And why go and dump him on our doorstep?'

Alan shrugged. 'A warning maybe?'

'Eh?'

'You know. This is what's gonna happen to Carla if we don't hand Oleg over to them.'

It was certainly a possibility and the only explanation that made any sense, but what about the video? What had that got to do with us?

Alan had had the same thought. 'And why the video? That's got fuck all to do with us.'

'Dunno,' I said. 'Perhaps they expect us to pass it on to the cops or MI5 or somebody so they don't get done for murder.'

But as soon as the words were out of my mouth, I knew that this was absurd. As I'd said myself only a minute ago, these Russians didn't seem to care too much about keeping it a secret that they were prepared to do whatever it took to kill Oleg. The only vaguely plausible reason for the video was that they wanted us to show it to Oleg to prove to him that his apparent protector was no longer up to the job. After all, they weren't to know that he wasn't actually with us and that we didn't have the ghost of an idea where he might be.

'You know one thing that's odd about that video?' said Sanjeev, who we hadn't heard a peep out of since the last time Alan had told him to shut his trap.

I could tell that he was about to do the same again, but I was desperate to hear any other opinion that may just throw some light on what the hell was going on, so I pre-empted him with a: 'What's that, Sanjeev?'

'Well,' he went on, 'if it's true that the Russians wrote the script for the guy, it strikes me that their English is damn near as good as a native speaker's. Better in many cases. "Liquidate"? "Honourable course of action"? Not the sort of language many foreign people would use if you ask me.'

It was a good point and one that hadn't occurred to me till then. 'So, if you're suggesting that it wasn't the Russians that tortured and killed him, who did?'

Sanjeev didn't answer and nor did anyone else, clearly because this was yet another piece in the puzzle that was becoming increasingly mind-bending by the day – almost by the hour.

I asked Alice to cover the body back up. There was nothing more we could do down here in the mortuary, and the stink of the place was playing serious havoc with my osmophobia.

'May as well go back up,' I said, but at the same moment, Scratch shouted down from the top of the steps.

'Hey, guys. Oleg's here.'

'*Here*? *Oleg*?'

I could scarcely believe what I was hearing. In fact, I wouldn't believe it until I'd clapped eyes on him myself, so I hurried towards the bottom of the steps.

'Turned up just now,' said Scratch. 'He's with a

couple of other people.'

'Other people? What other people? Not Russians, are they?'

By now, I'd reached the top of the steps, and Scratch spoke quietly in my ear. 'Dunno, Max. They didn't say. Don't think they're Russians, though.'

I looked past him and saw Oleg, large as life, who appeared to be browsing amongst the display coffins. There was a woman on one side of him and a man on the other, and if they were Russians, they definitely weren't the two agents we'd tangled with before. The woman had short mousey hair and was a fair bit taller than the female Russian agent, and the man was beardless with much darker skin than the male one.

As I got closer, I could see that Oleg had a black eye that was badly swollen, a sizeable bruise above his jaw and a nasty cut on his lower lip.

'Jesus, Oleg. What happened to you?' I said and couldn't help a suspicious glance at the people with him.

'Had a little disagreement with a friend of these two,' he said and lightly fingered the cut on his lip.

'Oh yeah? And who *are* these two?'

'That's not something that—' the woman began, but Oleg interrupted.

'Security Service. MI5.'

'And this friend that messed your face up?'

'The same. MI5.'

The woman tried again. 'OK, that's enough. So where's this coffin then?'

She'd directed the question at Oleg, but Alan answered it instead. 'Well, if it's a coffin you're after, you've certainly come to the right place.'

The glare she fixed him with would have melted

Teflon. She was obviously not in the mood for some gentle banter, and quite frankly, neither was I. What I really felt was anger at what these people – or a "friend" of theirs – had done to Oleg, mixed in with confusion and incomprehension as to why they had brought him back to the funeral parlour. But I didn't have to wait too long for an explanation.

Oleg had stopped wandering around the velvet-draped plinths that all of the coffins were displayed on and came to a halt in front of one which had nothing on it at all.

'It's gone,' he said, spreading his palms wide as if in amazement.

'Gone?' said the female agent. 'What do you mean "it's gone"?'

'As in it's not here any more.'

The woman bent forward slightly like she was inspecting the top of the plinth to make sure it was indeed empty. 'Well, where is it then?'

'How should I know? Why don't you ask the guys who run this place?'

Sanjeev took a step forward. 'Ah yes. You must be referring to the Windsor Royale. It's one of our most popular models. Elegant and beautifully crafted, it comes complete with—'

'Look,' said the agent, 'I don't want to buy the thing, so quit the sales pitch and just tell me where the fuck it is.'

'Um, it's occupied.'

'Meaning?'

'Meaning there's a body in it.'

She closed her eyes and very possibly counted to ten before opening them again. 'OK. So where is it now?'

'The coffin?'

'Yes, the bloody coffin!'

'In the hearse. The funeral's at four o'clock, and I was getting quite worried that Max and the others wouldn't be back in time to—'

'And is that the hearse that's parked out the front?'

It was the male agent who'd taken over the interrogation, possibly because he'd recognised the need to introduce a level of calm before his colleague totally lost her shit.

Sanjeev told him that it was the only hearse we had, so yes, this was the one with the coffin in it.

'You'll have to bring it back in so we can search it.'

'Search it?' I'd had more than enough of this bullshit and decided it was time to intervene. 'What is it you're looking for?'

The woman took over again. 'That's none of your concern.'

'You're kidding, right? You're talking about a deceased person who's been entrusted into our care, and you want to go rummaging through their coffin?'

'They're after a thumb drive I hid in the lining,' said Oleg, and the agent told him to shut up.

My guess was that this was the evidence he had of the MP's affair with a Russian woman, and I also assumed that he wouldn't want MI5 to get their hands on it before he could use it himself.

'You'll need a warrant then,' I said without knowing whether this was true or not, but the fleeting glance that passed between the two agents and the momentary hesitation seemed to indicate that it was.

The woman was clearly rattled. 'Not in the case of national security. We can search whatever we want.'

I suspected this may have been utter bollocks, but in the absence of any real knowledge, I didn't have a leg to stand on, so I tried another tack. 'Technically, the coffin and its contents are the property of the deceased's family, so you'll need their permission at the very least.'

'Coffin. In here. Now.'

'Or what?'

'Or you will find yourself in some extremely serious shit that's so incredibly deep that it'd make the Mariana Trench look like a sodding puddle.'

Was she bluffing? Judging by the narrowing of her dull grey eyes and the cold, piercing stare, I didn't believe she was, and I decided it wasn't worth the risk of finding out.

'Very well,' I said, 'but I shall be making a formal complaint to the relevant authorities.'

The male agent failed to suppress a snigger. 'Yeah, and good luck with that.'

He then followed Scratch and Alan out to the hearse while the woman, Oleg and I stood in stony silence.

Less than a minute later, her partner came rushing back in, flapping his arms around and seemingly about to piss his pants.

'It's gone!'

'The coffin?' said the other agent.

'No, the whole bloody hearse. It was there when we arrived, but now it's disappeared.'

'Oh dear, it must've been stolen,' I said. 'That's a bugger, isn't it? Mind you, I've been saying for ages that there'd be a lot less crime if all those coppers hadn't been taken off the streets.'

I couldn't resist giving the female agent the hint of a smirk, and if this had been a cartoon, there'd have been bursts of smoke coming out of her ears and jets of flame flashing from her eyes.

35

When the female agent had finally calmed down enough to speak coherently, she told her partner to use the tracking app to find out where the hearse was.

'You put a tracking device on our *hearse*?' I said. 'I don't suppose you had a warrant to do that either.'

Shit. After we'd found the tracker that the Russians had fitted to the hearse before we came over from France, why had it never occurred to me that MI5 might do the same thing?

The male agent was tapping away on his phone. 'Not too far away, according to this.'

'Good,' said the woman. 'Get after it and bring that bloody coffin back.'

Apparently the junior of the two agents, he was off out of the door without further discussion.

Left alone with his partner, I was about to continue voicing my outrage about the tracking device when Alice appeared at the top of the mortuary steps.

'So what do you want me to do with the CIA bloke then?' she said.

I'd intended to try and grab a moment when I could

have a discreet word with Oleg about the CIA agent previously known as Mr Mysterious, but the cat was now not only out of the bag but jumping up and down in front of the MI5 agent.

She spun round to face Alice. 'What did you say?'

Alice treated her to one of her famous withering scowls. 'What the fuck's it gotta do with you?'

'Almost certainly a whole lot more than you could possibly imagine.'

I could see that Alice was winding herself up to launch a blistering verbal attack on the woman, so I thought I'd nip it in the bud before it went nuclear. 'There's a dead man down in the mortuary who says he's a CIA agent.'

'A dead man,' the MI5 woman repeated.

'Uh-huh.'

'A dead man who speaks.'

'Well, no, of course not. That's what he said on the video.'

The raised eyebrow I got in response told me that more information was required, so I gave a brief explanation.

'And where is this video now?' she asked.

I looked to Alice for an answer, and she rolled her eyes at me. 'Where d'you think? Down in the mortuary where you left it.'

The agent was already striding towards the steps with her hand on Oleg's back to keep him in front of her. Evidently – and unsurprisingly – she had no intention of letting him out of her sight.

I checked the clock on the wall. Less than five hours till I had to hand Oleg over to the Russians. My chances had improved slightly since one of the agents was out of the way for now, but how was I going to get him away while the other was watching him like a hawk? I also had plenty of questions to ask him if I could get him on his own and, in particular, why he hadn't told us anything about the CIA being involved.

Before that, I had another question, and this one was for Scratch and Alan. 'Any idea what's happened to the hearse? Can't believe it's really been stolen.'

Scratch shook his head. 'Nah. I reckon Sanjeev's taken it. I spotted him slinking out when the MI5 people started on about searching the coffin.'

'Haven't I always said that lad's got much more to 'im than just being able to make a decent cuppa tea?' said Alan.

'No. You haven't.'

'What do you mean "No"? I'll have you know that…'

I left Alan and Scratch to their bickering and went to join Alice, Oleg and the MI5 woman down in the mortuary.

When I got there, Alice had pulled back the part of the sheet that was covering Mr Mysterious's face, but the agent was obviously far more interested in studying the video clip. Oleg was nearby, listening in with an expression that was somewhere between anger and consternation.

While the agent was so engrossed in the video, replaying it over and over again, I took him by the elbow and surreptitiously led him a few feet away. I had to stoop so that my mouth was close enough to his ear that I could speak quietly without being overheard.

'What the fuck's going on, Oleg? You know this guy or what?'

'Never seen him before in my life.'

'OK, maybe you've never *seen* him, but you know *of*

207

him, right?' Oleg didn't answer, so I pressed on. 'He mentioned you by name, for Christ's sake. Said he was trying to save your arse from the Russians.'

'Yes, Max, I heard.'

'Well?'

He had to lift his gaze to look me in the eye. 'Listen, I'll tell you all about it later, I promise you, but right now the number one priority is to get me out of here and away from these MI5 agents. Once they've done with me, they're just as likely to kill me as the Russians.'

Helping Oleg to escape was a top priority for me too but for rather different reasons.

'And how do you propose we do that when the woman hardly takes her eyes off you?'

'I've got an idea, but you'll need to distract her.'

'She's already distracted watching that bloody video.'

'Distract her *more*, then. But whatever you do, make sure she's got her back to her bag.'

He gave a sideways nod at a black canvas shoulder bag that was on the floor and about eighteen inches from her right foot. Presumably, she'd dropped it there when Alice had given her Mr Mysterious's phone.

I went up to her on her left side and pointed at the phone she was holding in both hands. 'CIA, is he?'

'Apparently,' she said, barely acknowledging my presence.

'Criminal Intelligence Agency.'

'Central.'

'Pardon?'

'*Central* Intelligence Agency.'

'Oh, right.'

Over her shoulder, I could see Oleg frantically

twitching his head to the left, which I guessed meant he wanted me to move her further away from the bag.

'Personally, I very much doubt that he committed suicide.'

'Uh-huh,' she grunted without showing any interest whatsoever and ran the video clip once again from the beginning.

'Pretty sure he was murdered.'

'Uh-huh.'

'And what's more, I think I can prove it.'

The absence of an "Uh-huh" and the merest turn of her head in my direction told me that I had finally got her attention.

'Here, I'll show you.'

There was a heavy sigh from somewhere down near her diaphragm, but she switched off the phone and followed me over to where Mr Mysterious's body was lying on the stainless steel table about ten or twelve feet away.

I pulled the sheet down to reveal the wrists. 'For a start, check out where the blood's dried. Not on the hands. On the inside of the forearms.'

'So?'

'So, how many people slash their wrists with their hands up in the air?'

As I spoke, I looked over to where Oleg was crouching beside her bag and ransacking its contents.

'And the girl told me you just found him on your doorstep?' said the agent.

In the background, Alice emitted a snort that suggested she didn't appreciate being referred to as "the girl".

'That's right.'

'But you've no idea how he—'

'Freeze!'

Bad as things had been over the last few days, I'd been under no illusion that it couldn't get any worse. But Oleg pointing a gun at an MI5 agent hadn't been high on my list of the kind of shit that was likely to happen next.

'*Well, what do you think he was looking for in her bag?*' said the voice in my head. '*Her packed lunch?*'

True enough. I suppose I should have expected something like this, but the MI5 woman clearly hadn't either.

'I'd put that back where you found it if I were you,' she said, her hands only half raised in surrender.

Oleg flicked the muzzle of the gun upwards a couple of times. 'Hands behind your head.'

There was a short delay while she seemed to be considering her options, but as soon as she'd done as instructed, Oleg turned to me. 'She'll have another weapon on her, Max, so you'd better frisk her.'

I'd seen how it was done in the movies and on telly, of course, and I wasn't too happy about running my mitts up and down a complete stranger's body, and especially a woman's, but before I could object, Alice was straight in with: 'I'll do it.'

Other than some fairly frequent sardonic grins, I didn't remember ever having seen her smile, but as she hurried over to the agent, her whole face lit up with a look of pure glee. And without a moment's hesitation, she carried out the search with an overly rough enthusiasm that more than once caused the agent to wince.

'Gotcha,' said Alice triumphantly and pulled a semi-automatic from a holster at the woman's waist.

'Excellent,' said Oleg, 'and now we need to be on

our way before the other spook gets back.'

I was still freaked out at the possibility of being an accessory to the cold-blooded murder of an MI5 agent, so I hoped this wasn't what Oleg had in mind when I asked him what we were going to do with this one.

His answer brought me instant relief. 'Got anything to tie her up with?'

'Oh, we've got even better than that,' said Alice, still beaming her uncharacteristic smile.

36

As far as Holly Gilmartin was concerned, the phrase "incandescent with rage" didn't even come close. She'd successfully completed the first part of her mission in capturing Oleg Radimov but then let him get the jump on her through a moment's lapse in concentration. Now she'd have to start all over again to find the little bastard, wherever the hell he might have got to.

Her gut-wrenching humiliation was compounded still further by having spent the last half hour flat on her back on a stainless steel mortuary table with her hands and feet tightly secured with thick leather straps. And why the fuck had they got straps fitted to a mortuary table anyway? Not that she really gave a damn, but when she'd asked the young woman in the white coat who'd stayed behind after the others had left, all she'd got in return was a flick of the finger and a widening of her stupid smirking grin.

It did nothing to improve her mood when the first words that Jonah said when he finally made his appearance were: 'Shit. What happened to you?', closely followed by: 'And where's Radimov?'

'Gone.'

'Gone?'

'Just get me out of these bloody straps, will you?' Holly snapped, and while he set about undoing the buckles, she asked him if he'd found the hearse.

'Yeah, it was only a few streets away. It wasn't stolen, though. It was one of the funeral people driving it. Sanjeev, I think his name is. Trouble was, he refused to pull over even though I kept blasting the horn and flashing the headlights behind him. I didn't think it would look too good if I'd shunted a hearse and forced him to stop, so in the end we were a couple of miles away before he eventually decided to park up. And you know what? When I asked him why he'd driven the hearse off when he knew full well that we wanted to search the coffin, he told me he'd taken it to the carwash to get it smartened up ready for the funeral. Total bollocks, of course. I mean, it didn't look any cleaner than when we first saw it outside on the street.'

Jonah undid the last of the four straps, and Holly slipped down from the mortuary table, massaging her wrists.

'Not that it matters now anyway,' she said.

'What doesn't?'

'Searching the coffin. Radimov lied about the thumb drive being hidden in the lining.'

'Oh?'

'Even had the nerve to wave it in front of my face before he buggered off. Seems he had it on him the whole time.'

'But I searched him when we were at the safe house.'

'Not thoroughly enough, apparently.'

'Well, unless he had it hidden up his arse, I don't

see—'

'You didn't *look*?'

'No, I—'

'Christ almighty. Didn't they teach you anything in officer training?'

'I haven't finished the course yet, and they haven't covered amateur proctology so far.'

Already in the foulest of tempers, Holly resisted the urge to demonstrate one of her most agony-inducing karate moves and settled instead for an icy glare and: 'Don't get sarky with me, sunshine. I'm not in the mood, OK?'

Desperate for a smoke, she went over to her bag and took out a packet of cigarettes.

Jonah frowned. 'Are you allowed to do that in here?'

'To be perfectly honest, I couldn't give a flying fuck right now whether I'm allowed to or not. And besides, her over there with a face like a pin cushion has been chain-smoking ever since I came down here.'

Jonah followed Holly's sideways nod at the young woman with the multitude of facial piercings, who was sitting on a high stool at a workbench near the far end of the room. She had a lit cigarette in one hand and a semi-automatic in the other that she was examining with casual interest.

'Who's she?'

'Supposed to work here, I believe. Or maybe she just volunteers. One of those weirdos that likes messing about with dead bodies probably.'

'So why's she got a gun?' Jonah asked.

'It's mine,' said Holly. 'And speaking of which…' She marched over to the woman with her hand outstretched in front of her. 'Give.'

She blew a smoke ring in Holly's face. 'What?'

'Give. Me. The. Gun.'

'A "please" would be nice.'

'You think?' said Holly and grabbed hold of the woman's wrist, twisting it harder than necessary so that she let go of the gun and it dropped into Holly's other hand.

'Jesus! Bloody hurt, that did. Take a bleedin' chill pill, will yer?'

'You know, I don't think I will, and you want to watch yourself or you'll seriously regret it.'

'Oh yeah? Says who?'

'Says an MI5 officer who has the authority to do whatever the hell she likes with you, and nobody will ever know.'

At long last, the young woman's grin vanished without a trace, which lifted Holly's mood, albeit by the minutest of degrees.

She holstered her weapon and turned back to Jonah. 'So, there are a few things I need to tell you about.'

'Perhaps you might want to start with how she ended up with your gun and why you were strapped down on a table. Oh yes, and how Radimov managed to escape.'

Holly didn't appreciate the rather condescending tone in Jonah's voice, but she proceeded to fill him in on what she considered to be the more pertinent details of what had happened, which didn't include dwelling too much on the parts that had most humiliated her.

'The dead guy's CIA?' he said when she'd finished and glanced at the partially uncovered body on the mortuary table. 'What's any of this got to do with the CIA?'

'Your guess is as good as mine, although it appears that he was meant to be protecting Radimov.'

She handed him the dead man's phone and told him

to watch the video.

After he'd played it for the third time, he let out a low whistle. 'I still don't understand why the CIA are involved and why they'd want to stop Radimov getting croaked.'

'Or why the guy says he's going to top himself when it's far more likely that he was murdered.'

'How'd you figure that out?'

She showed him the dried blood on the corpse's forearms and asked him how many suicides he thought would slash their wrists with their hands up in the air.

'Good catch,' said Jonah, nodding his admiration. 'I doubt I'd have spotted that myself.'

Holly saw no reason to mention that it wasn't her who'd first noticed the anomaly, and the woman in the white coat was too busy texting to bother contradicting her.

'It makes a lot more sense that the Russians murdered him instead of him killing himself,' she said, 'although the guy's fairly obviously reading from a script that the Russians wrote for him, but don't you think the English is a bit too perfect? And there's something else as well.' She played the video again and paused it just before the end. 'It's very quiet, but if you listen to the few seconds after the CIA guy stops talking, I'm almost sure that someone else says something in the background.'

She turned up the volume on the phone to maximum and restarted the video.

'There,' she said. 'You hear it?'

Jonah took the phone from her, holding it close to his ear, and played the clip again.

'Yeah, maybe you're right,' he said. 'Two or three words perhaps, but I can't make out what they are.'

'Nor can I, but does that sound like a Russian accent to you? In fact, if push came to shove, I'd lay odds that whoever's speaking is English.'

'English?'

'I'd say so, yes.'

Jonah shook his head as if to clear his fuddled brain. 'So now we've not only got the CIA putting their oar in, but one of their agents winds up dead and possibly murdered by person or persons who may not even be Russian. All this is really doing my head in.'

'Likewise,' said Holly, 'but I'll call Bendix later to see if he knows anything about what the CIA are up to. In the meantime, we need to find Radimov and get that thumb drive off him. He went off with Dempsey, and since the hearse is here now, I'm assuming they're in the Polo again, so check if the tracker's still working on that.'

Jonah began tapping on his phone, and less than a minute later announced that it was working fine. 'Hang on a sec, though,' he said, then suddenly brought the screen closer to his face.

'What is it?'

'Well, unless this app's on the blink, it looks like it's coming *towards* us.'

37

Oleg and I jumped into the Polo, and I drove off in a hurry without the least idea where we were heading, but the important thing was to get him away from the MI5 agents as fast as possible. He'd pissed me off big time, and if it hadn't been for Carla's kidnapping, I wasn't sure why I'd even bothered to help him escape.

'As if I wasn't already in enough shit because of you,' I said, 'you damn near made me an accessory to murder – of a fucking MI5 agent.'

'I wasn't going to *kill* her, Max.'

'Maybe not, but I can still get done for aiding and abetting a fugitive, or whatever they call it. God knows what they'll throw at me for that.'

'I'll tell them I forced you at gunpoint.'

'Oh yeah? And why are they gonna believe *you*? I bloody wouldn't. In fact, I don't believe a single word that comes out of your mouth.'

'OK, I admit I haven't been entirely honest with you about everything but—'

'Not entirely honest? For Christ's sake, Oleg, you've been lying to me ever since we were stupid enough to pick you up in France. MI6 had never heard of you, even though you claimed to be a defecting Russian spy. Then there's the dead CIA bloke who was dumped on our doorstep. He mentioned you by name in the video and said he was protecting you, yet you denied any knowledge of him. So, which are you? A defecting spy with CIA connections or just some chancer who's out to make a quick buck by blackmailing an MP?'

There was a pause before Oleg answered. 'I'm kind of both.'

'What do you mean, "kind of both"?'

'Well, I'm not exactly a chancer, as you put it, but the spy thing and the blackmail aren't unconnected.'

'You want to try being a bit less cryptic?'

Oleg shifted uneasily in his seat and sighed heavily. 'What I'm involved in is extremely... sensitive, you understand, so I can't go into too many details. Not yet, anyway.'

'All right, but as long as what you tell me isn't your usual bullshit.'

'If you remember, I told you a while ago that there was a suspected mole within the British intelligence services, which is why my contact hired you to smuggle me over from France instead of using any agents from MI5 or MI6. It's not yet clear which organisation the mole works for, so my contact didn't know who they could trust and decided it was wiser to outsource the job.'

'This contact of yours. You mean Mr Mysterious?'

'Who?'

'The dead CIA guy. Connelly.'

'I only knew him by his codename, Bluebird, and I wasn't lying to you when I said I didn't recognise him because we'd never actually met in person.'

'But if this mole's MI5 or MI6, what's that got to do with the CIA?'

'Well, without going into specifics, it was the CIA who first suspected there might be a mole. And as you can imagine, the Yanks weren't too happy that this mole could be passing on their own secrets to the Russians. The ones they shared with the Brits.'

'So you work for the CIA then, and everything you told us about defecting to MI6 was a load of bollocks, was it?'

'Yes, I'm sorry about that, but it was necessary, I'm afraid.'

'Necessary? Even to the extent of spending hours at a bloody police station when you knew all along it was going to be a complete waste of time?'

'I had to keep up the pretence until I knew I could trust you enough to tell you anything about why I was really here.'

'As an agent for the CIA.'

Oleg gave a wry smile. 'Let's just say I've been... seconded, specifically for this mission.'

'To find out who this mole is.'

'Correct. The CIA believes that this Hayes-Edlington MP is simply a go-between and there must be somebody in British intelligence who's feeding him the classified information.'

'So why did the CIA use you and not one of their own people?'

'Because I have certain information that they don't, and I wasn't prepared to hand it over to them as I have a personal interest in the matter.'

'You mean the stuff you've got on the MP's affair with the Russian woman?'

'Uh-huh.'

'So what's the "personal interest" part?'

'I can't tell you that yet, but what I will say is that I need to meet the MP face to face when I deliver the bad news. I haven't had much opportunity so far, but I need to get on with it as soon as possible.'

Before I could quiz him any further, Oleg made a show of checking his watch. 'Haven't you got a funeral to get to?'

My head was spinning with the effort of trying to make sense of everything Oleg had told me, and I'd completely forgotten about the funeral at four o'clock. Scratch's phobia about anything to do with death and dying meant that he refused to come into direct contact with any coffin that had a body in it, so it was unlikely that he and Alan would be able to manage without me.

'Shit,' I said. 'What time is it?'

'Couple of minutes past three.'

It was going to be close, but if I put my foot down, I might just make it. The only immediate problem was that I had to find somewhere to drop Oleg sharpish.

'Listen, Oleg. I think there's a kind of mini services about a mile up ahead. If I leave you there, you can get a coffee or whatever and wait till I can get back to you. OK?'

'Do you think they'll have vodka?'

'Who knows? Maybe you'll strike lucky.'

Five minutes later, I dropped him off at the services, then ignored most of the speed limits to make it back to the funeral parlour in time. But with less than a mile to go, it occurred to me that this wasn't the smartest of options. There was a reasonable possibility that the MI5 agents might still be there, and running into those two was to be avoided at all costs. I had a vague memory from a TV show about the Security Service that they didn't have any powers of arrest themselves but would have to call in the cops if they wanted to nick me. Perhaps that's what they *would* do, but even if they didn't, what was to stop them taking me some place and beating the crap out of me like they did with Oleg?

I pulled over and rang Alan, who told me that the MI5 agents hadn't left yet and they were looking decidedly hacked off. Hardly a big surprise, of course, but also confirmation that my turning up back at the parlour was out of the question. So I asked Alan to meet me round the corner from the bereaved family's house before he and Scratch went there with the hearse. I also checked with him that the two funeral cars we'd hired for the family were due to arrive at the same time and told him to bring my undertaker outfit to change into.

Satisfied that I'd done all I could – for now – to escape the clutches of MI5, I drove a little more sedately to my new destination, thinking about how I was going to arrange handing Oleg over to the Russians.

'*And what you gonna do if you find Oleg's done a runner when you get back to the services*?' said the voice in my head.

It was a fair point, but one I didn't want to dwell on too much. If Oleg *had* gone missing again and I couldn't deliver him to the Russians by seven o'clock, Carla was screwed.

38

Holly Gilmartin was pacing in amongst the display coffins while she waited for Max Dempsey to reappear. There was no chance that Oleg Radimov would still be with him, and finding him had become even more urgent than before. She'd put off phoning Bendix to ask him about the CIA involvement because then she'd have to admit that the Russian had slipped through their fingers once again and that she'd failed to retrieve the thumb drive. Her boss's reaction to this news would almost certainly make her ears bleed.

Dempsey would obviously know where Radimov was, but it was unlikely he'd give up the information easily unless she resorted to Bendix's barbaric methods of interrogation, and that was never going to happen.

'Looks like he's stopped,' Jonah called out from across the floor.

He was staring at his smartphone, and Holly hurried over to see for herself that the red dot in the middle of the screen was stationary but still blinking.

'Do you think we should go after him now he's not moving?' said Jonah. 'He's less than a mile away.'

'No, wait. Maybe he's just stopped for a pee and he'll carry on back here in a minute,' said Holly, recognising that this was unlikely so close to home unless he had bladder issues. The other possibility was that he'd found the tracking device and dumped it.

Seconds later, they both saw that the red dot was on the move again but not in the direction of the funeral parlour.

'OK,' said Holly. 'Now we go.'

Jonah pocketed his phone. 'What about the dead CIA guy down below? You reckon we should call the cops or what?'

'We'll deal with that later. It's not as if he's going anywhere, is it?'

She was already making for the door with Jonah hot on her heels when two of the other undertakers beat them to it – the big one with the shaved head and the shorter one in the padded neck brace – but now they were dressed in knee-length black coats and each was carrying a black top hat.

'Just the two of you?' said Holly.

'Yep,' said the tall guy.

'Don't you need the other one? Dempsey?'

'Nope.'

'And if you don't mind, we're in a bit of a hurry,' said Neck Brace.

Holly and Jonah stepped out onto the pavement and watched as they walked quickly towards the hearse. Before they reached it, the one they called Sanjeev came out of the funeral parlour carrying a top hat and with a black overcoat draped over his arm.

'So you're going as well, are you?' said Holly.

'Me? No. I have to stay here and mind the shop.'

'Who's the outfit for then?'

Sanjeev looked down at the coat and the top hat as if he'd no idea how they'd got there. 'Er, well, we always carry a spare in case of um… accidents, kind of thing.'

'Accidents? What sort of accidents?'

'Oh, you know. The usual.'

Holly raised an eyebrow. 'No, I don't know. Enlighten me.'

'Well, there was this one time when Scratch—'

'Scratch?'

'The big guy. That's what we call him on account of all these allergies he's got. Anyway, he was on a job a few weeks ago, and he'd eaten something – I can't remember what it was now – but it set off one of these allergies, and he puked his guts up into his top hat. He was almost at the church by then, so if he didn't have the spare, he'd have—'

'Sanjeev! Get a bloody move on, will you? We've got a funeral to get to.'

It was Neck Brace, shouting from where he stood beside the hearse, and Sanjeev scuttled towards him.

'What do you think then?' Holly asked Jonah when Sanjeev was out of earshot. 'Telling porkies or not?'

Jonah shrugged. 'I suppose the big bloke chucking up into his hat is fairly plausible – and actually quite amusing really.'

'No, Jonah, what I'm getting at here is whether they're lying about not needing Dempsey for the funeral. Have a look where his Polo is now.'

Jonah fished his phone out of his pocket and checked the screen. 'Seems he's stopped again. About three miles away. So we go after it, do we?'

'Change of plan. We'll stick with the hearse for now.'

Holly took a deep breath as she started the Mondeo's

engine. She'd have to contact Bendix sooner or later, so she might as well get it over with. Despite the inevitable bollocking she was bracing herself for, she was eager to hear what he had to say about the CIA's interest in Radimov. Jonah knew almost as much as she did by now, so the fact that he'd be listening in hardly mattered any more.

Bendix answered on the second ring.

Although she omitted certain details, such as how she ended up being strapped to a mortuary table, the verbal onslaught she got was even more savage than she could have imagined when she told him about Radimov's escape. But worse was yet to come.

'At least tell me you managed to get the thumb drive,' Bendix said when he eventually recovered enough of his composure to stop yelling.

'He lied to you,' said Holly, deliberately pointing the finger of blame. And why not? After all, it was Bendix himself who'd interrogated Radimov and got the information about the thumb drive being hidden in a coffin.

The gambit only partially did the trick. Holly had a few seconds' respite while Bendix presumably considered how he could make this her fault as well, and when he spoke again, his volume was as loud as ever.

'So where the fuck is it? I assume you searched him before I got to the safe house?'

'Certainly, sir.'

'Thoroughly?'

'Of course, sir.' No way was she telling him that Jonah had been rather less diligent than he should have been and that Radimov had the thumb drive on him the whole time.

'And you've no idea where the damn thing is?'

''Fraid not, sir.'

'Jesus Christ almighty. What a bloody shitshow.'

In the brief silence that followed, Holly decided this would be an opportune moment to shift the focus away from her cockup. 'There's something else, sir.'

'What?'

She could almost hear him running his fingers through his thinning sandy hair in anticipation of even more bad news.

'It's the CIA, sir.'

'CIA? What about them?'

Holly proceeded to tell him about the dead CIA agent at the funeral parlour, the video he'd left on his phone and how he claimed to be protecting Radimov. She finished by asking him if he was aware of the Agency's involvement and what their interest was in Radimov.

Bendix took so long to answer that Holly would have thought she'd lost signal if it hadn't been for the sound of his ragged breathing.

'Bit of a conundrum, that,' he said at last, suddenly striking a considerably softer tone.

'Do you mean that you didn't know anything about the CIA having an interest in—'

'I'll have to look into it. Cheerio.'

Then the line went dead.

Jonah puffed out his cheeks and exhaled slowly. 'Blimey, that was quite a roasting.'

'Not exactly unexpected,' said Holly and reached for her cigarettes on the dashboard, somewhat puzzled by Bendix's almost casual response to her news about the CIA and their dead agent.

39

The funeral had gone off without a hitch, and the bereaved family had seemed happy enough. Not about having to bury their loved one, of course, but the way we'd handled the whole thing. Much less gratifying, however, was the appearance of a pair of uninvited mourners in the shape of the two MI5 agents. They'd obviously followed Alan and Scratch and made no secret of watching me change into my undertaker garb on the roadside and climbing into the hearse. They had at least maintained a respectful distance at the funeral itself, but as soon as it was over, they pounced.

Naturally, they wanted to know where Oleg was, and I told them I had no idea, which might actually have been true, given that I couldn't be sure that he hadn't disappeared from the services where I'd dropped him. Also as expected, they threatened me with all kinds of unpleasantness for helping him to escape, so I pointed out that the only witness they had was Alice, and it was extremely doubtful that she'd be keen to cooperate. I was even bold enough to venture my half-baked theory that they had no powers to arrest me and that I wasn't prepared to hang around while they called in the cops.

They didn't outright deny this so, perhaps foolishly, I went a step further and added, 'Or are you going to drag me off some place and do an Oleg on me?'

Neither of the agents responded, and I may have misread their body language, but I had the impression that reminding them of how Oleg had been treated made them distinctly uncomfortable. This was despite the fact he'd told me himself that these two had had nothing to do with the beating and it had been delivered by someone else altogether.

'So,' I said, taking advantage of what I perceived to be a convenient, if temporary, stalemate, 'unless there's anything more I can help you with, I have a particularly important meeting to get to.'

The MI5 agents didn't seem to have an answer to this either, so Scratch and I headed for the now empty hearse. With just over an hour to go before we were due to exchange Oleg for Carla, I was beginning to get more than a little agitated that I still hadn't heard from the Russians about where the handover was supposed to happen. I'd also failed completely to come up with any workable plan how to get Carla released without sending Oleg to his inevitable death. The guilt was already eating away at me and made even harder to bear because I knew that I'd have to lie to him when I told him I was taking him somewhere safe where he could hide out.

As Scratch climbed in behind the wheel of the hearse, my phone rang. The Russians? No, it was Sanjeev.

'Max, there's something you ought to know.'

'Oh God. Now what?'

'Alice was listening in on what the MI5 agents were

talking about when they were here at the parlour, and it seems they've got a tracking device on your car.'

'The Polo?'

'Yes. And while you're at it, you should probably check out the hearse as well.'

I told him I already knew about the one on the hearse but had forgotten to do anything about it until now. I should also have guessed that there'd be one on the car too.

I thanked Sanjeev for the warning and hung up.

Since I'd found the Russian device – following Oleg's expert guidance – I at least knew the sort of thing I was looking for this time, and I slung my overcoat over the bonnet of the hearse and lay down on the tarmac, face upwards. I wriggled myself underneath in roughly the same position as I'd discovered the Russian device but couldn't see anything that remotely resembled a little black plastic box, so I slithered out again and went round to the back.

'You OK, Max?' said Scratch.

He'd got out of the hearse and was staring down at me as I resumed my horizontal position and took hold of the bumper to pull myself under.

'I'll explain in a minute,' I grunted, and I twisted my head from side to side as I carried on searching.

Once again I drew a blank, and I was about to heave myself back out when I spotted a small black box almost directly above my nose. It looked almost identical to the one the Russians had planted, so I gave it a sharp tug and the magnet gave way with only minimal resistance.

'Recognise this?' I said to Scratch when I got out from underneath the hearse and used the bumper to haul myself upright.

'One of those tracking things, isn't it? I thought we'd got rid of that when we—'

'This one's different, though. Courtesy of our MI5 pals, I believe, and there's another on my Polo from what I've been told.'

He held out his hand. 'Give it here and I'll smash the shit out of it.'

'No, wait,' I said. 'I've got a better idea.'

The nearest vehicle was one of the hired limos, so I slapped the tracking device under its rear end. If the MI5 agents were going to use it to follow us, they'd find themselves at wherever the bereaved family's funeral reception was being held. On the other hand, if they watched us leave in the hearse and were still keeping an eye on their tracking app, they'd clock that something was wrong and come after us anyway.

'Time to make our getaway,' I said, but suddenly realised that Alan wasn't with us. 'Where the hell's Alan?'

'Dunno,' said Scratch. 'He wandered off while we were with the MI5 people. Had something he needed to do, apparently.'

I scanned the area, and almost immediately I saw Alan scurrying towards us, grinning his head off and brandishing a small screwdriver.

'They'll not be going anywhere any time soon,' he said and jerked his thumb back over his shoulder.

On the far side of the church's small car park I could see the male MI5 agent crouching next to the dark grey Mondeo they'd been driving, and the woman was flailing her arms around like a drowning tarantula.

'Did you just do what I think you just did?' I said, fairly confident what Alan's answer would be.

His grin widened. 'Oh yes. "And why stop at the one

tyre?" I thought, so I did two of 'em. That way, they're buggered even if they're carryin' a spare.'

'Nice one,' said Scratch, which was about as close as he ever got to paying Alan a compliment, but then he added, 'I'm amazed you got the right car.'

40

Getting away from the MI5 agents had been our top priority, and next on the list was picking up Oleg from the services where I'd left him – assuming he was still there, of course.

Scratch pulled the hearse over to where I'd left my Polo, and the first thing I did was to look for the tracking device that Sanjeev had warned me about. The car being considerably smaller than the hearse, it took me no more than a few seconds to find it.

'Maybe we should take it to a bridge over the motorway and drop it onto a lorry or something,' said Alan. 'That'd fox 'em. 'Specially if it was on its way to Scotland – or France even.'

I had to admit that this had a certain appeal, but the nearest motorway was in totally the wrong direction from where Oleg was, and no way could we spare the time. Instead, Scratch did what he'd said he was going to do with the tracker on the hearse and smashed the shit out of it.

We set off in a convoy of two with me in the Polo and Alan and Scratch behind me in the hearse, heading for the services. But a couple of miles before we got there, my phone rang.

'Iss diss Meester Dempsey?'

At bloody last.

'Yes,' I said.

'And you haff Radimov?' said the Russian woman.

'Yes,' I lied.

'Goot, becoss your vife she hass been drifing us fucking crazy.'

If it hadn't been for the rapidly mounting stress, I might actually have laughed. 'Oh really?'

'So vee meet very soon ant you tek her avay, OK?'

'Sure,' I said. 'Just tell me where.'

She told me she'd text me the GPS coordinates and that the handover would now be at eight o'clock that evening instead of seven. When I asked her why, the line went dead. Not that I was going to argue. If Oleg *had* gone AWOL from the services, it would give us a little extra time to try and find him. We'd know soon enough.

I turned into the services and parked up. Alan and Scratch came alongside me in the hearse, and as they got out, I could tell that they were in the middle – or possibly the beginning – of one of their all too frequent arguments. From what I could make out, this one was about zoos, which was far and away from most of their usual topics to disagree on. Scratch's point of view seemed to be that keeping wild animals locked up in cages was cruel and inhumane, while Alan was insisting that zoos did a lot of good work in preventing certain species from becoming extinct.

As usual when they got into one of these bickering matches, I was only half listening, but I was glad I picked up the gist on this occasion since this was later to create the spark for my plan of how to save Carla without sacrificing Oleg. For now, though, they were just being bloody irritating.

'If I might interrupt,' I said, 'I think we have rather more pressing matters to deal with, like finding Oleg and getting him to the handover.'

The pair of them fell mercifully silent, so I told them that the Russians had been in contact at last and given me details of where and when to meet.

'Why eight o'clock?' said Alan. 'I thought it was supposed to be seven.'

'They didn't say,' I said, 'but it might be to our advantage.'

'Yeah, it means we've got time to grab something to eat in the caff.'

It wasn't quite what I had in mind, but I couldn't remember when I'd last eaten, so I didn't bother to contradict him.

The services consisted of a petrol station and two separate single-storey buildings, one of which was a kind of miniature shopping mall and the other a café that announced itself in gaudy neon lights as "Diner Mighty".

'Funny,' said Scratch, although I presumed he was being ironic.

The interior of the café was as gaudy as its neon sign. The colour scheme, if it was possible to imagine that the design had been given any thought at all, was predominantly red, yellow and blue, and the overhead lighting was ridiculously bright. As for the smell of frying foods, it came within a gnat's eyelash of my osmophobia threshold.

There were twenty or so plastic-topped tables, and since the café was so sparsely populated, it took less than a second to realise that Oleg wasn't at any of them.

'Perhaps he's in the bog,' said Scratch, and he went to the far end of the diner to check.

Fruitlessly, as it turned out.

'Fuck's sake,' I said. 'I knew this would happen.'

'What about the shop next door?' said Alan, and as he turned towards the exit, Oleg himself appeared carrying a brown paper carrier bag.

For once, I wouldn't have minded if it was stuffed full of vodka bottles. Better to be totally rat-arsed than go to his death stone cold sober. That there was no telltale sound of clinking glass from the bag may simply have meant that he'd restricted himself to the one bottle, which would probably be enough to do the job, even for a hardened drinker like Oleg. Alternatively, the morose look on his face tended to imply that he may have failed to score any vodka at all, as he quickly confirmed.

'Stupid bloody shop,' he said. 'No vodka.'

He set his bag down on the nearest unoccupied table, and glancing inside it, I could see it was more than half full with cans of beer. 'Didn't they have whiskey or anything then?'

Oleg muttered something that was inaudible apart from the word "vodka" and sat down.

'Right, I'm gonna get some food,' said Alan. 'Anybody else want anything?'

Scratch declined, saying that he doubted they'd have anything that didn't set off one of his allergies, so he'd stick with the supply of bananas he almost always brought with him. Oleg shook his head, and I ordered a cheese sandwich, adding, 'And don't go getting a massive fry-up for yourself unless you want to tip me over the edge and bring on an osmophobia attack.'

As Alan made his way to the food counter, which ran the length of the wall on the far side of the diner, I decided I could do with some fresh air anyway. And besides, I needed to check out Google Maps without Oleg knowing and find out where we were supposed to be meeting the Russians.

On my way out, Scratch caught up with me and said he was going to fetch his stash of bananas from the hearse. He was far better than me at messing about with smartphone apps as I'd only made the reluctant transition from my trusty ancient mobile a couple of months ago, so I asked him to hang on and give me a hand first.

'We're still going ahead with it, are we?' he said. 'Giving Oleg up, I mean, even though we know what's gonna happen to him.'

'Believe me, I wish we didn't have to,' I said, 'but I can't see any way round it.'

I gave him my phone, and his thick, prodding fingers finally had the location up on the screen. The red pin on the map looked to be roughly in the middle of the wooded area of an extensive park that was part woodland and part meadow.

I asked Scratch how far it was from where we were, and he zoomed out on the map.

'Not too far. Twenty minutes? Half an hour max.'

No great rush then, which was OK by me. The longer I could put off betraying Oleg to the Russians, the better.

Scratch walked off to get his bananas from the hearse, and I went back inside the café. Alan and Oleg were deep in conversation – about animal welfare from what I could gather. Alan had clearly developed an obsession about the subject, but at least the pair of them seemed to be agreeing with each other.

In between voicing their opinions, both were glugging on cans of lager, and there were already two empty cans on the table next to a cheese sandwich, which I guessed was what Alan had got for me as requested. Also as requested, he'd been considerate enough to limit himself to just a single bacon roll, albeit a pretty enormous one.

I sat down, opened the plastic sandwich pack and took a bite. Not unexpectedly, the bread was limp and damp from spending too long in a fridge, and as far as the cheese was concerned, I'd have got more taste out of the plastic packaging itself.

'So then, Oleg,' I said when there was a gap in the conversation and studiously avoided any eye contact with Alan. 'We need to get going fairly soon and take you somewhere where you'll be safe.'

Oleg nodded and swallowed a generous mouthful of lager. 'You know a place?'

'Uh-huh.'

'Good, because you thought the boat on the canal would be safe.'

'Yes, but since then we've got rid of the tracking devices the MI5 agents planted.'

Oleg smiled and raised his can of lager as if in a toast. 'I've obviously taught you well, my friend.'

Oh God. "My friend"? He's calling me his friend when I'll soon be betraying his trust in the most unforgivable way imaginable. Instead of answering, I forced another bite of the sandwich.

'Hello, hello,' said Alan. 'And here comes Dr Dolittle.'

Scratch sat down at the remaining empty seat at the table, munching on a banana.

'Dr who?' said Oleg.

'No. Dr Dolittle. Scratch here reckons that keeping wild animals in captivity amounts to cruel and unusual punishment and that all zoos should be banned.'

'That's not exactly what I meant,' said Scratch, and I was about to intervene before they resurrected the same old argument when the spark of an idea I'd begun to have earlier suddenly burst into flame.

'I need to make a call,' I said and headed for the exit.

41

Alan and Scratch led the way in the hearse while Oleg
and I followed on in the Polo. According to Google
Maps, there were dozens of interweaving footpaths
through the park but no access for vehicles, so we had
to leave ours in the only parking area, which looked to
be about half a mile from where we were due to meet
the Russians.

'Here?' said Oleg when we got out of the car, gazing
at the open space with a heavily wooded area beyond.
'This is the safe place you meant, is it? You expecting
me to sleep out under the stars or what?'

'No, not at all,' I said, forcing a smile. 'We're
meeting someone in the woods who'll be taking you to
this cottage I know of that's quite remote and very
secluded.'

'Oh? And who is this "someone"?'

'Friend of mine. Don't worry, though. I trust him
completely.'

'So why can't *you* take me?'

It was a question I should have anticipated but
hadn't. 'Er, well, the thing is that um… the cottage kind

of… Well, it belongs to this guy, you see, and he has all the keys and stuff.'

Christ, if Oleg hadn't already figured out I'd been lying to him, this latest piece of blathering would surely have convinced him. Apart from anything, spies like Oleg were probably trained to spot when somebody was bullshitting them.

But to my amazement, Oleg simply shrugged and said, 'OK then. Let's go, shall we?'

I hated all this subterfuge, but I didn't feel quite so bad about it now that I at least had some sort of plan worked out. There was no guarantee that it would turn out how I hoped, of course, and if I was being entirely honest, I'd have to say that the chances of a successful outcome were slim at best. This had certainly been Scratch and Alan's opinion when Oleg had gone to the gents back at the services and I'd told them what I had in mind. In fact, if anything, they'd been even more pessimistic than me and thought the whole idea was utterly crazy and would more than likely end up in a bloodbath.

I guessed we'd find out soon enough, and with map at the ready, I set off towards the woods with Oleg beside me and leaving Scratch and Alan at the car park to wait for Sanjeev's call.

It was fortunate that we'd allowed plenty of time to get where we were going by eight o'clock because Oleg was hardly light on his feet, and I had to slow down to match his pace. Something else I was grateful for was that he didn't ask me any more questions, and we reached the edge of the woods in silence.

Carrying straight on along a dirt pathway for about fifteen yards, we then took a fork to the right, and it grew noticeably darker as the overhead canopy of leaves became more and more dense. My knowledge of different types of trees was virtually non-existent, although I could recognise the huge oaks and the pale grey trunks of the beeches, but other than these, I hadn't a clue.

A sudden memory came to me that Carla and I had brought the kids here once when Emma must have been about seven and Brad about five. They'd already been to all kinds of adventure parks with us and other kids' parents, but I just wanted them to experience a bit of Nature before I lost them forever to the likes of Peppa Pig World or whatever the equivalent was in those days. I should have known better, though. They'd been distinctly unimpressed with the deer and other wildlife, the variety of trees and the carpets of bluebells, complaining constantly at the absence of anything they could actually "do". Not to be thwarted, I'd suggested that there were plenty of trees they could climb, but this was met with an immediate veto from Carla. The result? I wound up spending a small fortune at a crappy amusement arcade back in the town.

'Not too far now,' I said to Oleg, consulting the map on my phone and taking a path to our left. Besides having got even darker as we ventured further into the wood, it had also become spookily quiet, so I was glad to break the silence between us.

But all I got in return was a 'Good', so then I began to get seriously worried that he'd sussed I was leading him into a trap. On the other hand, he'd been unusually grumpy ever since we'd picked him up at the services, but maybe that was just because he'd been pissed off at not being able to top up his vodka levels.

The dirt path took a sharp bend to the right, and straight away we found ourselves in a small clearing among the trees. I checked my phone again, and if the red pin on the map was accurate, we were exactly where we were supposed to be. The little digits at the top of the screen also told me that we were five minutes early, but apparently so were the Russians.

'Stop there and put the hands in the air.'

The female agent stepped out from behind the trunk of a massive oak tree, a pistol pointing directly at us.

I did as instructed and assumed that Oleg had done the same. "Assumed" because I didn't dare to turn my head to the side and witness the look of bitter contempt he'd no doubt fixed me with.

The next order was for us both to lie face down on the ground, and once the woman had finished searching us for weapons, she told us to get to our feet again. I could see that Oleg's bulk was causing him quite a struggle to get himself upright, so I held out a hand to help him. This time, however, it was impossible to avoid looking him in the eye, and I was astonished to find no trace of the animosity I'd anticipated. On the contrary, there was the hint of a smile on his lips, and I was almost sure he winked at me. Was he forgiving me for my treachery, or was he just calmly resigning himself to his fate? Or perhaps I wasn't the only one with a plan and he had a trick of his own up his sleeve.

The woman shouted something in Russian over her shoulder, and her partner appeared instantly from behind another oak tree, prodding Carla in front of him with the barrel of his gun. Her hands were tied behind her, and there was a strip of silver duct tape across her mouth. Not that this stopped her from yelling her head off, even though the words were unintelligible. Her eyes popped wide open when she saw me, and her expression was most definitely not one of gratitude to the man who had come to save her life.

Making sure that the Russians didn't notice, I had a quick surreptitious glance around the immediate area for any sign of Sanjeev and the others, but there was nobody in sight and not even the sound of a broken twig or rustling of leaves.

'That's a good thing, though, isn't it?' said the voice in my head. *'If the Russians happened to clock them, your whole plan would be down the toilet, wouldn't it?'*

This was true, but the same applied if they were late or didn't turn up at all.

'So they kidnapped your wife, eh?' said Oleg.

'Yes,' I said. 'Well, ex-wife, strictly speaking.'

The male agent barked at us to be quiet, then grabbed Carla by the shoulder and forced her down onto her knees with the muzzle of his gun against the back of her head.

Jesus. After all this, they're going to kill her anyway.

I shouted at the guy to let her go and launched myself forward but without the slightest idea what I was going to do by the time I got to him. Not that I had the opportunity to find out because I'd covered only five paces when I felt a sharp stabbing pain in the outside of my right thigh. The next moment, my knees buckled and I crumpled to the ground, my head swimming and my vision rapidly fading from a psychedelic blur to an impenetrable black.

42

My head was pounding a lot harder than from one of my osmophobia attacks and definitely more brutal than the worst of all hangovers. My eyelids felt like they had been glued shut, and when I managed to prise them open, all I could see around me were weird fuzzy shapes that could have been humans or alien beings from the planet Zog.

I was sitting on hard ground with my legs stretched out in front of me and my back against something solid with a rough surface. As my vision began to clear, I glanced behind me and realised it was the trunk of an oak tree.

'So you're back with us, are you?'

I recognised Alan's voice, and I could dimly make out his face as he bent over me.

I blinked hard a few times to try and get my eyesight functioning properly. 'What the hell happened?'

'You were out cold, mate.'

'Yeah, I kinda got that. How long for?'

'Twenty minutes or so.'

'Is everyone OK? What about Carla? They didn't

kill her, did they?'

My vision was almost back to normal, and I could see the grin on Alan's face. 'No, Max, she's fine. Well, not *fine* exactly. Seriously pissed off but alive and kicking. Quite literally, as it happens.'

'What?'

'The Russians. My God, that woman can really put the boot in when she's a mind to.'

None of this was making any sense. The last thing I'd seen was Carla on her knees with a gun at her head, so how come she'd ended up kicking shit out of the Russians?

'And what about Oleg?' I asked.

'He's fine too,' said Alan, and he held out his hand to help me to my feet. 'You wanna see for yourself?'

He needed all his strength to pull me upright, and when I got there, he had to keep hold of me until my giddiness faded and I could support myself unaided. Surveying the scene around me, I saw the two Russian agents sitting as I had been with their backs against separate trees about three or four yards apart. Unlike me, though, they were tied to the trunks with their hands behind their backs, their heads slumped forward with their chins on their chests.

Standing close to the centre of the clearing, Scratch, Oleg, Sanjeev and Carla seemed to be deep in conversation. There was another person too, and it took me a moment to clock who it was. Oh yes. It was all coming back to me now. Philippa Buckland, MRCVS, and various other letters after her name that I couldn't remember. She was in her late forties and skeletally thin. She was wearing a dark green bush hat and khaki safari jacket as if she'd just walked out of an Amazonian jungle. She'd also been instrumental to my plan for saving both Carla and Oleg, which appeared to have turned out rather well.

With a little help from Alan, I tottered over to them, and Philippa was the first to speak. Despite her stick insect physique, her voice was deep and booming.

'Oh, hello, Max. How are you feeling?'

'Groggy and with a blinding headache.'

'Yes, I'm afraid that's to be expected. Sorry about that, but unfortunately you walked in front of one of the Russians at the precise moment I pulled the trigger.'

'You shot me?'

'Lucky it was a tranquilliser dart and not a bullet, eh?'

Her roar of laughter was equally as booming as her voice, but I failed to see what was quite so hilarious. Nor did anyone else in the group for that matter, although I noticed Carla having a quiet smirk.

'OK,' I said. 'Since I obviously missed out on all the fun, perhaps somebody would care to fill me in.'

Everyone started jabbering at once, so I clasped my hands over my ears, which clearly got the message across because they all immediately clammed up. As Sanjeev had been in on the plan from the outset, I elected him as spokesperson and the words spewed out of him in a torrent of overenthusiasm.

When I'd called him from the services where we'd picked up Oleg, he'd done as I'd instructed and contacted Philippa. She's the resident veterinarian at a local zoo, and Alan had known her since they were kids growing up in the same street. We'd also done her a favour not so long ago when a lemur she'd been treating at the zoo had died, and since she was particularly fond of this animal, she'd asked Alan if he could help. What she'd wanted was a proper funeral for

247

it, which included Scratch, Alan and I all dressed up in our undertaker togs and a hearse to bring the deceased primate to its final resting place in her back garden. I don't know what the zoo's policy is on this sort of thing, so maybe she'd had to smuggle it out. Anyway, we did the whole thing for next to nothing and she'd been delighted – although understandably tearful – and told us to let her know if there was anything she could do for us in the future. So that was why she'd hardly batted an eyelid when Sanjeev phoned her and, without giving her too many details, asked her to meet him at the funeral parlour and bring her rifle and a bunch of tranquilliser darts.

They'd then linked up with Alan and Scratch at the edge of the park, and the four of them had skirted the woods before picking their way through the trees till they found the perfect spot on a slight incline above the clearing. They were far enough away so as not to be seen by the Russians but close enough for Philippa to have line of sight for a clean shot.

'So,' she said, taking up the story, 'as soon as I saw the woman shoved down onto her knees with a gun at her head, I let one go.'

'And got me in the leg,' I said.

Philippa shrugged. 'Wrong place, wrong nano-second, as I told you. On the plus side, though, the Russians were so distracted when you hit the deck that I had time to reload and take the pair of them out.'

My getting KO'd by a tranquilliser dart had never been part of the plan, of course, but apart from that, everything had worked out better than I could possibly have imagined. Carla and Oleg were alive, and both the Russian agents were spark out and totally incapacitated. They were also still in the land of the living, which was exactly the result I'd intended. Actually killing the Russians had never been part of my plan and hence the need for Philippa and her tranquilliser gun. One thing puzzled me, though, so I asked Philippa why they were still out cold when I was already back on my feet.

'Antidote,' she said with a beaming smile. 'I gave you one, but I haven't bothered with theirs yet. They'll come round soon enough.'

'And speaking of which,' said Scratch. 'What we gonna do with 'em? Leave 'em here to rot or get eaten by wolves or whatever?'

Alan snorted his derision. 'Wolves? This is England, mate. Not fucking Siberia.'

Aside from the eaten by wolves thing, Scratch had a point. I hadn't given a second's thought to what we'd do with the Russians if we did manage to get them safely trussed up, but it was Oleg who came to the rescue.

'I'm sure those MI5 people would be quite interested in having a word or two with them,' he said.

'Excellent idea,' I said, and as they were bound to still have Mr Mysterious's phone, I texted them the coordinates of where they could find the Russian agents.

Carla tapped me on the shoulder. 'I'd quite like to go home now if it's all the same to you.'

The quiet, calm voice was not at all what I'd been expecting. What I'd expected was a ferocious tirade about what an utter bastard I was for putting her in a position where she'd been kidnapped and might very possibly have ended up dead. Maybe she was simply relieved that her ordeal was over or that she'd expended all her energy on inflicting her revenge on the Russians and had nothing left in the tank. But whatever the reason, I was grateful to have been let off the hook – for the time being at least. Who knew what might lay in store for me when Carla eventually got her shit back together again?

I asked Alan and Scratch if they could take her home right away, and she didn't even complain when I told her it would have to be in the hearse.

Once the three of them had left the clearing with Sanjeev and Philippa following on behind, Oleg took me by the arm. 'I must admit that you had me worried for a while.'

'You thought I was going to betray you?'

'It crossed my mind. But only for a moment. I knew you'd never do that and you'd probably have some kind of plan in place.'

'I'm just glad it all came together,' I said, not daring to confess to him that there hadn't always been a plan and that until Alan and Scratch's argument about zoos had given me the idea, betrayal had seemed to be the only option.

Oleg clapped his hands, and the sound reverberated through the trees. 'So then. Unless there are other Russian agents after me – and I'm not convinced there are – I need to get on with the job you brought me over from France for. I'm sure it won't be too difficult to find out where Mr Hayes-Edlington is likely to be during the next day or so.'

The two Russian agents were almost completely conscious by now and Oleg bid them a cheery '*Do svidaniya*' as we left the clearing.

43

'What's that smell?'

Jonah Wilson was leading the way to the wooded area half a mile from the edge of the park.

'Fresh air,' said Holly. 'Countryside.'

Jonah grunted his disdain and checked the map on his phone. 'So what are we going to do with the Russians when we get there?'

It was a question Holly had been considering ever since she'd received Dempsey's text on the dead CIA guy's phone: "2 RUSSIAN AGENTS SECURED AND WAITING FOR YOU AT…" and then the GPS coordinates. She'd almost dismissed it as a hoax that wasn't worth following up on, but why would he bother? Then there was the issue of how a simple undertaker had managed to take down a pair of hardened Russian agents. Not on his own, that was for sure, so most likely Radimov had had a hand in it. And where the hell *he* was right now was anyone's guess. There was the slimmest of chances that the Russians might know where he was heading next and she had precisely zero other ideas, so what had she got to lose?

'One step at a time,' she said in answer to Jonah's question. 'Let's see if they're actually there first.'

Although the moon was almost full, only the occasional ray found its way through the canopy of leaves once they'd entered the wood, so they switched on their torches and Jonah guided them along a series of footpaths until they came to a small clearing of about twenty feet by ten. On one of the longer sides two figures were sitting on the ground, each tied to the trunk of a beech tree three or four yards apart. Both were gagged, and both looked up with their eyes full of hope, but the light quickly dimmed when they realised who their supposed rescuers were.

'So we meet again,' said Holly and ripped the duct tape gag from the female agent's face. 'You want to tell me what happened?'

The woman stretched her mouth in every direction to ease the stiffness, then spat in the dirt. 'Fuck you.'

'OK, if that's the way you want to play it, we'll just leave you here to rot, shall we? Still, you might get lucky and some kind soul could wander by and set you free, but I wouldn't bank on it. Come on, Jonah. We're leaving.'

Holly gave a sideways nod towards the path where they'd entered the clearing but had gone no more than half a dozen paces before the Russian woman called her back.

'Good decision,' said Holly as she retraced her steps and stood over her. 'A little cooperation is all I'm after, and if I get what I want, you and your boyfriend can be on your way.'

'He iss not my boyfriend.'

'Really? Is that so?' She shone the beam of her torch directly into the woman's face. 'Well, to be perfectly honest, I couldn't give a flying fuck whether he's your boyfriend or your uncle's cousin's illegitimate love-child. What I *do* want to know is where I can find Oleg Radimov.'

The agent squinted against the light from the torch. 'I don't know. He vent with the uzzer people.'

'What other people? You mean the undertaker and his pals?'

'Undertaker?'

'Buries dead bodies. You were chasing him on a motorbike yesterday, remember?'

'Him. Yes.'

'And you've no idea where they were going?'

The woman squeezed her eyes shut and turned her head to the side. 'Take light off my face and I tell you vot I heard.'

Holly swung the torch to point it at the ground. 'Go on.'

'Radimov say he vonts to find the man who iss Member of the Parliament. The man who vee are here to protect. It iss him who—'

She was interrupted by her fellow agent, who was frantically trying to shout through his gag, his eyes wide in horror as he wrestled pointlessly against his bonds.

The female agent twisted her head to face him. 'Vot does it matter now, Nikolai? These two vill kill us anyvay.'

'Not at all,' said Holly. 'Tell me everything I want to know and you can walk away. Keeping your mouths *shut* is what'll get you killed.'

She had no intention of killing either of them whether they talked or not. Bendix might well have done, but this was her call, and cold-blooded murder wasn't going to achieve anything.

Despite her reassurance, however, there was no let-up in Nikolai's ranting, and although it was getting on her nerves, she persisted with questioning the woman. 'So, what about this MP then? You say you were protecting him?'

'Yes.'

'From Radimov?'

'Ve theenk he iss trying to kill him.'

'Why?'

From what Bendix had told her, the only reason MI5 wanted Radimov dead was to stop him revealing the MP's sexual indiscretions and causing a scandal that would seriously embarrass the government. There'd been nothing about Radimov planning to *kill* the guy.

The agent took a deep breath and paused for several seconds before answering. 'He iss haffing affair with woman called Natalia Makarova.'

'Yes, we know that. – Well, not the name, but certainly the affair.'

'She iss daughter of a best friend of President Putin, and the MP hass been giving her the knowledge of things that are top secret.'

Holy shit, thought Holly. It was what she'd suspected for quite some time now. The mission wasn't simply about avoiding a scandal, but why would Bendix want Radimov dead? Maybe he didn't know that this MP had been passing secrets to the Russians, but if he did, why was he so desperate to defend him? What was clear, though, was that these Russian agents had been sent to liquidate Radimov before he could sabotage what was presumably a highly useful flow of information.

'You have a name for this MP?' Holly asked.

'He hass two names. Hayes and Edlington.'

'Double-barrelled, you mean? Hyphenated?'

The Russian woman frowned. 'I don't understand.'

Holly didn't waste time explaining but called out to Jonah to check Google for an MP called Hayes, Edlington or Hayes-Edlington.

Seconds later, she had her answer.

'Peter Hayes-Edlington,' Jonah read aloud from the screen of his phone. 'Member of Parliament for Upton and Hornbury. Junior minister for Agriculture and Rural Affairs.'

'Nothing to do with national security then? Doesn't sit on any defence or intelligence committees? Anything like that?'

'Doesn't look like it, no.'

'So where's he getting his intel from?' Holly muttered to herself, barely aware that she'd spoken the words aloud, but the female agent answered her question anyway.

'You haff a mole.'

'What?'

'In your MI5. It iss this mole who iss telling the secrets to the MP.'

The other Russian – Nikolai – dramatically upped the volume of his attempt to be heard through the gag, and with a nodded cue from Holly, Jonah took out his gun and whacked him across the side of the head with the butt. The agent's chin dropped to his chest. Not quite unconscious but silent at least.

With order restored, Holly turned her attention back to the woman sitting beneath her. 'And the identity of this mole? Do you know who it is?'

The agent shook her head. 'Vee neffer meet. Vee haff only a code name.'

'Which is?'

'Angel.'

'To the Russians, maybe.'

'Excuse me?'

'Never mind. So, do you get your instructions from him… or her?'

'Sometimes, but mostly from our own people.'

'How do you communicate with this Angel if you never meet?'

'Vee use… Vot do you call it? A dead drop?'

'How often do you use it?'

'Not often.'

'When was the last time?'

'Three days ago.'

'And you can tell me where it is?'

The woman shrugged. 'If you vont. But it iss difficult to explain. I vill haff to show you.'

Holly allowed herself a faint smile as a plan began to develop in her mind. Exposing an MI5 mole had never been an objective of her mission, but if the Russian agent was telling the truth, it certainly was now.

44

The headache had mostly gone, and my vision was back to normal, but I was still a little groggy even four hours after Philippa had zapped me with the tranquilliser dart. I guessed it was a small price to pay for not only saving Carla's life but also not having to follow through with my betrayal of Oleg.

'*Saving Carla's life?*' said the voice in my head. '*Let's not forget it was your fault that Carla's life had been put in danger in the first place.*'

I couldn't deny it, of course, and I had no doubt whatsoever that I'd be getting it in the neck from her as soon as she'd recovered from the shock of almost having her brains blown out. But not tonight and not tomorrow either since I wasn't going to be within tongue-lashing range as long as I didn't answer any of her calls.

As soon as we'd got back to the funeral parlour, Sanjeev had fired up his computer to check on the forthcoming whereabouts of Peter Hayes-Edlington MP, which turned out to be remarkably straightforward. He'd done a couple of quick Google searches and found an online local newspaper which carried a brief article about a village fête that was due to be officially opened by the man himself. The only slight problem was that the fête was due to kick off at twelve noon on the very next day, and given that the village of Linton-in-Ashdale was about half way between Sheffield and Manchester, it would mean a pretty early start if we were going to make it in time. Turning up in the hearse was definitely out of the question, and I wasn't at all confident that the Polo could cover that kind of mileage without at least one major breakdown, so the train was the only realistic option.

'There's one that leaves St Pancras at 7:32 in the morning that gets you into Sheffield at 9:45,' Sanjeev had said after a few minutes' online research, 'but then you'd need to get a local train and a taxi to the village, so that'd be cutting it a bit fine even if there aren't any delays. Maybe you'll need to catch the 7:02 instead.'

Since we'd also have to allow a good hour to get to St Pancras, an early night would have been the sensible thing to do, but by the time we'd got back to the funeral parlour, that ship had already sailed. Besides, Scratch had grumbled on about being sick of eating bananas and needed something rather more substantial or he wouldn't be able to sleep.

And so it was that he, Alan, Sanjeev, Oleg and I were now lounging around in my flat above the parlour and tucking in to a variety of Indian takeaway dishes. The delivery had been impressively swift, but placing the order had taken the best part of half an hour. This was because we'd left this up to Scratch, who'd insisted on asking for the precise ingredients of every single dish in case there was anything that might set off one of his allergies. It was also noticeable that every ingredient was listed on the cardboard lids of each of the tin foil cartons as per his instructions.

'Where's my paneer pasanda?' Alan had asked after he'd inspected all of the lids.

'I didn't order it,' Scratch had said. 'It's got cashews in it.'

'So?'

'So, I'm allergic.'

'Well, you didn't have to bloody eat it yourself, did you, you selfish prick.'

After a few more acrimonious exchanges, even Alan and Scratch fell silent as they began stuffing their faces, and peace was restored.

Predictably enough, Oleg was much less interested in the food and far more intent on guzzling his way through the bottle of vodka he'd demanded we stopped to buy on the way back from the woods.

'You don't all have to come, you know,' he said after everyone but Alan had finished eating. 'Tomorrow, I mean, when I go to find this MP.'

'Wouldn't miss it for the world,' said Scratch. 'After all the shit we've been through over the past four days, I reckon we all want to be there for the grand finale.'

'Too right,' said Alan through a mouthful of curried something-or-other. 'But what exactly are you gonna do when you meet him face to face?'

Oleg shrugged. 'Same as I'd planned from the beginning. Tell him I have evidence of his affair with Natalia Makarova, which I'll deliver to the relevant authorities or the media unless he gives me the name of the British agent who's been giving him the secrets to pass on.'

'But I thought you said there wasn't any real

evidence that the guy *had* been doing that.'

Once again, Oleg shrugged. 'It's what the CIA believe, and it's my job to find out one way or the other.'

'And speaking of which,' I said, 'have you got anyone else at the CIA you're in contact with since Mr Mysterious turned up dead on our doorstep?'

'I only ever dealt with Bluebird – Connelly, I mean – so no, I haven't yet, but nothing's changed as far as I'm concerned. I don't suppose the CIA are going to abort the mission just because my handler's died.' A faint smile crept across his lips. 'And as I may have mentioned before, I also have a personal interest in the matter.'

'Yes, you did, but you wouldn't tell me what it was.'

'Perhaps tomorrow all will become clear.' He drained his glass of vodka and checked his watch. 'And if my calculations are correct, we have less than five hours before we have to head off to catch this train, so I think a little sleep might be a good idea.'

'We'd better all crash here then,' I said. 'No point anybody going home now, except Sanjeev if you want. You'll have to man the fort here tomorrow, I'm afraid.'

Sanjeev's face fell, and he began to protest, but Alan interrupted by telling him we'd bring him back a toffee apple from the village fête. This did nothing to lighten his mood.

After he'd left, I busied myself finding any spare bedding that Alan and Scratch could use to make them a little more comfortable sleeping on the floor. Oleg was already spark out on the settee and snoring loudly.

'I doubt we'll get so much as a wink of sleep if that racket goes on all night,' said Alan.

'Maybe we should stay awake in case the Russians

turn up,' said Scratch. 'I mean, I know that the two that were after Oleg probably aren't a threat any more, but he did say that there might be others.'

'Well, Sleeping Beauty doesn't seem to think so now, does he? But if you want to stay up and stand guard, that's entirely up to you, mate. As for me, I'm gonna get whatever kip I can.'

With that, Alan wrapped himself in a blanket on the floor and shoved a cushion under his head. 'Oh, and if it's not too much trouble, scrambled eggs and coffee for brekkie would definitely hit the spot.'

'Twat,' said Scratch and let out an enormous fart in rather close proximity to Alan's face.

I left them to it and climbed into the relative luxury of my own bed, but even though I was knackered beyond belief and my head was still fuzzy from the lingering effects of the tranquilliser, sleep didn't come easily. But I must have dropped off eventually because the next thing I knew I was jolted awake by my phone. At first, my fogged-up brain assumed it was the alarm I'd set to make sure I got up in time to catch the train, but the persistent noise told me it wasn't that at all. It was an incoming call.

I stretched out a sluggish arm and picked up the phone from the bedside table. 'Yes?'

'Hi, Max. Sorry, did I wake you?'

It was Sanjeev, and I didn't bother to answer.

'The thing is,' he went on, 'when I got home, I decided to double-check the details I gave you. About the train times and all that. And guess what. It seems I may have made a bit of a boo-boo.'

'Uh-huh.'

'Yeah, this fête that the MP's gonna be at isn't tomorrow. It's the day *after*. So that means you don't have to catch the early train and you can get a much later one and then stay somewhere local overnight. Good thing I double-checked, eh, or you'd hardly be getting any sleep at all.'

By way of thanks, I yawned loudly into the phone and hung up.

45

Last night's phone call had been even more awkward than any of Holly's previous conversations with Bendix. She'd hardly been expecting him to shower her with compliments when she'd told him that they'd captured the two Russian agents, but he'd been remarkably cool in his response.

'That's all well and good, Miss Gilmartin, but your mission is and always has been the neutralising of Oleg Radimov and nothing to do with capturing Russian agents.' He'd then lowered his voice and added, 'Get anything useful out of them?'

Until she discovered the identity of the MI5 mole, nobody was above suspicion, and that included Bendix himself, so the only information she gave him was that the Russians had told her Radimov was intent on finding Hayes-Edlington and was probably planning to kill him. This was when Bendix had totally lost it.

'Well, damn well get to him before Radimov does or I'll nail your arse to the fucking wall. Do I make myself clear?'

'Perfectly, sir, but what do you want us to do with

the Russians?'

'What?'

'The two Russian agents. Shall we get someone to come and pick them up while we go after Radimov?'

There was a lengthy pause before Bendix had answered. 'Let them go.'

Holly had almost dropped her phone. She couldn't believe she'd heard him correctly and said so, but Bendix had claimed that they were probably too low level to be any use in terms of intelligence gathering, and if they were free, there was still a chance that they could be saddled with the blame for Radimov's death.

Despite Bendix's dire warning what would happen to her if she failed to protect the MP from Radimov, there was no way she'd been going to pass up the opportunity of catching an MI5 double agent. Jonah had tried to convince her otherwise, but she'd been adamant, and besides, as far as they could discover, Hayes-Edlington's next public appearance was the following day when he was due to open a village fête in his constituency. More than likely, this was where Radimov was intending to make the hit, so there was plenty of time to stake out the dead drop and travel up the night before.

True to her word, the female Russian agent had taken them to the dead drop site which she and her partner used to communicate with their MI5 mole. This turned out to be the drastically neglected graveyard of a small church that had long since been abandoned to nature and the worst excesses of the elements. The church building itself was almost entirely roofless, and although most of its walls remained largely intact, much of the stonework was obscured by the spreading expanses of ivy and brambles. The graveyard had fared no better and was choked with all manner of thriving weeds and patches of dead and dying grass that was nearly waist height in places.

It was amongst one particularly dense area of grass that Holly and Jonah had positioned themselves so as to have a perfect view of the dead drop whilst being almost invisible from anyone approaching it.

As the Russian woman had shown them, the drop site was immediately in front of one of the few cracked and fallen gravestones on which the inscription was still just legible after the passing of the decades: "In Loving Memory of Albert Henry Rollinson. Died 8th October 1932, aged 56". Barely visible at its base was a short piece of thin leather which was attached to the top of a black aluminium tube of about half an inch in diameter and five inches long. It was inserted into the earth by means of a sharp spike at its bottom end, and unscrewing the cap at the top revealed a hollow interior.

'It's vot vee use for passing messages ant uzzer small things,' the Russian had said.

Holly had sniffed. 'Yes, I do know what a dead drop spike is, thank you.'

'You vont to put a message in? Angel will be expecting something.'

'Not necessary. I'm only interested in who comes to check it out.'

The Russian agent had previously explained that she and the mole alerted each other when they should visit the dead drop by texting each other's burner phones simply with a date and time when there'd be something to pick up. However, as an extra level of security, six figures were added to both, so, for instance, "13th July 3 p.m." really meant 7th July at 9 a.m. In this case,

Angel had been told to go to the graveyard at one o'clock that day.

It was now getting on for four, and so far nobody had shown up. Sitting, squatting, kneeling, lying on her side or on her front, it didn't matter how often Holly shifted her position, there was hardly any part of her body that wasn't complaining about the increasingly intolerable aches and pains. The only difference between her and Jonah was that she hadn't been griping and groaning about it every few minutes since they'd first arrived.

'Doesn't look like anybody's coming,' he said for the umpteenth time, grimacing as he rolled from his left side onto his front.

'Give it a bit longer,' said Holly, her eyes still fixed on Albert Henry Rollinson's gravestone.

'We've been here three bloody hours already. If you ask me, we'd be far better off cutting our losses and going after Radimov before he gets to this MP guy. That's what Bendix told you to do, wasn't it?'

'But he doesn't know what the Russians told us about the mole, and that information stays between you and me till we find out who it is, OK? Until then, everyone's a suspect.'

'Even Bendix?'

'Even Bendix,' Holly said with rather more conviction than she genuinely felt.

The man was a pompous, overbearing, misogynistic bastard, for sure, but a traitor? From what she knew of him, he was far too much of a "company man" to go down that road, although some of his behaviour had been highly questionable. There was his unwavering insistence that the only reason for killing Radimov was to prevent a scandal, his strangely casual response when she'd told him about the CIA's involvement, and his latest decision to set the Russian agents free had been especially hard to swallow.

'Maybe whoever this mole is didn't get the message the Russians sent,' said Jonah, 'or maybe they tipped him off after we turned them loose.'

'Him?'

'Yeah, or her. It could be a her.'

'We dumped them in the middle of nowhere and took their phones off them. How are they gonna tip anyone off?'

'All I'm saying is that—'

'Yes, I know what you're saying, Jonah, but has it actually occurred to you that every time you open your mouth, you're giving away our position to anybody who might be within earshot?'

But the ensuing silence was short-lived and interrupted, not by Jonah, but by a rustling sound in the undergrowth a few feet behind them. They both spun round, and as Holly reached for her gun, she heard: 'And what exactly do you two think you're doing?'

46

Soon after leaving the outskirts of Sheffield, the two-carriage train trundled its way through open rolling moorland and some increasingly spectacular hills towards a day that could very easily end in tears or worse.

The city centre hotel we'd stayed in the night before had been basic and reasonably cheap but a vast improvement on the shithole we'd been forced to stay at in Calais almost a week before. At least the en suite bathrooms had hot running water and a complete absence of black mould or mould of any other colour for that matter. There was nothing at all to set off my osmophobia, and Scratch was delighted to find that all of the bedding was guaranteed hypoallergenic. The downside? The MI5 agents who were after Oleg were also staying at the same hotel.

Alan had gone down to reception to get more sachets of coffee soon after we'd checked in and spotted them making their way across the parking area. Fortunately, we'd already eaten, and Oleg had an almost full bottle of vodka, so nobody had any reason to complain about having to shut ourselves away in our rooms until it was time to leave the next morning. Alan, however, had been seriously pissed off that he'd had to miss out on the ten quid all-you-can-eat breakfast in the hotel restaurant and was still moaning about it as our train squealed to a halt at the tiny station of Tidsdale.

Perhaps not surprisingly, there was no sign of a taxi, but Scratch saw a notice for a local cab company and dialled the number.

'Off to the fête then, are you?' said the cabbie when he picked us up and we told him where we were going.

'That's right, yes,' I said from the passenger seat beside him.

The cabbie snorted. 'Waste o' time if you ask me. Fête worse than death, I always say. Only good thing is it's not slashing it down with rain like it does most years.'

'So, we're lucky then.'

Another snort. 'If you count the possibility of bumping into our local arsehole of an MP "lucky", yeah.'

'Oh?'

'Supposed to be doing the grand opening is what I've heard. Useless upper-class prick couldn't open a can of bloody baked beans if you ask me. Never done sod all for people round 'ere. All he's interested in is climbing up the greasy pole and lining his own pockets while he's at it. And you know what makes my blood really boil?'

It was obviously a rhetorical question, so I didn't feel the need to answer. Instead, I let him chunter on about a whole range of things that made his blood boil until we finally arrived at our destination. I paid him his fare and added a not ungenerous tip, even though the voice in my head strongly advised me against it: '*You give him any more than what he's owed and all you're doing is telling him how much you enjoyed his stream of monotonously annoying bullshit. Still, on your head be it if you ever get him again.*'

As we walked away from the taxi, the cabbie wound down his window and called out after us, 'And if you see that twat of an MP, give him a right good kick in the bollocks from me, yeah?'

'Oh, I think I can do better than that,' muttered Oleg, quietly enough for the cabbie not to hear.

Although the grand opening wasn't due to happen for another hour, the fête was already in full swing. There were plenty of people who clearly didn't share our cabbie's opinion of the event as they meandered happily round the twenty or thirty stalls set up on the green in the centre of the village. Several of the stalls were selling cakes, jams and other homemade produce, while the most popular appeared to be the standard village fête games and activities like hoopla, coconut shy and splat the rat.

On the far side of the green, a quaint-looking country pub was doing a roaring trade with a temporary bar set up in front of it to cope with the extra demand, and a little further along, a group of Morris dancers had attracted quite a crowd.

'Never did understand what that was all about,' said Alan. 'Eight blokes all dressed up with flowers in their hats and bells on their legs prancing about, waving handkerchiefs and pretending to whack each other with sticks.'

'That's because you're a total philistine,' said Scratch.

'Yeah, I might have known *you'd* be into this kinda

stuff.'

'Not 'specially, but the music's all right.'

It wasn't really my kind of thing, but the accordion and fiddle players seemed to be pretty adept at bashing out their traditional folk tunes. Either way, we weren't here to discuss the merits or otherwise of Morris dancing.

'OK,' I said. 'We need to concentrate on the job in hand. Maybe it'd be best if we split up and make sure we know the minute the MP gets here. We also need to keep an eye out for the MI5 spooks. Sure as hell they're gonna try and grab Oleg as soon as they spot him.'

Alan chuckled. 'Oh, I don't think we need to worry too much about those two just yet.'

47

Holly hadn't been bothered about breakfast, but Jonah had insisted that all-you-can-eat for ten quid was too good to miss out on. Besides, it had been the only way she could stop him from moaning about how cheap and crappy the hotel was when they'd checked in the evening before, but her part of the deal was that they'd have to be at the restaurant as soon as it opened in the morning. Not that this had worked out too well as Jonah had forgotten to set his alarm, and she'd had a hell of a job waking him either by phone or hammering on his door. The earplugs, he'd claimed, had been essential to cut out the noise of the traffic if he was to get any sleep at all.

'We need to get going,' Holly said, taking a sip of her coffee and wincing as she watched him stuff yet another chunk of heavily buttered croissant into his mouth.

'Just want to get my money's worth, that's all.'

'It's not even your money. It's the Service's.'

'So how come if we're on expenses, we didn't stay at a decent hotel instead of this dump?'

'Cutbacks.'

'Yeah, right,' said Jonah, spraying croissant crumbs down his shirt as he spoke.

Holly finished her coffee and got to her feet. 'Anyway, I'd say that two bowls of cereal, three yogurts, four slices of toast and God knows how many croissants and juices means you're well up on the deal.'

With a bit of luck, this might turn out to be the last day she'd ever have to spend with the irritating prat, she thought as she picked up her overnight bag and strode out of the restaurant. Not that luck had been on her side a whole lot lately, and she still hadn't a clue who the MI5 mole was. Three hours hanging around in some bloody graveyard only to end up getting told off by some snooty jerk in his mid seventies with a tweed cap and a ridiculously large handlebar moustache.

'And what exactly do you two think you're doing?' he'd said in a plummy headmasterish kind of voice.

Holly had returned her gun to its holster before he'd spotted it. 'Er, just admiring the old church. Such a pity it's been left to fall apart like this.'

The man grunted. 'Don't believe a damn word of it. More like a bit of hanky-panky, I'd say.'

'Excuse me?' Holly had said with strident indignation and more than a hint of repugnance at the very idea of her and Jonah getting up to anything even remotely sexual.

'Go on, the pair of you. Clear off out of it before I call the police.'

'And who the hell are you, ordering us about?' Jonah had said, standing up and eyeballing the old man.

'If it's any business of yours,' he'd said, pulling himself up to his full height and puffing out his chest, 'I happen to be chairman of the SBCPS – the Saint

Barnabas Church Preservation Society.'

'Oh yeah? Well, I have to say you're doing a pretty shit job at it. I mean, look at the place. It's a fucking wreck is what it is.'

Jonah had vaguely waved a hand in the direction of the derelict church, and he and Holly had headed for the car, leaving the chair of the SBCPS huffing and puffing and with his already gammon face turning a dangerous shade of crimson.

The dead drop had been their best chance of finding out the identity of the MI5 mole, but Holly knew that she'd have to put that out of her mind for now and focus on today's priority – saving Peter Hayes-Edlington MP from a possible assassination attempt. First, though, there was a fairly major problem to overcome.

Her dark grey Mondeo was sitting in the middle of the hotel's crowded car park, and it was only when she got close to it that she saw that both of the rear tyres were completely flat. She dropped her bag and walked round to the front.

'Jesus!'

Not that it made any difference that all four tyres were buggered, but the end result was precisely the same. The Mondeo wasn't going anywhere any time soon.

'Oh, shit. Not again,' said Jonah, who'd followed Holly's route to the front of the car. 'How the hell did they know where we were?'

'Doesn't really matter, does it?' said Holly, taking a fresh packet of cigarettes from her jacket pocket. 'What does matter is that we need to get to this bloody village before Radimov can take out the Honourable Member for Wherever-the-Fuck, so why don't you make yourself useful and get us a taxi?'

48

Oleg and I had positioned ourselves at one end of the green and Scratch and Alan at the other. Apart from a secondary road at right-angles to it, there was only one main road in and out of the village, and it bisected the green into two roughly equal parts. In order to preserve the lives of the fête-going public, both roads had been closed to traffic, but it was highly likely that the MP's car would be waved through by the stewards, so it shouldn't be too difficult to spot his arrival. There was also the probability that the MI5 agents could arrive at any time despite Alan having seriously immobilised their Mondeo.

Oleg had attempted to persuade me that he and I would be far more comfortable sitting outside the pub than on the bone hard ground at the edge of the green, but he'd soon capitulated when I pointed out that there'd be no clear view of the road. I'd tried to placate him with a generous slice of homemade lemon drizzle cake from the nearest stall, but he'd accepted it with bad grace and immediately tossed it to a passing Staffordshire Bull Terrier. The dog's owners had not been best pleased, but Oleg had simply smiled at them and said something in Russian, which he afterwards translated to me as: "Your dog has more brains in its arse than either of you two put together, and I hope it shits in your soup." Apparently, this is a fairly traditional and common insult in Russia, or so Oleg claimed.

Minutes afterwards, a large black Mercedes with tinted windows pulled up at the flimsy makeshift barrier. A young woman in a hi-viz yellow vest hurried over to the driver's side, and after the briefest of exchanges, she beckoned to one of the other stewards to lift the barrier.

'That's gotta be him,' I said and with a considerable degree of effort, helped Oleg to his feet.

We followed the car along the road until it pulled up near the middle of the green and almost opposite the pub. Straight away, a small group of two women and two men scurried towards it. All in their fifties, they were dressed in their Sunday best and were presumably the MP's designated welcoming committee. It was obvious from their exuberant expressions that they could scarcely contain their excitement as they waited for the Merc's driver to open the first of the rear doors.

When he'd done so, out stepped a woman wearing a floral summer frock and one of those tiny little flouncy hats that perch precariously on top of the head. Fascinators, I think they're called, but to me, the only thing fascinating about them was how the hell they managed to stay in place. I guessed she was the MP's wife, and I briefly wondered if she had any idea about hubby's extramarital liaison.

As soon as she was out of the car and upright, the welcoming committee hurried forward and did the expected glad-handing, while Mrs Hayes-Edlington returned their beaming smiles with one that looked rather more dutiful than sincere.

By now, the driver had gone round to the other side of the car, but Peter Hayes-Edlington was already out and smoothing the creases from the trousers of his dark blue suit. He was instantly recognisable from the TV appearance that Oleg and I had watched a few days ago. Dark hair greying at the temples and a razor sharp parting, rimless spectacles and a smugly supercilious grin.

I don't follow politics that closely myself, but Sanjeev had done some research and filled us in on some of the more basic details. Educated at Eton and Oxford, Hayes-Edlington was about as far to the right of the Tory party as you could get without actually being classified as a neo-Nazi. According to his voting record in the House of Commons, he had consistently opposed any law that promoted human rights and virtually anything that smacked of helping the poor and underprivileged. He'd also been a keen supporter of the stricter enforcement of immigration laws and increasing the mass surveillance of the general public's communications and activities.

'Not a nice man at all,' Alan had said when Sanjeev had read out the results of his research, except those may not have been his exact words.

'Good morning to you,' boomed the MP as the welcoming committee almost fell over themselves in their rush to greet him. 'And I must say what a splendidly delightful village you have here.'

'Yes indeed, sir. We're very proud of it,' said one of the female members of the committee.

Hayes-Edlington airily brushed the remark aside.

'Oh, tosh to all the "sir" business. "Peter" will do just fine.' Then he winked. 'Unless I become Prime Minister, of course.'

There was somewhat over-enthusiastic laughter all round, but I'm fairly sure that someone in the small crowd that had gathered said, 'Well, we'll all be even more fucked than we are now if that ever happened.'

The welcoming committee then led the MP and his wife towards a small platform in front of the pub and close to where the Morris dancers had since completed their performance. It was a makeshift affair of about a foot high and constructed from wooden pallets covered with wide strips of artificial grass. A canvas-topped frame to shield the VIPs from the sun was bedecked with Union Jack bunting, and on the platform itself were four chairs and a microphone on a stand that stood front and centre.

I rang Alan to check if he knew that the MP had arrived.

'Yeah, we saw,' he said. 'You want us to come over?'

'Might as well,' I said, 'but remember we still need to keep an eye out for those MI5 people.'

'Sure. Give us five minutes or so and we'll be there. Scratch should be finished by then.'

'Finished? Finished what?'

'The welly boot throwing competition. He's next up for his last attempt, but he's already well ahead of anybody else. Mind you, he did almost get disqualified after his second throw when he got it a bit wrong and the welly hit some bloke on the head.'

'Christ, Alan. We've got all this going on with Oleg and the MP and MI5, and Scratch is chucking welly boots around?'

'Keep yer hair on, Max. It doesn't mean we haven't still been keeping a lookout. It was just something to do to pass the time.'

'Well, maybe you could pass the time by getting your arses over here right now, OK?'

I hung up, and at the same moment, Oleg grabbed me by the arm.

'It's him,' he said, his voice barely above a whisper. 'The guy talking to the MP.'

I looked over to where Hayes-Edlington was deep in conversation with a tall, broad-shouldered man in a three-piece suit and a dark brown trilby hat. 'You recognise him?'

'He's the one who roughed me up when he was interrogating me.'

'MI5?'

'Yes, and fairly senior from what I could gather.'

'Right. In that case, we need to make sure he doesn't see you before you get a chance to corner the MP.'

But Oleg had other ideas.

49

Oleg had no intention of hiding from the MI5 guy in the trilby hat. Quite the opposite, in fact.

'You sure about this?' I said when he told me his plan.

He shrugged. 'I don't know how else we're going to get him away from the MP long enough so I can have my little chat with him.'

'All right then. So, as long as Alan and Scratch agree to—'

'Did I hear our names taken in vain?'

I turned to see the pair of them grinning at me and Scratch clutching an enormous teddy bear to his chest.

'I won it,' he said. 'In the welly boot competition. I was streets ahead of everybody else.'

'Really? That's fantastic,' I said. 'Your mum would be so proud of you.' Scratch had no problem recognising the heavy sarcasm, and his triumphant grin instantly morphed into a dejected frown. 'So, if you two have quite finished pissing about, perhaps you might like to focus your attention on the reason we're actually here today.'

Alan and Scratch muttered their apologies, and I got Oleg to tell them his plan.

When he'd finished, they asked a couple of questions and then dutifully walked round the side of the pub to the back.

The MP and the trilby hat guy were still deep in conversation near to the makeshift platform, and I followed Oleg as he sauntered past and wished them a jaunty 'Good morning.'

Trilby Hat's reaction was instantaneous. His mouth hung open part way through a sentence, and his face erupted into a peculiar blend of consternation and rage. He gestured to the MP to stay where he was and went after Oleg, who had disappeared round the corner of the pub.

The back yard of the pub was bordered on three sides with high wooden fencing and was reserved for industrial-sized garbage and recycling bins along with empty beer barrels, crates of empty bottles and a few items of broken furniture. There was no sign of Alan or Scratch, but Oleg had stopped in the middle of the yard and turned to face his pursuer.

'So, we meet again,' said Trilby Hat, 'and to be honest, I'm not sure whether to admire your nerve in showing your face like this or marvel at your extraordinary stupidity.'

'Well, I think we're both going to find out the answer to that little conundrum any second now,' said Oleg with a self-satisfied smirk.

The man glowered at him and prodded a finger at his chest. 'You listen to me, you little—'

Whump!

There was a dull thud, and Trilby Hat's eyes popped wide open, then rapidly fluttered closed before he

281

dropped to his knees and fell forward onto the ground with a muffled groan, his hat nestling beside him.

Towering above him, Scratch held a short plank of wood in one hand and tapped it rhythmically onto the palm of the other. 'Job done, I reckon.'

50

As soon as Alan and Scratch had half dragged and half carried Trilby Hat out of sight behind a wall of empty beer barrels and set to work with whatever they could find to tie him up with, Oleg and I went back round to the front of the pub. The MP was still standing close to the small platform and apparently being harangued by half a dozen of his unhappy constituents.

'Your lot's been promising that ever since you got elected, and so far you've done bugger all about it,' a middle-aged woman with long grey plaits was saying as we came within earshot.

Hayes-Edlington was giving her his trademark supercilious grin, tinged with an imitation of compassionate understanding. 'Yes indeed, madam, and whilst I fully understand your concerns, I can assure you wholeheartedly that my government is working tirelessly to—'

'Oh, don't give me that crap,' the woman interrupted and jabbed a finger at him. 'The only thing your lot work tirelessly at is lining your own pockets and dishing out nice fat government contracts to all your upper-class mates.'

'No, I'm afraid I'll have to contradict you there. You see, during the last fiscal year, my government has—'

This time, the interruption was from Oleg. 'Morning, Peter. Just thought I'd drop by and let you know that Natalia sends her regards.'

The MP's grin vanished in an instant. 'What? Who?'

'Natalia Makarova. Oh, please don't tell me you've forgotten her. She'll be terribly upset when I tell her.'

'Now, look here, little man. I have absolutely no idea who you think you are, and I have no knowledge whatsoever of anyone by the name of… What was it again?'

'Natalia Makarova. She's the daughter of a close friend of the Russian president. Remember now?' The MP simply glowered at him in response. 'No? Well, perhaps the Grosvenor Hotel or the Savoy might ring a few bells. Then there was that rather shabby cheap motel outside—'

'Is everything all right, dear? You're looking a little… flushed.'

Out of nowhere, Mrs Hayes-Edlington had appeared at his side.

The MP struggled to force a smile. 'Yes, I'm fine, thank you, Margaret. Just having a bit of a chat with some of my constituents. I tell you what, though. I'm absolutely gasping for a cuppa. I don't suppose you'd mind…'

He let the sentence hang, and his wife took the obvious hint.

'Coming right up, dear,' she said and trotted off in search of a refreshments stall.

'Nice woman,' said Oleg and produced a thumb drive from his trouser pocket. 'I'm sure she'd be intrigued to have a look at what's on this little stick.'

By now, the small group of dissatisfied constituents had begun listening intently, muttering to each other and seemingly having lost all interest in launching further attacks on their Member of Parliament.

Hayes-Edlington must have noticed too. 'Perhaps we could go somewhere rather more private before we continue this discussion,' he said, stooping to speak quietly into Oleg's ear.

'Excellent idea,' said Oleg and led the way into the pub.

The interior was admirably traditional, by which I mean it hadn't been turned into one of those dreadful gastro-pubs where every nook and cranny had been destroyed to make way for a single open space and all the staff wore identical polo shirts and uselessly tiny aprons. No, this pub had personality. There was dark wood panelling on the walls, a well worn flagstone floor, an inglenook fireplace, and old wooden settles. The layout was roughly L-shaped with a bar taking up one wall of the shorter leg to the left of the entrance, and the man and two women behind it were working their socks off to keep up with the never diminishing queue of thirsty customers.

The rest of the pub – the longer leg of the L – was entirely empty, and Oleg headed for the far end where he turned and faced Hayes-Edlington.

'Well,' he said, taking the thumb drive back out of his pocket, 'now that I've got your attention, I expect you're wondering what I intend to do with this extraordinarily explicit evidence of your rather sordid affair with Ms Makarova. I could, of course, hand it over to the scandal-hungry tabloid newspapers and very probably receive quite a handsome payment.'

'So, that's what you're after, is it?' scowled the MP. 'A grubby little blackmail scam to extort money from me in return for keeping your mouth shut.'

Oleg pursed his lips and exhaled slowly. 'Blackmail? Certainly. Money? No, not at all.'

'I don't understand. If it's not money, then—'

'Information. You tell me what I want to know and all this… unpleasantness goes away.'

Beads of sweat were beginning to form on the MP's brow, and he took off his spectacles and carefully wiped the lenses with a pristine white handkerchief from the top pocket of his jacket. 'What information exactly?'

'The name of whoever it is in British intelligence that's been giving you state secrets to pass on to the Russians.'

Hayes-Edlington almost choked on an unconvincing laugh. 'Oh, for goodness' sake. You can't be serious, surely.'

'Unfortunately for you, I am totally serious.'

'Me? Passing secrets to the Russians? Utterly preposterous. Who *are* you anyway?'

Oleg ignored the question, and without turning to me, waved the thumb drive in my direction. 'What do you think, Max? *The Sun*? *The Mail*?'

'One of the Sunday papers perhaps?' I said. 'Any one of them would give their eye teeth to get hold of such a juicy scandal as this. I can see the headlines now. "MP in sordid love affair with Russian spy temptress." I doubt Mr Hayes-Edlington's parliamentary career would last very long after that.'

There was a lengthy pause while the MP appeared to be considering his options.

'And how do I know what's really on that thumb

drive?' he said at last. 'How do I know that this isn't just an almighty bluff?'

Oleg sighed, reached inside his jacket pocket and pulled out a single photograph. 'In the absence of any means of showing you the complete contents of the drive right at this moment, perhaps you'd settle for one of the highlights.'

Hayes-Edlington took one glance at the photo, and his complexion paled to an ashen grey.

'Jesus Christ,' he said quietly and slumped down onto the nearest chair.

51

Another twenty minutes had gone by between Jonah's phone call and the taxi arriving at the hotel to pick them up. Then, according to Jonah, the cabbie must have been the slowest driver on the planet, and Holly had doubted that her sidekick's frequent outbursts of 'Get a bloody move on, will you?' and 'Are you sure the handbrake isn't still on?' had done much to help the situation. When the cabbie finally dropped them at the edge of the village, Jonah paid the "exorbitant" fare, and pointedly refused to give the man a tip.

Holly checked her watch. There was only a little over half an hour until Hayes-Edlington was due to officially open the fête.

'Right, we need to find the MP first and then see if we can spot Radimov.'

They threaded their way through the variety of stalls until they reached what was roughly the centre of the village green.

'Over there probably,' said Jonah, pointing towards the pub. 'Seems to be some kind of platform, which I'd guess is where the MP is likely to make his speech.'

But when they got there, there was no sign of Hayes-Edlington.

'Maybe we're too late and Radimov got to him already,' said Jonah.

'Yeah? And whose fault would that be?' said Holly, not daring to even contemplate that he might be right.

A young guy was testing the microphone on the platform – 'One two. One two' – so she asked him if he'd seen the MP around anywhere.

'I think that was him going into the pub just now,' he said, his voice booming out of the twin loudspeakers mounted on stands in front of the platform. 'He was with a couple of other blokes. One of 'em was a dead ringer for Danny DeVito.'

Holly thanked him and went into the pub, her heart racing as she began to fear that the worst really had already happened.

It took her less than two seconds to recognise the three men at the far end of the pub. The MP, Radimov and Dempsey, the undertaker. She stopped in her tracks, thrusting out an arm in front of Jonah to prevent him going any further.

The MP was sitting on an upright wooden chair, his face deathly pale, and gesticulating wildly with both hands. Radimov was standing over him – or rather, given his lack of height, staring at him almost on the same eye level. Dempsey was close by and listening attentively. All three of the men were sideways on from Holly's perspective, so she risked taking a couple of steps forward to hear what was being said.

Hayes-Edlington was clearly struggling to lower his voice below shouting level. 'For the last time, I haven't got a clue what his name is. All I can tell you is I met him once every two weeks on the same park bench, but we rarely spoke. Then, when he got up to go a few minutes later, he'd leave behind a folded newspaper that had my latest instructions in it.'

'The secrets he wanted you to pass on to Natalia Makarova,' said Radimov, and the MP nodded briefly, gazing down at the stone-flagged floor between his feet. 'And did this man ever tell you which organisation he was from? MI5 or MI6, for instance?'

'No.'

Holly was so focused on hearing every word of the conversation that she was hardly aware that she'd taken another step forward. So it was true. Hayes-Edlington *was* leaking secret intel to the Russians, and now she also had cast iron confirmation of the existence of a mole in British intelligence. At the same time, she was aware that Bendix's orders had been to get whatever evidence Radimov had of the MP's affair and "neutralise the Russkie bastard", and here she had the opportunity to carry out both objectives right in front of her. She could see that Radimov was periodically waving a thumb drive in the MP's face, which very probably contained the evidence that Bendix was after, and if she took out her gun, she'd have a perfectly clear shot at the Russian. But was he intending to kill the Member for Wherever-it-was? There was no weapon in his hand, but that didn't mean anything. Russian agents had all kinds of death-dealing devices at their disposal that were disguised as innocuous everyday items. Maybe he had a fountain pen loaded with a lethal poison or a watch that squirted cyanide gas.

She grasped the butt of the semi-automatic in the holster at her waist. If Radimov made any sudden moves, she'd be ready. In the meantime, though, all she wanted to do was listen. Less than twenty-four hours earlier, she'd given up on staking out the churchyard dead drop, convinced that this had been her only chance of finding out the identity of the MI5 mole, and now it might be handed to her on a plate. As to why a Russian spy was so keen to get the same information, that was a complete mystery, but if he got the answer she was looking for, his motivation was of little concern.

Radimov was still probing. 'OK, so if you don't know the man's name or even whether he's MI5 or MI6, perhaps you could describe him to me.'

Hayes-Edlington raised his eyes to meet the Russian's, and as he did so, Holly heard Jonah attempt to stifle a cough. The MP instinctively glanced in his direction and was beginning to look back at Radimov again when what appeared to be a spark of recognition lit up his face. He leapt to his feet, knocking over his chair as he did so, and pointed directly at Jonah.

'That's him!' he shouted. 'He's the one. He's the one who—'

Holly was momentarily deafened by the gunshot about two feet from her right ear, and her peripheral vision caught the sudden flash of flame from the muzzle of Jonah's pistol as Hayes-Edlington clutched at his chest and staggered backwards before crashing to the floor with a heavy groan.

With her hand clasped to her damaged ear, Holly whirled round to see a wisp of smoke still drifting upwards from the barrel of Jonah's semi-automatic. 'What the fuck?'

Jonah lowered the weapon to his side. 'Holy shit. I was aiming at Radimov. Saw him reach inside his jacket. Thought it must be a gun.'

Holly had seen no such movement, and Radimov and the MP hadn't been so close to each other that Jonah could have hit the wrong man, especially with the level of firearms training he must have had. And then, of course, there was the MP's unmistakeable identification of him as the MI5 mole. But that didn't make any sense either. Jonah of all people. Surely he was far too junior in the Service to have any kind of intel that would be of interest to the Russians.

52

My lips were flapping like they wanted to say something, but my brain was refusing to form any words. Even the voice in my head was having problems: *'What the...? I mean how the...? Did he just...? Is he...?'*

The MP was lying on his back, his legs at weird angles and his eyes closed, but the rapid rise and fall of his chest indicated that he was still breathing.

I felt Oleg grab me by the arm. 'We need to leave.'

'What?'

'The cops could be here any minute, and there's also the matter of those two MI5 agents.'

He nodded towards the woman and the young guy who'd fired the shot. Behind them, a crowd of people had begun to gather, eager to find out what the gunshot was all about.

There was a door at the back of the pub, next to where we were standing, and Oleg led me through it to the yard where we'd left Alan and Scratch keeping a watchful eye on Trilby Hat. He was conscious now and sitting up behind a wall of empty beer barrels, trussed up and with a handkerchief rammed in his mouth. He glared wild-eyed at Oleg, and whatever he was shouting was totally incomprehensible through the gag.

Alan and Scratch were firing questions at us, but I was too much in shock to answer coherently, and Oleg told them he'd explain later once we'd got away from the place.

'So what do we do with him?' said Scratch, picking up the trilby hat and setting it on the man's head at a particularly jaunty angle.

'After what he did to me?' said Oleg, then paused for several seconds while he stroked his chin and stared down into the man's bloodshot, raging eyes. 'Let him go, I suppose.'

Alan raised an eyebrow. 'You sure about that? I mean, he looks like he'd kill you at the drop of a hat. Trilby or otherwise. In fact, I reckon he'd do us all in, given half a chance.'

'Not if we just untie his feet. By the time he's got himself up and stumbled around trying to find someone to undo his wrists, we'll be well away.'

'OK, if that's what you want,' said Alan and crouched down to loosen the rope from around the man's ankles.

A moment after he'd finished the job, we could all hear the sound of rapidly approaching sirens. Whether it was the cops or an ambulance or both didn't make any difference, and we legged it round the side of the pub at the double with Trilby Hat having already wedged his back against the beer barrels to help lever himself upright.

All we knew was that we had to put as much distance between ourselves and the village as quickly as possible, and when Scratch checked his phone, he found there was another slightly larger village no more than a mile away. The public footpath between the two was mostly uphill, and we had to stop a couple of times for Oleg's little legs to catch up. On the second occasion, Scratch dialled the number of the taxi company that had picked us up from Tidsdale station. The driver himself answered almost immediately. Clearly, it wasn't so much a "company" as a one-man band.

'Well, you didn't last very long,' said the cabbie when Scratch told him who we were. 'Told you you'd hate it.'

As it happened, though, he was about to drop somebody else at the fête – presumably with the same dire warnings he'd inflicted on us – so he could be with us in less than ten minutes. It turned out to be more like twenty since he'd spent longer at the village than he'd intended because he'd wanted to find out what all the commotion was about. And we'd scarcely climbed into the cab when he began to regale us with a somewhat exaggerated version of what had taken place, involving a terrorist attack and at least six people dead.

'Not so bloody boring after all then,' he said. 'Be back to normal again next year, I s'pose. Probably piss with rain as well.'

53

As soon as she realised what had happened, the pub's landlady had gone straight outside to the platform microphone and asked if there were any doctors who'd be willing to attend to a "minor medical emergency".

Three of them – two women and a man – were now bending over the stricken MP, and having stemmed the flow of blood from just below his left shoulder, all agreed that the gunshot wound was not life-threatening, but the bullet would have to be surgically removed.

The only police officer on duty at the fête had ushered the gawping crowd out of the pub and appeared to have been satisfied with Holly and Jonah's MI5 credentials.

'I've already called it in,' he'd told them with a disapproving scowl, 'so you can expect somebody from CID to be here any time now, and they'll be wanting a detailed statement from the pair of you.'

After that, he'd left them to it and marched back out of the pub.

Jonah had refused to answer any of Holly's questions and had sat himself down as far away from his victim as possible, his elbows on his knees and his head in his hands.

'He'll need some serious painkillers the minute the ambulance gets here,' said one of the doctors, checking the MP's pulse for a final time. 'You want us to stay till it does?'

'No, I'll be here,' said Holly, 'but thanks for what you've done.'

Left on her own and looking down at the semi-conscious Hayes-Edlington, her brain whirled as she tried to make sense of what had happened. In her mind, she went through everything she could remember of what Jonah had said and done since the beginning. Anything that might have given her a clue that Jonah was an MI5 mole. But there was nothing she could put her finger on.

There was a groan from the MP at her feet and a grimace of pain flashed across his face. At the same moment, she heard a loud banging noise at the back door of the pub behind her and muffled shouting from beyond it. She threw open the door and took a step back.

Wyatt Bendix was hovering on one leg, about to give the door another kick, a handkerchief stuffed in his mouth and his dark brown trilby hat perched rakishly on top of his head.

Holly gasped. 'Jesus. What are you doing here? And what the hell happened?'

Bendix bellowed at her through his gag, and his eyes filled with fury.

If it hadn't been for the horror of the recent events, Holly might have laughed, but instead she took hold of the handkerchief in his mouth and pulled it free, releasing a torrent of expletive-ridden outrage.

'And don't just stand there, woman!' he roared. 'Do something about my fucking hands.'

He turned his back to her, and Holly could see that his wrists were bound together with what she was fairly sure was his own Eton College tie.

The moment she'd released his hands, he shook them vigorously to restore the circulation, then pointed at the prostrate Hayes-Edlington. 'You want to tell me what in the name of holy Christ has been going on here? Not fucking dead, is he?'

'No, sir,' said Holly and told him it was Jonah that had shot the MP.

Bendix spun round and glowered venomously at Jonah, who was still sitting with his head in his hands close to the pub's entrance. '*He* shot him?'

'Told me he was aiming at Radimov, but I'm not so sure.'

'Oh?'

'For one thing, he claimed he saw Radimov reaching for a weapon, but I didn't see that myself. I also don't buy that his aim was so badly off.'

'So, what are you saying? That he shot Hayes-Edlington deliberately? Why on earth would he do that?'

Holly took a deep breath. This would be the first time she'd spoken to her boss about even the *possibility* that there was a mole in MI5, and she'd no idea how he'd react. He'd never said anything to her about the MP passing secrets to the Russians, and the only reason he'd given her for this assignment was to prevent his affair being exposed.

'Well, sir,' she said, 'Hayes-Edlington had admitted to Radimov that he'd been passing state secrets to the Russians via the woman he was having the affair with and had just pointed out Jonah as his contact. That's when he fired. My guess would be that he was trying to stop the MP from identifying him as the mole but was a couple of seconds too late.'

Bendix took off his hat and ran a hand over his thinning sandy-coloured hair. 'But that's absurd. I've been pals with Peter Hayes-Edlington since we were at Eton together. The chap's as patriotic as they come, so there's absolutely no way he'd ever betray his country like that. Never. Always been a bit of a philanderer, of course, so his affair with the Russian woman is totally in keeping, but a traitor? Never in a million years. It's all a load of utter poppycock, if you ask me. The boys in blue on their way, are they?'

'I believe so, yes.'

'In that case, you'd better stay here and deal with them when they arrive. In the meantime, I'll take... What was his name again?'

'Jonah, sir. Jonah Wilson.'

'Very well. I'll take him somewhere quiet for a little chat. See if I can get to the bottom of this fucking shitshow.'

He planted his trilby hat back in its proper position and strode down the length of the pub towards Jonah. As he went, he called back over his shoulder, almost as an afterthought. 'I presume somebody's called an ambulance?'

'Should be here any minute now, sir, but three doctors have already attended to Mr Hayes-Edlington and said the wound isn't life-threatening.'

'Glad to hear it,' said Bendix, although there was something in his tone that Holly felt wasn't entirely convincing, given that he and the MP were supposed to be such good friends.

54

Despite the extra cost and the additional half hour or so of having to endure the taxi driver's incessant griping about everything from the price of diesel to "the immigration problem" and why there was no such thing as global warming, we told him to skip the local rail station and take us straight to Sheffield. Then it was a quick dash into the hotel to grab our overnight bags and a train to Lincoln. If the cops or MI5 were after us – which in all probability they would be – they'd be expecting us to head back to London, so Lincoln seemed as good a place as any to lie low for a day or two.

Alan and Scratch were naturally champing at the bit to hear all about Oleg's encounter with Hayes-Edlington, the shooting and all the rest of it, but Oleg, for obvious reasons, hadn't wanted to say a word about it while we were in the taxi. So it was only after we'd settled into our seats on the Lincoln train, and far enough away from any other passengers, that he and I filled them in on everything they'd missed.

'Bloody hell,' said Scratch when we'd finished. 'So

is Hayes-Whatshisface dead then?'

'Dunno,' I said, 'but he was still breathing when we left the pub.'

'And it was the MI5 bloke who shot him?'

Oleg nodded. 'The moment he fired, I thought it was meant for me, but he was trying to stop Hayes-Edlington identifying him as the mole, of course. Unlucky for him, he was a couple of seconds too late, but luckily for me, my job's almost done.'

'Tell the CIA who the mole is, you mean?' said Alan. 'But what are you gonna tell them when you don't even know the MI5 guy's name?'

'I do, as a matter of fact. His first name anyway. While I was being interrogated at the safe house, I heard his partner call him Jonah. With that and a physical description, it shouldn't be too hard to track him down. And besides, his partner witnessed the whole thing in the pub, and she seems straight enough to me that she's not going to let him get away with it. Mind you, I have my doubts that he's the only one involved.'

'How'd you mean?'

Oleg turned his head to gaze out of the carriage window at the passing countryside and spoke as if he was thinking out loud. 'Young guy like him? Clearly the other agent's subordinate. I reckon he'd be too low level in the Service to be able to get his hands on anything the Russians would be interested in. More likely he's just a cutout.'

'A what?' I said.

He switched his attention back from the window and smiled. 'Sorry. Spy talk. Basically, a cutout is simply an intermediary. A go-between, if you like, but usually they don't know the identities of who's feeding them the information and who they're passing it on to. That way, if they're caught, they can't put the finger on anyone else. In this case, though, this Jonah guy *does* know who the MP is but maybe doesn't know who his source is. Still, that's up to the CIA and MI5 to figure out. As I said, apart from telling the Agency who the mole is, there's nothing else for me to do.'

'Yeah,' said Scratch, 'but just now you told us that your job's "almost" done. What else is there?'

Oleg went back to staring out of the window, and it was several seconds before he spoke again. 'I don't know if you remember, but I think I may have said at some point that this assignment wasn't only about tracking down a mole in the British intelligence agencies and that I had a personal interest in it as well.'

'You did, yes,' I said.

'Well,' said Oleg, turning back to face us. 'Very much against my will, my daughter Oksana was always determined to follow in her father's footsteps, and however much I tried to dissuade her, she eventually became a member of the SVR – Russia's Foreign Intelligence Service. She was a true patriot and was passionate about serving Mother Russia in whatever way she could, so what prompted her to turn a couple of years later remains a complete mystery to me. But that's what she did. Became a double agent, working for both the SVR and your MI6.'

'So she really did follow in her father's footsteps,' said Alan.

'In a sense, yes, but even though we were in frequent contact, I had no idea what she'd done until eight or nine months ago when she suddenly vanished off the face of the Earth. She'd only returned from a mission in the UK two days before, and we were due to meet for dinner that evening in Moscow. But she never showed up, so the next morning I started to make enquiries, although without much success. Nobody I spoke to had any knowledge of what had happened to my daughter, or if they did, they weren't going to tell me.

'No way was I going to give up, though, and some days later I hit upon an SVR agent that was willing to talk. According to him, Oksana had been identified as a double agent by a mole in the UK secret services, and the information had been passed on to the head of her directorate through one of the several channels the SVR uses for intelligence gathering.' Oleg took a slow deep breath before continuing. 'And this particular channel happened to be Natalia Makarova and her lover, Peter Hayes-Edlington MP, so now I think you'll understand why I had a personal interest in the job.'

'Christ,' I said. 'If that'd been my daughter, I'd have wanted to murder the bastard.'

Oleg's smile was tinged with bitterness. 'That was indeed my intention, Max, and believe me when I tell you that I became obsessed with devising all kinds of ways I would do it. A life for a life, if you like.'

'So your daughter is actually…' and I hesitated to use the word, 'dead, is she?'

'I don't suppose I'll ever know for sure, but given the way in which my country has usually treated its traitors – and even those it merely *perceives* as traitors – I can only assume that she's either been executed or sent to rot in some hellhole of a prison.'

It was Scratch who finally broke the pin-drop silence that followed. 'And are you still planning to kill the MP? If you get the chance, that is.'

Oleg almost imperceptibly shook his head. 'It's a bit of a cliché, I know, but in the end I decided that a quick death was too good for him. As things have turned out, I've not only destroyed his career but also, I would imagine, sentenced him to spending the rest of his miserable life behind bars. For someone like him, death would probably have been preferable.'

'What about this Jonah bloke?' said Alan. 'Surely you want to get your revenge on the man who ratted out your daughter in the first place?'

'What's that expression you have about monkeys and organ grinders? No, as I said, I'd be amazed if he was anything more than a go-between. If I was going to kill anyone, it would be whoever's been feeding him the intelligence.'

'But you don't know who that is.'

'I could make an educated guess.'

'The guy in the trilby hat that we nobbled at the fête? If it's him, you could've done him in right there and then.'

Oleg shrugged, and with a faint grin, shifted his gaze to staring out of the window again. 'I don't kill people based on an educated guess.'

55

Once the paramedics had taken Hayes-Edlington away in an ambulance and she'd finished giving her statement to the two detectives who'd arrived shortly afterwards, Holly was desperate for a cigarette. She grabbed a pack from her shoulder bag and headed for the door. But no sooner had she stepped out into the back yard than she froze.

Twenty feet away, Jonah was lying face down on the ground with his head turned to the side. Bendix was crouching beside him, and he quickly stood upright when he heard Holly's footsteps approaching.

'Little bastard tried to kill me,' he said, taking off his trilby hat and brushing the dust from its brim.

Holly could tell straight away from the neat round hole and the trickle of blood in the middle of Jonah's forehead that he was already dead. She bent down and felt the barrel of the semi-automatic that was lying close to his right hand with a silencer attached. It was still warm.

She picked up the gun and showed it to Bendix. 'He was going to shoot you with this?'

Bendix rolled his eyes. 'What do you think? Yes, Miss Gilmartin. With that very weapon.'

'How very odd.'

'Nothing odd about it, my dear. I was quizzing him about why he'd shot Hayes-Edlington, and he pulled his gun on me, so I didn't have any choice. Self defence, clear as day. So what's your point?'

'Well, sir, this is a Glock 19 and Jonah carries a Glock 17. And how do I know that? Because I have it right here.' She produced a semi-automatic from her bag. 'I took it from him right after he'd fired it. – Would you mind showing me *your* gun, sir?'

Bendix glared at her with indignant fury, but almost immediately his expression reshaped itself into a broad smirk. 'Oops. Slipped up there, didn't I? Rather a rookie mistake, I'm afraid. Still, no harm done, eh?'

'No harm done? What the hell are you talking about? You fucking killed him. In cold blood.'

Holly leapt to her feet and took a couple of steps backwards, aiming the Glock at Bendix's chest.

'I say, steady on Miss G,' he said, throwing up his hands in mock surrender while the smirk remained fully intact. 'Let's not be too hasty, eh? Put that thing down before there's a horrible accident, and I'll explain everything.'

'Oh really? Or maybe I can spare you the trouble and tell you what *I* think.'

Even though Holly's gun was still pointed at him, he slowly lowered his hands to his sides and shrugged. 'Be my guest. Quite frankly, I'm all agog to hear what your half-baked theories could possibly be.'

'Well, first off, I'd lay a pound to a penny that you're the real MI5 mole and you've been using Jonah as a go-between to pass highly secret intelligence to your old school chum, Peter Hayes-Edlington MP, so that he could pillow-talk them to his Russian mistress. This assignment was never about saving him from a scandal. That may have been part of it, but what it was really about was saving your own arse. You were terrified that Radimov would somehow manage to expose you as a traitor, so he had to be neutralised before he could do anything about it. On the money, so far?'

Bendix pursed his lips. 'Plausible, I suppose.'

'You killed Jonah just now because he was threatening to squeal on you, but one of the things I don't understand is how you got him to be your stooge and why you needed one at all. If you're such great pals with Hayes-Edlington, why not simply give the intel straight to him?'

'You honestly expect me to answer any of this?'

'Well, the way I see it,' said Holly, lighting a cigarette, 'it wouldn't be much use me going to the Director General and informing on you, would it? I mean, I don't have any hard evidence, so it would be your word against mine, and I'm pretty certain which of us she'd believe.'

'Excellent point. Mind if I blag one of your ciggies? Normally a cigar man myself but left mine in the car.'

Holly tossed him the packet. No way was she going to close the distance between them and give him any opportunity to grab her gun.

Bendix took a cigarette from the pack and lit it from an expensive-looking lighter he produced from his trouser pocket. He took a tentative drag and exhaled slowly with apparent satisfaction. 'Not a patch on a good Havana, of course, but beggars can't be choosers, eh?' He threw the packet back at Holly far harder than necessary, and she had to dodge her head to the side to avoid being hit in the face. 'Oops. Sorry about that. Don't know my own strength sometimes. But I digress. Remind me where we were with our little confab.'

'You were going to tell me how you got Jonah to be your go-between and why you didn't just deal with the MP yourself.'

'Was I? Not sure I was, but as you say, your word against mine, so why not. Truth be told, it was a piece of the old proverbial cake to get the lad on board, and I collared him very soon after he'd started his training. He'd already caught my eye as being somewhat on the malleable side, and it was simply a matter of telling him I'd discovered he had a criminal record. In itself, that doesn't necessarily preclude someone from joining the Service, and Jonah's crime was relatively minor, but the big no-no is failing to declare the conviction in your application. More than enough grounds for instant dismissal if it's discovered after the fact.'

'But I've been through the vetting process myself, and I know the kind of detail they go into, so how come they never spotted something like a criminal record?'

'Because there was never one to find.'

'What?'

Bendix sighed theatrically. 'You really must learn to listen more carefully, my dear. What I said was that I *told* him I'd discovered he had a criminal record. Naturally enough, he denied ever having been convicted of anything in his life, which was perfectly true because I'd already checked. However, that's when I delivered my *coup de grâce* and said I could get one created as easy as wink. Not difficult at all for someone in my position. Really put the willies up him, that did, but the point is, I must have presented a jolly convincing case because he fell for it hook, line and sinker.'

'So you blackmailed him.'

'It's rather an unsavoury term, but yes, that's about the up and down of it.'

'But I still don't understand why you needed him at all. Or didn't Hayes-Edlington know that the intel Jonah was giving him was actually coming from you?'

'Oh, he knew all right. In fact, it was me who introduced him to the Russian floozy. That was after he'd confided in me that he was on the verge of bankruptcy. Bit of a gambling problem, poor chap, so of course I was more than happy to help him out.'

'You mean you paid him to turn traitor.'

Bendix dropped his half-smoked cigarette and left it to burn itself out on the ground. 'We Old Etonians have to stick together, you know. *Floreat Etona*. Old school motto. May Eton flourish.'

'And ordinary people like Jonah are expendable, are they?' she said.

'A little harsh, but yes. If Peter had been caught, he would have fingered him as the mole and kept me out of it. That's why I made sure that the method of passing the intel was deliberately amateurish. Face to face meetings on a park bench are almost unheard of these days, but it meant that Peter would have no problem identifying Jonah if it came to it. And that's precisely what's happened and why the lad had to meet his untimely end before he could pass the buck on to me.'

Holly could feel her blood pressure soaring. Privileged toffs like Bendix and Hayes-Edlington always seemed to believe they could do whatever they pleased without any repercussions. In Bendix's case, he appeared smugly confident that this even included murder.

'Oh, and by the by,' he said. 'Why do you think I assigned young Jonah as your partner? So he could keep me up to date on whatever you were up to. No coincidence that nobody turned up at the dead drop, eh?'

'Although every time I was in contact with you, you were adamant that Jonah shouldn't hear a word of it.'

The smirk that had never left Bendix's face widened further. 'The important thing was that you should trust him, so it was essential that you believed he was simply a know-nothing lackey, but I kept him in the loop about anything pertinent after you and I had finished our chats.'

'And did that include the fact that you'd tortured and murdered the CIA agent?'

'Oh, you knew that was me, did you?'

'There were a couple of clues on the video that suggested it wasn't the Russians, but I couldn't be certain until now that you've admitted it.'

'A tad sloppy, was I? Oh well, never mind. Water under the bridge, as they say.'

'I presume you killed him because he was here to protect Radimov, and you didn't want anyone getting in the way. But why dump his body at Dempsey's funeral parlour?'

'Ah, rather amusing that, I thought. You see, I was well aware that the undertaker chaps had taken our Russian friend under their wing, so it was inevitable he'd get to see the video. It was only an outside chance, of course, but it occurred to me that it might put the frighteners on him when he knew he'd lost his babysitter and call the whole thing off. Unlikely, as I say, but worth a shot, I thought.' He checked his watch. 'Anyhoo, I've thoroughly enjoyed our little *tête-à-tête* and would love to carry on chewing the fat with you, but I really should be making tracks, so if you don't mind, I'd rather not leave without my gun.'

As he held out his hand, Holly adjusted her aim and took another step back. 'Go fuck yourself.'

'Oh, how charming. I'm guessing *you* didn't go to Roedean.'

'Correct.'

'So, unless you're going to shoot me…'

Bendix moved towards her, his hand still outstretched in front of him.

Putting a bullet in the bastard was definitely tempting, and unlike him, maybe *she* could get away with claiming self defence. All she'd have to do was shoot him with her own gun, then fire another shot into the air from his silenced Glock 19 and leave it close to his body. The weapon would easily be traced to him through MI5 records, so to all intents and purposes, it would look very much as if he'd killed Jonah and then fired at her when she'd tried to stop him.

Whether to carry out her plan or not was a decision Holly didn't have to make, however, because while she was considering the possible consequences, the on-duty copper she'd met earlier appeared round the corner of the pub.

'Christ give me strength,' he said, eyeing Jonah's body on the ground. 'Not another one.'

'Nothing to concern you, dear boy,' said Bendix. 'More Security Service business, I'm afraid.'

He turned to Holly, and this time, under the watchful gaze of the cop, she felt she had no option but to give him his gun.

'Your word against mine, remember,' he whispered and pocketed the weapon before taking the officer gently by the arm and guiding him back the way he'd come.

'Perhaps I could leave you to… tidy up here, Miss Gilmartin,' he called over his shoulder as he went. '*Bonne chance* and *au revoir*, my dear. And don't do anything I wouldn't do, eh?'

Holly's hands were trembling as she took a cigarette from her packet and took several attempts to light it. She took a deep lungful of the smoke and fought back the urge to be suddenly and violently sick. If only she'd been wearing a wire.

56

Another night, another hotel. This time in Lincoln, but the same chain as the one we'd stayed at in Sheffield, so the rooms were almost identical. The only problem was that when we'd checked in, we were told that there was only one twin room available, so we'd had to pay extra for two singles. Oleg had tossed a coin, and he and I had ended up in the singles with Alan and Scratch in the twin-bed room. I had an idea that there was a bit of sleight of hand with the coin toss, but Alan and Scratch hadn't seemed to have noticed, and I wasn't about to complain.

After we'd all showered, Scratch had spent several minutes perusing the hotel restaurant's menu and eventually pronounced it a potential death trap for someone with his vast assortment of allergies. We then scoured the streets of the city until we found a restaurant that met with his approval, and even Alan didn't kick up a fuss and said it was fine with him.

Nobody spoke much while we ate. I, for one, was still in shock from the events at the village fête, despite having heard the news that the MP had survived the attack and had been taken to hospital. I was also mulling over the story Oleg had told us about his daughter. Although he'd done his damnedest to dissuade her from joining the SVR, she'd gone ahead anyway and with tragic consequences. No wonder he'd been so consumed with wreaking his revenge on whoever was responsible for knowingly sending her to her almost certain death. If it had been one of my kids, I'd have wanted to slaughter the bastard, so I'd been rather surprised that Oleg had been content to spare Hayes-Edlington's life. I understood his reasoning that a quick death would have been too good for him and that his ruined career and a lengthy prison sentence would amount to a far more severe punishment, but I didn't think I could have been quite so restrained in the circumstances.

I pushed away my half-eaten plate of food and looked up at Oleg on the opposite side of the table. 'I suppose that now the MP's been exposed for what he is, there's not much point handing over the evidence of his affair to the media.'

'Ah yes. The evidence,' he said, giving me one of his beaming smiles and fishing in his pocket for the thumb drive. He held it between finger and thumb and turned it this way and that as if it were some kind of inconsequential bauble. 'To be honest, I very much doubt that even your British tabloids would be terribly interested in a couple of hours' worth of Russian cartoons. Especially as they're not very good ones either.'

'You're joking, right?'

Oleg shook his head. 'Sorry, but I never did have any video of the MP and his mistress caught in the act. The important thing was that Hayes-Edlington *believed* that

I had.'

'Wait a minute, though,' I said. 'You showed him a photo of him and the woman to prove what was on the video.'

He sat back in his chair and folded his hands across his belly. 'I happen to know someone who's an absolute genius when it comes to faking that kind of thing, and I made certain that the MP only got a quick glance at it. In any case, he knew perfectly well what he'd been up to with Ms Makarova, so probably didn't need much convincing. Of course, if he'd called my bluff, I'd have had nothing at all to blackmail him with. Diddly squat, as I believe the expression goes.'

Scratch, Alan and I all stared at him in stunned silence. Ever since we'd picked Oleg up from France, he'd told us so many lies I'd lost count, but this was a real bombshell. After all we'd been through to protect him and his precious "evidence", this felt like the ultimate betrayal of our trust, and I was about to tell him so when Scratch suddenly brought his meaty fist hammering down onto the tabletop, making everything on it jump an inch into the air.

'Oleg, that's fucking brilliant,' he said, his words almost unintelligible through his roar of laughter.

Almost immediately, Alan joined in as well and slapped Oleg heartily on the back. 'Love it, mate. Bloody love it.'

It took me a few more seconds to see the funny side of Oleg's confession, weighing it up against the betrayal of our trust, but the voice in my head told me not to be such a humourless prick, and I found myself laughing like a drain along with the rest of them.

* * *

Scratch and Alan were already in the hotel restaurant when I came down for breakfast the next morning. Alan was happy because this time he had all the time in the world to make the most of the all-you-can-eat buffet, while Scratch was munching on what appeared to be his third banana.

'No Oleg?' I said, pulling up a chair.

'Not seen him yet,' said Scratch. 'Mind you, he was pretty pissed last night, so maybe he's having a lie-in.'

This was true. Oleg had had several vodka nightcaps before the rest of us had decided to turn in, and he'd probably had a few more after he'd gone back to his own room.

I walked over to the buffet bar and helped myself to coffee, juice and a bowl of cereal, then went to rejoin the others, passing Alan on his way to replenish his plate.

Scratch was peeling his fourth banana. 'Oleg had better get down here soon or there'll be nothing left to eat if Alan keeps at it like he has been.'

I doubted that the absence of solid food would bother Oleg too much, but even so, I had a nagging feeling that something might be wrong. It was unlikely, but perhaps the cops or MI5 had managed to track us down and dragged him off in the middle of the night. If that was the case, though, they'd presumably have grabbed all of us at the same time. Still, I needed to reassure myself that Oleg was OK and simply sleeping off a pig of a hangover, so I called his mobile.

When there was no answer, I told Scratch I was going to check on him in his room, and without waiting for the lift, took the stairs two at a time up to the second floor. I was about to knock on his door when I realised it was very slightly ajar. Shit. This wasn't good. All the rooms were en suite, so he'd hardly have nipped down the corridor for a pee.

'*I wouldn't go in there if I were you,*' said the voice in my head. '*You've no idea what you're gonna find, and you know how squeamish you get over the sight of blood. Or maybe there's a couple of Russian assassins or MI5 agents ready to put a bullet in you the moment you step through the door.*'

I decided the voice was overdramatising the situation but couldn't entirely ignore the possibility or the pounding in my chest as I slowly eased the door open with my foot.

So far, so good. No gunshot, and from where I was standing, no Russian assassins or MI5 agents. Also, no Oleg.

I crept further into the room and saw that the bed was a mess of tangled sheets and discarded pillows, so it had obviously been slept in. Maybe he was taking a shower. The door to the bathroom was closed, although there was no sound of running water.

I knocked three times but softly enough not to cause him any alarm.

'*Oh, nice one,*' said the voice. '*Warn whoever's in there that you're on your way in and give 'em time to take aim. You never seen any Bond films?*'

I'd seen most of them, of course, but unlike 007, I didn't have a gun, so there didn't seem to be much point in kicking the door in to take my would-be killers by surprise. Instead, when there was no response to my knocking or my follow-up of 'Oleg, are you in there?', I opened the door like a normal person, and it took no more than a second to clock that the bathroom was empty.

Returning to the bedroom, I wondered if Oleg had

gone down in the lift while I was coming up the stairs, so I rang Scratch, but he still hadn't shown up in the restaurant.

I sat down on the edge of the bed and began to fear the worst. Whether it was Russian assassins or MI5 agents, he'd clearly been abducted some time during the night, but whoever it was, Oleg was well and truly fucked.

I returned one of the pillows to its proper place at the head of the bed and lay back, trying to figure out how anybody had been able to find where we were. As I did so, however, I turned on my side, and that's when I noticed the sheet of paper on the bedside table. It was one of the hotel's letterheads and was filled with cramped writing in green ink.

I snatched it up and read quickly:

> My dear Max, Alan and Scratch. First of all, I must apologise most sincerely for my sudden departure and without thanking you in person for everything you've done for me. I'm sorry also for not being entirely truthful with you along the way, but this was mostly unavoidable. My greatest regret is the danger I have put you all in, even to the extent of putting your very lives at risk, which is why I've decided that it's time to end our association for your own safety. There can be no doubt that Moscow – and probably others – will not rest until I am dead, so for your own sakes, the less you are in my company, the better.
>
> I would have liked to have told you all this to your faces instead of stealing away like a

318

thief in the night, but I was concerned you might try to change my mind, and besides, I hate goodbyes and might even have got quite tearful!

OK, and now I must go, but not before repeating my very sincere thanks to you all and assuring you that the memory of your help and friendship will remain with me for as long as I have left.

Oleg

P.S. I've asked my new CIA contact to make sure you're paid the second half of the fee that you're owed.

P.P.S. And thanks for all the vodka!

I skim-read the note again, then absent-mindedly folded it in half. He was right, of course. Since picking him up in France, he'd consistently lied to us and put us through all kinds of hell, including almost getting us killed, but I was still going to miss our vodka-swilling Danny DeVito lookalike more than I could ever have imagined.

'*Jesus, you're not welling up, are you?*' said the voice in my head.

'Fuck off,' I said and went back down to the restaurant to tell Alan and Scratch the news.

57

Wyatt Bendix hummed softly to himself as he almost swaggered along the brightly lit hospital corridor, swinging a brown paper bag of grapes at his side. There was no difficulty finding which of the private rooms his friend was in as it was the only one with someone sitting on a chair outside the door. He was in his early thirties with short dark hair and a neatly trimmed beard, and was leaning forward slightly, engrossed in the screen of his smartphone. So engrossed, in fact, that he almost dropped the phone when Bendix came within six feet of him and ostentatiously cleared his throat.

'Just you, is it?'

The young MI5 officer jumped to his feet. 'Yes, sir. We're taking it in shifts.'

'Know who I am, do you?'

'Yes, sir. Of course.'

'Anyone been in to see the patient recently?'

'Doctor and a nurse about half an hour ago.'

'Well, while I'm in there, you're to stop anybody coming in. I don't care who they are, but tell them they'll have to come back later. Clear?'

'Perfectly, sir.'

Bendix held the officer's gaze for a few seconds, then stepped into the room, quietly closing the door behind him. He cast his eyes around and took in the beige walls, blue carpet and large, heavily curtained window at the far side of the room. The head of the bed was roughly central along the wall to his left and next to it was a high-backed chair upholstered in a similar blue to the carpet.

Peter Hayes-Edlington was dressed in a standard issue hospital gown and lying on his back on the bed, his head and upper body raised with the aid of three thick pillows. His eyes were closed, but the lids flickered faintly every now and again. There was a plastic clip attached to his left index finger and a cannula inserted into his forearm. His nostrils were plugged with the twin prongs of transparent plastic tubes that passed back behind his ears and joined again beneath his chin.

The regular bleeping sound was coming from a monitor above and to the far side of the bed. Bendix glanced up at the screen, and although he knew next to nothing about such things, all vital signs seemed to be normal.

He shuffled the high-backed chair so it was at right-angles to the bed and sat.

'So, how are you, old chap?' he said, bringing his face to within a couple of feet of the MP's. 'Rather sozzled with sedatives, I imagine. Oh well, not to worry. Just thought I'd pop by and check up on you. Make sure you were still in the land of the living, eh?'

Bendix opened the bag of grapes. 'Thought I'd bring you a few of these. Can't say I'm a big fan myself. Much prefer them when they've been squished and turned into a nice bottle of claret, what?' He put a grape in his mouth and chewed slowly. 'These are rather tasty, though, I must admit.'

He sat back in the chair and sighed heavily. 'Anyway, dear boy, I don't know if you can hear me or not, but *nil desperandum*. Just wanted to get a couple of things off my chest really. First off, I have to share some responsibility for your current tragic situation. Not for the shooting itself, of course, but for enlisting your help in acting as a conduit between myself and our Russian friends, which has undeniably resulted not only in an attempt on your life but also your meteoric fall from grace.

'However, in my defence, if it hadn't been for your terrible gambling addiction, you would probably never have agreed. On the other hand, I'm sure you must have had lots of fun making the two-backed beast with young Natalia. Oodles of cash and plenty of horizontal jogging? Not a bad recompense for your trouble, eh?'

Bendix chuckled and popped another grape into his mouth.

'As you know, my own decision to betray my country was almost as self-serving as yours in terms of the extremely generous financial rewards I've received – albeit without the sexual "fringe benefits" you yourself enjoyed. What I never told you, though, was what motivated me most of all – by far, in fact – was the *personal* betrayal I had experienced at the hands of the very nation I had faithfully served for so many years.

'When the last Director General of MI5 retired, the job was mine by rights. I was the clear and obvious choice, but what did the Home Secretary do? Appoint a bloody woman over my head. She'd far less experience than I had, but given that the Home Secretary was also of the female gender, I could only conclude that it had been some kind of girlie stitch-up, or political correctness gone mad, if you like.

'To say I was beside myself with rage would have been the understatement of the century, and it wasn't long before I hatched my plan to undermine our new DG in the most destructive way possible. Make her ultimately responsible when it was eventually discovered that her organisation had been leaking top secret intelligence to the Russians, and she'd utterly failed to do anything about it. Yes, she now knows all about you and the Jonah lad, but I'm still in the clear, and I have every intention of keeping it that way.'

Realising that his voice had risen dramatically in volume, he reduced it to little more than a whisper.

'Sorry for the rant there, Peter old chap, especially when I know that all you really want is a bit of peace and quiet. Anyway, I shan't keep you much longer, but suffice it to say, the bitch is still the DG, and now that you'll be *hors de combat* I'll have to find alternative means to continue my communications with the Russians. Never say die, though, eh?'

As he spoke, Bendix pulled on a pair of disposable latex gloves and took out a small plastic phial from the same jacket pocket. The phial was half filled with a transparent viscous liquid, and he held it up to the light before smiling to himself and removing the cap.

'Many apologies, old man, but I hope you'll understand. Can't have you blabbing your mouth off to all and sundry, can we? And in any event, this will be a damn sight less painful than spending the rest of your days rotting in some godawful prison.'

Hayes-Edlington's eyes were now almost fully open, and he tried to speak, but no words came.

'Hush now, Peter. Try not to exert yourself,' said Bendix and removed the twin prongs of the breathing tube from the MP's nose. Then he took a cotton bud from his waistcoat pocket, dipped it into the phial and dabbed a tiny drop of the viscous liquid into each nostril.

He glanced up at the monitor. All vital signs still appeared to be showing as normal.

'Excellent,' he said, replacing the plastic breathing tube. 'Should be at least five minutes before this stuff does its work and all manner of alarms start kicking off. Plenty of time for me to make my exit, as indeed I must do *tout de suite*.'

He patted Hayes-Edlington gently on the arm and stood up, carefully placing the gloves, phial and cotton bud into a sealable plastic wallet, which he returned to his jacket pocket.

'Farewell, my dear friend, and may flights of angels sing thee to thy rest.'

Bendix closed the door behind him as he left the room, and the young MI5 officer sprang up from his chair.

'Everything OK, sir?'

'All tickety-boo, thank you, um… What's your name?'

'Mowbray, sir.'

'Signed the Official Secrets Act, have you?'

'Of course, sir.'

'Well, Mowbray, this is one of the very things covered under that act.'

The officer frowned. 'Sir?'

'My visit here is more top secret than any secret you're ever likely to come across, yes? In fact, I was never actually here at all, if you catch my drift.

324

Understood?'

'Yes, sir. Certainly, sir. Never here at all.'

'Good man. Keep up the good work,' said Bendix and strode off down the corridor, quietly humming the tune of the *Eton Boating Song* as he went.

EPILOGUE

I knew how quickly the British press considered a story to be "old news", so only a little over two weeks after Peter Hayes-Edlington's death, it was as if it had never even happened. At the time, though, the media had been full of it. The tabloid papers especially had a field day – or several field days, in fact – with headlines like "GOOD RIDDANCE TO SCUM MP" and "MYSTERIOUS DEATH OF TRAITOR MP".

The mystery surrounding the MP's demise was due to the inconclusive findings of the autopsy. According to his doctors, the bullet wound had not been life-threatening at all and he'd been making steady progress towards a complete recovery, so his sudden death was totally unexpected. Rumours abounded, of course, and by far the most popular was that he'd been murdered by Russian assassins using some kind of poison or nerve agent that toxicology tests were unable to detect. However, as the more responsible elements of the media pointed out, Hayes-Edlington's room had been guarded day and night by members of the Security Service, so any access to the man would have been impossible.

Then, almost immediately after the furore over the MP's treachery had begun to subside, the nation's media launched its demand that heads should roll at the highest level. More specifically, it was MI5's Director General who became their primary target, since she was deemed to have had overall responsibility for failing to contain the leaking of top secret intelligence to the Russians. It therefore came as no surprise when the Home Secretary accepted her resignation with almost indecent haste and the usual "thanking her for her service" kind of platitudes. What did come as a massive shock to us, though, was the announcement of her successor. None other than Oleg's hot tip for the real MI5 mole, Wyatt Bendix.

'That's just crazy,' Scratch had said when the news was announced. 'Oleg should have killed the bastard when he had the chance.'

Neither Alan or I had disagreed, but in the days that followed, the matter was all but forgotten. The possibility that we might be getting a visit from the police or the Security Service for our part in Oleg's activities seemed increasingly unlikely to transpire, and things got pretty much back to normal at the funeral parlour.

There was one slight difference, however, and this was that Sanjeev had been relieved of one of his usual duties, which was opening and sorting through the daily post. Not a particularly demanding task, you'd imagine, but even so, Sanjeev managed to cock it up big time, and we only came to realise it when our electricity supply was cut off without warning. I rang the company straight away to complain, only to be told that we were seriously in arrears with paying our bills.

Further investigation revealed that, for reasons best known to himself, Sanjeev had believed that the logo on the envelopes meant that they were begging letters from some charity or other and had simply binned all of them unopened. As to why he hadn't thought it strange that we hadn't received a single electricity bill in months, he had no answer.

So this was why I was sitting at the reception desk just inside the front door of the funeral parlour and sifting through the day's mail delivery. There was the regular batch of glossy junk mail leaflets, half a dozen envelopes – none of them bills on this occasion – and roughly in the middle of the stack, a large format picture postcard.

Who the hell sent postcards these days?

I took little notice of the image on the front of the card but vaguely clocked the words "Greetings from Santorini" and flipped it over. Most of the left side of the back was filled with tiny cramped handwriting in green ink, but I skipped to the end first: "Take care and all the best, Oleg".

So that's who sent postcards these days.

I started to read from the top:

> Dear all. Decided to take a short holiday on the beautiful Greek island of Santorini, and by an amazing coincidence (ha ha!) discovered that a certain person of our mutual acquaintance must have had the same idea and is even staying at the same hotel. How about that, eh? Receptionist told me he's here for the rest of the week, so I've decided to pay him a visit and have a little chat before he leaves. (Seems he's swapped

his trilby for a panama hat. Must be the heat.) Wish me luck! Take care and all the best, Oleg.

* * *

Three days later, I got a second postcard. Identical to the previous one and with the instantly recognisable cramped handwriting on the back. So cramped, in fact, that I almost needed a magnifying glass to read it:

Dear all. Me again. As I told you I would, I was on my way to see you-know-who and I'm half way along his corridor when the door to his room opens and out steps this woman. Big floppy hat pulled low over her forehead and enormous sunglasses but wearing exactly the same outfit and carrying the same shoulder bag as the last time I'd seen her. Also caught a glimpse of mousey hair as she hurried away towards the far end of the corridor. Almost certain it was our other secret friend! Naturally, I had a quick peek inside the room and there he was, stone dead on the floor with a pool of blood by his head. Anyway, thought I'd let you know as you might want the job of picking up the corpse. Ha ha! Oleg.

THE END

DEAR READER

Authors always appreciate reviews – especially if they're good ones of course – so I'd be eternally grateful if you could spare the time to write a few words about *The Undertaking* on Amazon, Goodreads or anywhere else you can think of. It really can make a difference. Reviews also help other readers decide whether to buy a book or not, so you'll be doing them a service as well.

MAILING LIST

If you'd like to be kept informed of new posts on my website, my new books, special offers on my books and other relevant information, please click on the link below and add your details.

Don't worry, any emails I send you will be few and far between, and I certainly won't be sharing your details with any third parties. You can also easily unsubscribe at any time.

http://eepurl.com/cwvFpb

AND FINALLY...

I'm always interested to hear from my readers, so please do take a couple of minutes to contact me via my website at **https://rob-johnson.org.uk/contact/**

ACKNOWLEDGEMENTS

I am indebted to the following people for helping to make this book better than it would have been without their advice, technical knowhow and support:

Rob Johnson (a different one); Penny Philcox; Colin Ritchie; John Rogers; Dan Varndell; Chris Wallbridge; Nick Whitton; Patrick Woodgate.

And last but not least, my eternal gratitude to my wife, Penny, for her unfailing support, encouragement and belief.

COVER DESIGN

Special thanks as always to Penny Philcox for the cover artwork and to Patrick Woodgate for the original design.

ABOUT THE AUTHOR

'You'll have to write an author biography of course.'

'Oh? Why?'

'Because people will want to know something about you before they splash out on buying one of your books.'

'You think so, do you?'

'Just do it, okay?'

'So what do I tell them?'

'For a start, you should mention that you've written four plays that were professionally produced and toured throughout the UK.'

'Should I say anything about all the temp jobs I had, like working in the towels and linens stockroom at Debenhams or as a fitter's mate in a perfume factory?'

'No, definitely not.'

'Motorcycle dispatch rider?'

'You were sacked, weren't you?'

'Boss said he could get a truck there quicker.'

'Leave it out then, but make sure they know that *The Undertaking* is the seventh book you've written. And don't forget to put in something that shows you're vaguely human.'

'You mean this kind of thing: "I'm currently in Greece with my wife, Penny, three cats and three rescue dogs and working on a new novel and a couple of screenplays".'

'It'll have to do, I suppose, and then finish off with your website and social media stuff.'

'Oh, okay then.'

- visit my website at
  http://www.rob-johnson.org.uk

- follow @RobJohnson999 on Twitter

- check out my Facebook author page at
  https://www.facebook.com/RobJohnsonAuthor

- follow me on Amazon at
  https://viewauthor.at/Rob_Johnson_Author

OTHER BOOKS BY ROB JOHNSON

LIFTING THE LID

(Book One in the 'Lifting the Lid'
comedy thriller series)

**"The twists and turns kept me on the edge of my seat,
laughing all the time."** – San Francisco Review of Books

http://viewbook.at/Lifting_the_Lid

**Also available as an audiobook from
Amazon and Audible**

**Read on for the opening chapters
towards the end of this book.**

HEADS YOU LOSE

(Book Two in the 'Lifting the Lid'
comedy thriller series)

**"Masterfully planned and executed... It tickled my
funny bone in all the right places."** - Joanne Armstrong
for Ingrid Hall Reviews

http://viewbook.at/Heads_You_Lose

DISHING THE DIRT

(Book Three in the 'Lifting the Lid'
comedy thriller series)

**"A real romp through the criminal wiles. A great way
to take your mind off your own troubles."** – Suzi
Stembridge (Author of the *Greek Letters* and *Jigsaw*
series of books)

https://viewbook.at/Dishing_the_Dirt

CREMAINS

(A comedy crime caper.
Book One in the "Cremains" series)

"A hilarious comedy that keeps you on the edge of your seat... and there are loads of twists and turns as the story hurtles towards an explosive ending." - Anne-Marie Reynolds for Readers' Favorite

http://viewbook.at/Cremains

QUEST FOR THE HOLEY SNAIL

(A time travel adventure)

"Fans of Douglas Adams' *Hitchhikers' Guide to the Galaxy* will enjoy *Quest for the Holey Snail*." - Awesome Indies

http://viewBook.at/Quest

A KILO OF STRING

(Non fiction: A British expat in Greece)

"Witty and very funny. I really enjoyed this book. The author clearly has a love for the country and the people." - *USA Today* bestselling author Kathryn Gauci

http://viewbook.at/A_Kilo_of_String

Also available as an audiobook from Amazon, Audible, Google Play, Apple and Spotify

"LIFTING THE LID" OPENING CHAPTERS

I hope you've enjoyed reading *The Undertaking* and that you might be interested in reading one of my other novels. To give you an idea what to expect, these are the opening chapters of *Lifting the Lid*, which is the first in my comedy thriller series. It's similar in style to *Cremains* and *The Undertaking* but with completely different characters.

However, if you've already read *Lifting the Lid*, many thanks, and you can now skip the next few pages and check out the very exciting Copyright page at the end.

LIFTING THE LID
CHAPTER ONE

Trevor stood with his back to the fireplace like some Victorian patriarch but without a scrap of the authority. Although the gas fire wasn't on, he rubbed his hands behind him as if to warm them. His mother sat in her usual chair by the window, staring blankly at the absence of activity in the street outside.

He knew exactly what her response would be. It was always the same when he told her anything about his life. Not that there was often much to tell, but this was different. This was a biggie. Almost as big as when he'd told her about Imelda's—

'It's of no concern to me.'

There we go. And now for the follow-on. Wait for it. Wait for it.

'I'm seventy-eight years old. Why should I care? I could be dead tomorrow.'

Trevor screwed up his face and mouthed the words of his mother's familiar mantra, but it became rapidly unscrewed again when she added, '…Like Imelda.'

'Don't,' he said. 'Just don't, okay?'

'No concern to me,' said the old woman with a barely perceptible shrug.

In the silence that followed, Trevor became aware of the ticking of the pendulum clock on the mantelpiece behind him. It had never been right since his father had died, so he checked his watch instead. 'You won't be… ' and he hesitated to say the word, ' … lonely?'

If his mother had had the energy or inclination to

have laughed – derisively or otherwise – she would have done, but she settled for the next best option and grunted, 'Hmph.'

Trevor knew from experience that the intention was to pick away at his already tender guilt spot, and he looked around the room as if he were searching for the nearest escape route. His mother still referred to it as "the parlour", perhaps in a vain attempt to attach some kind of outmoded elegance to a room which, to Trevor's eye at least, was mildly shabby and darkly depressing even on the brightest of days. It was festooned with fading photographs of people who were long since dead, interspersed here and there with pictures of his more recently deceased brother and his very-much-alive sister. Of Trevor, there was only the one – an unframed snapshot of him and Imelda on their wedding day.

He became aware of the clock once again and cleared his throat. 'So... er... I'll be away then.'

This time, the shrug was accompanied by the slightest tilt of the head. 'No concern to me,' she said.

Again, he glanced at his watch. 'It's just that I have to—'

'Oh get on if you're going.'

Trevor stepped forward and, picking up his crash helmet from the table next to his mother, kissed her perfunctorily on the back of the head. For the first time, she turned – not quite to face him, but turned nevertheless.

'Still got that silly little moped then,' she said, repeating the comment she'd made when he had first arrived less than an hour before.

'Scooter, mother. It's a scooter. – Anyway, how could I afford anything else?' He was thankful she couldn't see the sudden redness in his cheeks or she would have instantly realised that he was lying.

He kissed her again in the same spot, and this time she seemed to squirm uncomfortably. For a moment, he followed her line of vision to the outside world. – Nothing. He tapped his helmet a couple of times, then turned and walked towards the door. As he closed it behind him, he could just make out the words: 'Your brother wouldn't have gone.'

Out in the street, he strapped on his helmet and straddled the ageing Vespa, eventually coaxing the engine into something that resembled life. He took a last look at the window where his mother sat and thought he saw the twitch of a lace curtain falling back into place.

'Oh sod it,' he said aloud and let out the clutch.

At the end of the road, he turned right and stopped almost immediately behind a parked camper van. Dismounting the Vespa and still holding the handlebars, he kicked out the side stand and was about to lean it to rest when he decided that some kind of symbolic gesture was called for. Instead of inclining the scooter to a semi-upright position, he looked down at the rust-ridden old machine, tilted it marginally in the opposite direction and let go. With the gratingly inharmonious sound of metal on tarmac, the Vespa crashed to the ground and twitched a few times before rattling itself into submission. Trevor took in the paltry death throes and allowed himself a smirk of satisfaction.

Pulling a set of keys from his pocket, he kissed it lightly and walked round to the driver's door of the van. The moment he turned the key in the lock, a lean-looking black and tan mongrel leapt from its sleeping position on the back seat and hurled itself towards the sound. By the time Trevor had opened the door, the dog was standing on the driver's seat, frantically wagging its tail and barking hysterically.

'Hey, Milly. Wasn't long, was I?' said Trevor, taking the dog's head between both hands and rocking it gently from side to side. 'Over you get then.'

Milly simply stared back at him, no longer barking but still wagging her tail excitedly.

'Go on. Get over.' Trevor repeated the command and, with a gentle push, encouraged her to jump across to the passenger seat. Then he climbed in and settled himself behind the steering wheel. 'Right then,' he said, rubbing his palms around its full circumference. 'Let's get this show on the road.'

LIFTING THE LID
CHAPTER TWO

The lift was dead. The grey-haired guy in the expensive suit wasn't, but he looked like he was. Lenny had him pinned against the wall by leaning his back into him as hard as he could to keep him upright – no mean achievement since, although built like a whippet on steroids, Lenny was little more than five feet in height and well into his fifties.

'Come on, Carrot,' he said. 'What you messin' about at?'

Carrot – so called because of his ill-fitting and very obvious ginger toupee – jabbed at the lift button for the umpteenth time. 'Lift's not working. We'll have to use the stairs.'

'You kidding me? With this lard-arse?'

'So we just leave him here, do we?'

Lenny's heavily lined features contorted into a grimace. 'How many flights?'

'Dunno. Couple maybe?'

'Jesus,' said Lenny, taking a step forward.

The laws of gravity instantly came into play, and the Suit slid inexorably down the wall and ended up in a sitting position, his head lolled to one side and his jacket bunched up around his ears. Not for the first time, Carrot wondered why he'd been paired up with a dipshit like Lenny and even why the whining little git had been put on this job at all.

'Well you'll have to take the top half then,' Lenny said. 'Back's playing me up.'

Carrot snorted. Here we go again, he thought. The old racing injury ploy.

Lenny pulled himself up to his full inconsiderable height and shot him a glare. 'And what's that supposed to mean? You know bloody well about my old racing injury.'

'Doesn't everyone?' said Carrot.

Although Lenny's stature – or lack of it – gave a certain amount of credibility to his countless stories about when he used to be a top-flight steeplechase jockey, nobody in the racing business ever seemed to have heard of him. It was certainly true that he knew pretty much everything there was to know about the Sport of Kings, and most of his tales of the turf had a ring of authenticity about them, so he must have been involved in some way or other but more likely as a stable lad than a jockey. Hardly anyone bothered to doubt him to his face though, probably because his vicious temper was legendary and so was his ability with both his fists and his feet. For a little guy, he could be more than handy when it came to a scrap.

He looked like he was spoiling for one right now, so Carrot diverted his attention back to the Suit.

'Grab his ankles then,' he said and manoeuvred the man's upper body forward so he could get a firm grip under his armpits from behind.

Halfway up the first flight of concrete stairs, Lenny announced that he'd have to have a rest. Even though Carrot was doing most of the work, he decided not to antagonise him and eased his end of the body down onto the steps. Truth be told, he could do with a short break himself. He was already sweating like a pig and, besides, he needed at least one hand free to push his toupee back from in front of his eyes.

Lenny leaned back against the iron handrail and started to roll a cigarette.

Carrot's jaw dropped. 'Lenny?'

'Yeah?'

'What you doing?'

'Er…' Lenny looked down at his half completed cigarette and then back at Carrot. 'Rollin' a fag?'

His expression and tone of voice rendered the addition of a "duh" utterly redundant.

'We're not in the removal business, you know.' Carrot nodded towards the Suit. 'This isn't some bloody wardrobe we're delivering.'

Lenny ignored him and lit up. He took a long drag and blew a couple of smoke rings. Putting the cigarette to his lips for a second time, he was about to take another draw when he hesitated and began to sniff the air. 'What's that smell?'

'Er… smoke?' Two can play the "duh" game, thought Carrot.

'It's like…' Lenny's nose twitched a few more times and then puckered with distaste. 'Ugh, it's piss.'

'Dumps like this always stink of piss.'

'No, it's more…' Lenny carried on sniffing, his eyes ranging around to try to identify the source of the smell. 'Oh Jesus, it's him.'

Carrot looked in the direction he was pointing and, sure enough, the dark stain which covered the Suit's groin area was clearly visible despite the charcoal grey of the trousers. 'Oh for f—'

'Bugger's wet 'imself.'

'I can see that.'

Lenny took a pull on his cigarette. 'Fear probably.'

'Don't be a prat. The man's out cold. He doesn't know if it's Christmas Day or Tuesday.'

'Maybe it's like when somebody has their leg cut off – or their arm. They reckon you can still feel it even though it's not there any more.'

Carrot stared at him, unable to discern any logical connection between amputation and pissing your pants.

'You know,' Lenny continued, apparently aware that further explanation was necessary. 'It's like your subconscious, or whatever, doing stuff behind your back without you realising.'

'I think it's far more likely it's a side effect of the stuff we injected him with.'

'Could be,' said Lenny, and he took a last drag on his cigarette before lobbing it over his shoulder into the stairwell.

'Ready now?' Carrot made no attempt to disguise the sarcasm in his tone.

'I'm not taking the feet this time though. My face'll be right in his piss.'

Carrot squeezed his eyes shut and counted to three. 'You want to swap?'

'Not necessarily. We could try taking an arm each.'

Because of the substantial difference in their heights, Carrot knew that this meant he would be taking most of the weight again, but he also realised there was no point in arguing. The priority was to get the guy up the stairs and into the flat before somebody spotted them.

LIFTING THE LID
CHAPTER THREE

The time wandered by, and the miles slid comfortably under the tyres at a steady fifty-five. Battered though it was, the converted Volkswagen Transporter was only twelve years old and could have gone faster, but Trevor was in no particular hurry. He was enjoying the ride, happy to be away and with the road stretching before him to an unknown destination. Milly seemed equally contented and alternated between sitting upright on the passenger seat, staring fixedly ahead, and curling up to sleep in the back.

It was Trevor's first real trip in the camper, and he liked the idea of having no fixed itinerary. After all, he reasoned, wasn't that the whole point of having one of these things?

To say that he had bought it on a whim would have been a gross distortion of the truth. Trevor didn't really do whims. His idea of an impulsive action was to buy an item that wasn't on his list when he did his weekly shop at the local supermarket. Even then, there would have to be a pretty convincing argument in favour of dropping the quarter-pound packet of frozen peas, or whatever it might be, into his trolley. Half price or two-for-one were minimum requirements.

The camper van hadn't fulfilled either of these criteria, and to begin with, he'd toyed with the idea of a motorbike. Something a bit flash, like a Harley. He'd have needed a halfway decent tent of course. A simple bedroll and sleeping out under the stars were all very well in Arizona or wherever but totally inadequate over here – unless you were one of those rufty-tufty outdoor survival types with an unnatural fixation about the SAS. He'd never understood the attraction of deliberately putting yourself in a situation where it was more than likely you would either starve or freeze to death or be attacked by a large carnivore or stung by something so venomous you'd have seconds to live unless you applied the appropriate antidote in time or got your best friend to suck out the poison. No, Scottish midges were about as much as he was prepared to tolerate, but even then he'd make damn sure he had a plentiful supply of insect repellent with him.

A hermetically sealable tent and a good thick sleeping bag would be indispensable as far as Trevor was concerned and, if space permitted on the Harley, an airbed – preferably with a pump which operated off the bike's battery. It had all started to make perfect sense until a small problem finally occurred to him. What about Milly? She was too big to ride in a rucksack on his back, and as for the only other possible option, the very idea of a Harley with a sidecar made him squirm with embarrassment.

A car was far too ordinary for his purposes, so a camper van had seemed to be the next best thing if he couldn't have a Harley. It still had a kind of "just hit the open road and go where it takes you" feel to it, and he'd once read a book by John Steinbeck where he set off to rediscover America in a camper with an enormous poodle called Charley.

The whole decision-making process had taken months of what Imelda would have called "anally retentive faffing", but which Trevor preferred to consider as an essential prerequisite to "getting it right". In his defence, he would have argued that it wasn't just about buying a van. There had been much greater life choices involved, such as whether to pack in his job at Dreamhome Megastores.

As it turned out, that particular decision had almost made itself for him. The company was in a bit of financial bother and was having to make cutbacks, so he and several of his colleagues had been offered voluntary redundancy. Although not exactly generous, the severance package was certainly tempting enough to cause Trevor a run of sleepless nights. But it wasn't until his annual staff appraisal that he'd finally made up his mind.

He had sat across the desk from the store manager and studied the thin wisps of hair on top of the man's head while he read out a litany of shortcomings and misdemeanours from the form in front of him.

'This simply won't do, Trevor. Really it won't,' Mr Webber had said, finally looking up and removing his glasses. 'I mean, there have been more customer complaints about you than any other member of staff.'

'I don't know why. I'm always polite. Always try and give advice whenever I—'

'But that's exactly the problem, Trevor. More often than not, the complaints are *about* your advice. We've had more goods returned because of you than... than...' The manager had slumped back in his chair. 'Good God, man, have you learned nothing about home maintenance and improvement in all the... What is it? Fourteen years since you've been here?'

'Fifteen.' And in all those long years, he'd never once heard Webber use the phrase "do-it-yourself", let alone its dreaded acronym.

'Quite honestly, I'm at a loss as to know what to—'

This time, it was Trevor who had interrupted. He couldn't be sure that he was about to be sacked, but he'd already had his quota of verbal and written warnings and thought he'd get in first with: 'About this voluntary redundancy thing...'

And that was that. Decision made and not a bad little payout. Added to what he'd squirreled away over the last couple of years or so, he could buy the van and still have enough left to live on for a few months as long as he was careful. He'd have to look for another job when the money did run out of course, but he was determined not to worry about that until the time came. At least, he was determined to *try* not to worry about it.

'What the hell, eh, Milly? This is *it*,' he said and shoved a tape into the cassette player.

He caught sight of the dog in the rear-view mirror. She briefly raised an eyebrow when the opening bars of Steppenwolf's *Born to be Wild* bellowed from the speakers above her head. Then she went back to sleep.

Trevor tapped the steering wheel almost in time with the music and hummed along when the lyrics kicked in. A song about hitting the open road and just seeing where it took you seemed particularly appropriate for the occasion, and when it got to the chorus, he'd begun to lose all sense of inhibition and joined in at the top of his voice.

Moments later, the van's engine spluttered and then abruptly died.

LIFTING THE LID
CHAPTER FOUR

Carrot and Lenny hauled the Suit to his feet and, with an arm slung around each of their shoulders, half carried and half dragged him up to the first floor landing. As Carrot had predicted, Lenny's contribution amounted to little more than providing a largely ineffectual counterbalance, and by the time they'd lurched and staggered to the top of the second flight of steps, every muscle in his neck and back was screaming at him to stop whatever he was doing.

'I'm gonna have to... have a break for a minute,' he said, fighting for breath as he altered his grip and lowered the Suit to the ground.

'Come on, mate. We're nearly there now,' said Lenny, but his words of encouragement were meaningless, given that he did nothing to prevent the Suit's descent.

Carrot groaned as he sat him down against the frame of the fire door and so did the Suit.

''Ang on a sec. He's not coming round, is he?' Lenny squatted like a jockey at the start gate and brought his face to within a few inches of the Suit's. 'He is, you know.'

The muscles in Carrot's back grumbled as he crouched down to take a closer look and spotted the faintest flicker of the eyelids.

'You can't have given him enough,' said Lenny.

'What?'

'The injection.'

'Yeah, stupid me,' said Carrot, slapping his palm against his forehead. 'I should've allowed extra time for all your fag breaks.'

Even though he resented Lenny's accusation, he'd

worked with him on several other jobs and was used to getting the blame when things went wrong. Not that this was surprising since Lenny always avoided making any of the decisions, so any cockups were never his fault.

'We'll have to give him another shot,' said Lenny.

"We" meaning "you", Carrot thought and shook his head. 'Stuff's still in the van.'

'Jesus, man. What you leave it there for?'

Carrot bit his lip, aware from his peripheral vision that Lenny was staring at him, but he had no intention of shifting his focus to make eye contact. The Suit's eyelids were twitching more rapidly now and occasionally parted to reveal two narrow slits of yellowish white. Maybe the guy was just dreaming, but it was two hours or more since they'd given him the shot, so—

'Better bop him one, I reckon,' said Lenny.

It was Carrot's turn to stare at Lenny. 'Bop him one?'

'Yeah, you know…' He mimed hitting the Suit over the head with some blunt instrument or other and made a "click" sound with his tongue. 'Right on the noggin.'

Carrot continued to hold him in his gaze while he pondered which nineteen-fifties comedian Lenny reminded him of, but he was shaken from his musing by a strange moaning sound. The Suit's eyes were almost half open now.

END OF FIRST FOUR CHAPTERS OF 'LIFTING THE LID'

To read on, please go to:

http://viewbook.at/Lifting_the_Lid

Printed in Great Britain
by Amazon